Praise For Maggie James

"For me, this book was a gritty and intense read and the characters work so well together in this book, plenty of twists and turns and an unexpected ending too..." **Donna Maguire – Donnas Book Blog**

"Great psychological suspense from Maggie James. A recommended read." **Mark Tilbury – Author**

"A truly electrifying read that delivered twist after twist and kept me turning the pages." **Babus Ahmed – Goodreads**

"A thoughtful and clever story with plenty to get your psychotic teeth into." **Colin Garrow – Goodreads**

"Overall a very twisty tale with a complicated web of relationships." **Lorna Cassidy – On The Shelf Reviews**

"The plot here is hard hitting with a few twists you won't see coming." **Joanne Robertson – My Chestnut Reading Tree**

"The plot is outstanding, highly recommended for suspense, action and thrilling entertainment. Pure Magic Maggie James!" **Susan Hampson – Books From Dusk Till Dawn**

"There are twists and turns and unexpected events that build on the intrigue and suspense to such a level that you just keep turning page after page." **Jill Burkinshaw – Books n All**

"I thought it was a genuine page turner and the kind of book that is right up my street – I loved it!!!" **Donna Maguire – Donnas Book Blog**

"An excellent ending (one of my big must have's to achieved 5*) , a brilliant plot, served with empathy and guts to achieve a thought provoking read." **Misfits Farm – Goodreads**

"A great psychological thriller from Maggie James that I highly recommend." **Deanna – Goodreads**

"WOW!! Seriously WOW!! I just loved The Second Captive!" **Laura Turner – PageTurnersNook**

"...The Second Captive by Maggie James is an excellent psychological thriller that will appeal to many readers." **Rebecca Burton – If Only I Could Read Faster**

"...told from different viewpoints a gripping hearwrenching tale...that you won't be able to put down till the last page is turned ..." **Livia Sbarbaro – Goodreads**

PROLOGUE

My mobile pinged in my handbag, causing my heart to pound, my pulse to skyrocket. With shaking fingers, I pulled out my phone.

A text message. *Hello, friend. Long time no talk.*

I forced myself not to respond. He'd soon tire of goading me if I ignored him, surely?

Another arrived after a few minutes. *Aw, have I upset you? You're not my friend anymore?*

I dug my nails into my palms, my hands clenched into tight fists.

A third ping. *Remember what I told you. You don't want to piss me off. I'm not always Mr Nice Guy.*

After my phone beeped a fourth time I hurried to the drinks cabinet and poured myself a whisky. Fuelled by the courage it provided, I read the latest message.

What, no more threats about the police? You're no fun these days.

I wouldn't reply. No way in hell.

I know lots about you, friend. More than you think.

Screw not replying. *OK, fucker. So what's my name?*

You've got me there, I admit. But I'm working on it, trust me. My shortlist of possibilities is down to two.

A final ping.

And when I find you, and I will, you're dead, bitch.

CHAPTER 1

SEVERAL WEEKS EARLIER

'Can you get the next available flight? She's conscious, but refusing to talk.' Exhaustion hovered in my mother's voice, along with terror. I clutched my mobile, my palm sweaty, the surrounding air hard to breathe.

'I'll come right away. Once I've landed, I'll call you.' My brain whirred with a list of things to do: pack a bag, lock up the gallery, make the hour-long drive to the airport. I'd go standby for the next plane out. Thank God the UK was only a short flight from Spain.

'I'm worried sick about her, Lydia.' Mum's last words before we wrapped up the call. She wasn't the only one.

I glanced at the clock on the kitchen wall: 8.30am. The temperature was already scorching its way to dizzy heights, the August sun a fierce blaze over the hills. Sweat dampened my body - and not just from the heat. I tried to reassure myself. With luck I would be in Bristol by the afternoon. Despite the two years I'd lived in this sleepy coastal town, I still considered good old Brizzle to be my home. I didn't care to examine what that said about my new life in Spain.

Right then my old existence was calling - no, demanding - me to return.

I took twenty minutes to pack. By the time I shut up the gallery and walked to my car, it was just after nine. With any luck, I'd be airborne by midday.

My chest clenched tight with tension all the time I drove, made worse by the broken air-conditioning in my car. I dragged in lungfuls of hot sticky air in an attempt to calm myself, my brain assessing the facts. My sister, from what our mother had told me, had tried to kill herself. Again. First she'd phoned Mum, saying she no longer wanted to live. Then she'd shut herself in her bedroom and lain down with a half-full bottle of antidepressants in her hand, a glass of water on her bedside cabinet. By the time she'd finished, both were empty. Her life had been saved by our mother, who had driven over straightaway, letting herself in with the key she possessed. She'd discovered my sister unconscious and phoned at once for an ambulance. I closed my eyes, imagining her opening the door to Ellie's bedroom, calling her name, terror in her voice. The horror on finding her daughter's limp body, an empty pill bottle by her side. Not the first time Mum had faced such an awful scenario.

Ellie, oh Ellie, I thought, as I turned into the airport car park. Would my sister ever slay her demons?

To my relief, I grabbed a seat on the eleven forty flight. That gave me a little over an hour after I'd checked in to get my head in order. I pulled out my mobile.

Caroline answered on the first ring.

'Hey, Lyddie.' Mum was the only person who called me Lydia. Or referred to Ellie as Eleanor. 'It's great to hear from you.'

She sounded surprised, as well she might. I didn't normally phone her. Most of our communication took place via Skype or text.

'How are you?' she continued. 'Everything okay your end?'

'I'm fine. But Ellie's not. I'm flying back to Bristol today.'

'Has something happened? Is she all right?'

My throat closed, refusing to say the words. I shoved a finger in one ear to block out the thrum of noise around me.

'Lyddie?'

'She ...' The tears I'd been choking back all morning flooded my eyes.

'Has she ... oh, God. I can't think how best to ask this. Did she try to kill herself again?'

I swallowed hard. From somewhere, I found the words I needed. 'Yes. She's back at the mental health unit at Southmead Hospital. Medicated and undergoing psychiatric evaluation.' My voice rose high, cracked a little, as I spoke. Damn it, I'd hoped I was holding everything together, until Caroline's concern sounded in my ear.

'But she was doing so well, wasn't she? Mentally, I mean.'

'We all thought so.' A tear slid down my cheek. 'Seems we were wrong.'

'I'm so sorry, lovey.'

Such empathy in her voice. Caroline Maston and I had been best friends for twenty years. She was as much my sister as Ellie was.

'Can we meet up?' I asked. 'Tonight, if possible?'

We arranged I'd go to her house after I'd visited Ellie in Southmead and spent some time with Mum. 'No idea when that'll be,' I told her. 'I'll call you later.'

***

My plane landed in Bristol to a welcome of steady drizzle. The contrast with my life in sun-soaked Spain couldn't have been starker. Once I'd collected my luggage, I rented a car at the airport and drove straight to Southmead Hospital, breaking the speed limit most of the way. Four years had passed since I'd last visited the psychiatric unit there, an overdose by Ellie the cause back then too. Before that, she had tried to hang herself in our family garage. Three suicide attempts: the first at eighteen, the next at twenty-one, and this, the most recent, at twenty-five. The motive for her latest one seemed obvious, even if my sister hadn't yet voiced the words. Pain rose within me, fierce enough to be almost physical, as my thoughts skated over the events of seven years ago. The night a phone call changed everything for the Hunter family.

Don't go there, I warned myself. *You need to be strong, for Ellie's sake.*

Once I entered the psychiatric unit, the twin odours of disinfectant and bleach hit my nostrils, along with the chilly temperature against my skin. Mum was waiting for me by the door to the locked ward when I arrived. Her complexion was dough-like in its pallor, the skin around her eyes creased with worry. She had aged five years in the three months since my last visit home. Mostly in the past twenty-four hours, no doubt.

'Lydia,' she murmured, before she pulled me into a hug. Her body was stiff with worry against mine. 'Thank God you're here.' Her voice shook, and tears pooled in her eyes. With one hand, she brushed them away, the movement angry, hurried, and reproach squeezed my heart. I should have stayed in England, not left her to cope with Ellie on her own. But my sister had seemed so positive, as though she'd turned the proverbial corner. She'd even mentioned she'd met a man, that they were dating, when we'd last spoken on the phone. A monumental step forward for her. No wonder I'd assumed she was on the road to recovery.

'How is she?' I asked.

Mum shook her head. 'About the same.'

'Still not talking?'

'She keeps asking for you. Apart from that, not a word.'

At that moment a doctor appeared. 'Mrs Hunter,' he said, his gaze on my mother. He flashed her a perfunctory smile, then another at me. 'And you must be Lydia.' He tapped in the entrance code to the ward, Mum and I following him through the double doors. To my left, I glimpsed my sister, lying in bed, her back to us. She made no attempt to turn around when we entered.

'We can talk later, after you've had a chance to speak with her,' the doctor said. 'I'll leave you to it.'

I walked around the bed, leaving Mum on the other side. Ellie's appearance shocked me, even though I didn't expect bright eyes and rosy cheeks. I'd seen her after her two earlier suicide attempts and I knew she'd look rough. Her blonde hair was a tangle of pale straw, her skin dry and sallow. Dark bruises of exhaustion sat under her lower lids. She seemed shrunken, curled in on herself, as if to occupy the least amount of space possible. I'd always felt something of an Amazon beside my petite sister - an impression heightened by the small figure under the bedsheets. What I wasn't prepared for were her eyes. They were blank, a dark nothingness in her soft brown irises. Fear squeezed my lungs, wouldn't let go.

I knelt before her, took her hands in mine. 'Why, Ellie?' As if I didn't already know.

She dropped her gaze, for which I was thankful. That deadpan expression scared me to the bone. In my peripheral vision, I saw Mum draw up a chair beside her daughter, a sigh of weariness escaping her. She knew better than to interrupt, aware my sister might talk more readily to me than to her. If Ellie talked at all, that was.

My fingers slid over her clammy hands, noting the contrast between them and mine. Over the years she'd chewed her nails into tiny nubs, the skin around them raw and ragged.

'Talk to me.' I wouldn't mention the car crash, not yet. The words would have lashed my sister like a whip. Wasn't she already in enough torment? Nevertheless, the image of Alyson's bloodied body forced its way into my mind.

'Please, Ellie.'

She didn't say a word. A thick cloak of tension hung around us, my sister's eyes shut tight, her defences locked in place. I shot a glance at Mum. Her mouth was thin, the lips pressed together, as if to keep in check the multitude of questions that yearned to burst forth. Thank God. She wasn't always so restrained.

'I'm sorry, Els.' A sob escaped me. 'I wish I'd been there for you.' Still no response. Ellie remained silent, closed off. My one consolation was that neither Dad nor any of her grandparents were alive to witness her in a psychiatric unit again.

Despite my efforts, she didn't respond or even acknowledge my presence. After our allotted visiting time was up, we left her curled in her foetal huddle. Our mission was to find her doctor.

When we did, I didn't waste my energy on preamble. 'How long must she stay here?'

What he told us wasn't reassuring. Given Ellie's history of suicide attempts, her refusal to talk, she'd need to remain at the unit for the foreseeable future, until she no longer posed a threat to herself.

***

'I'm heading your way,' I told Caroline over the phone, after I'd kissed Mum goodbye.

'I'll rustle up some chocolate and crack open the wine. I'm guessing you could murder a drink.'

'Amen to that.' In the background, I heard movement, the sound of something being dropped. A muffled curse, the voice male. I stiffened. 'Richie's not with you, is he?'

A slight pause. 'Don't worry, lovey. He's on his way home. He'll be gone before you get here.'

Thank God. I was too shattered to deal with Caroline's brother. Or the bittersweet memories he evoked.

Within half an hour, I'd parked my rental car outside my friend's house in Bishopston. As I walked towards the front door it opened and Caroline appeared in the gap. She rushed towards me, engulfing me in a hug. Always the demonstrative one out of the two of us, Caroline with her easy-going warmth posed a contrast to my typically British reserve. For a long moment, I soaked in her embrace, allowing her arms to wash away my sister's blank gaze. Then, all too soon, the horror of it swept over me again.

She pulled back to look at me, and I drank her in. She was my opposite in so many ways, more like Ellie than me. A pixie to my Amazon, the strength of her personality belied by her physical fragility. Our only similarities lay in our chocolate-hued eyes and wayward hair, although hers was a dark caramel, mine more honey-toned.

'You're the spitting image of my friend Lyddie.' She flashed me a grin. 'That miserable cow deserted me for Spain, though.'

I laughed. 'Driven there by your nonsense, you daft bat.'

'I miss you so much.' Affection shone from her eyes. 'It's fecking good to see you.' Although Bristolian to the core, Caroline had acquired a few speech tics from her Irish grandfather. 'You're here now, though, so you are. Come in, lovey.'

I followed her into her living room, noting the bottle of Malbec on the coffee table, the two glasses. Our houses were as dissimilar as our personalities; Caroline's an explosion of African wood and Oriental textiles in shades of brown, blue and red, a sharp contrast to my penchant for furnishings that came in white and silver from Ikea. I poured us both a generous measure of wine, knocking mine back in one go. Then I refilled my glass.

From the corner of my eye, I spotted a leather jacket slung over an armchair. Not my friend's - her tastes ran to silk, velvet, cashmere. Richie's, I presumed, left by mistake when he hurried off home. As keen to avoid me as I was him.

I clamped down hard on that line of thought.

'Make yourself comfy.' Caroline sank into one of her huge armchairs, her feet tucked under her bottom, gesturing at the sofa opposite. I followed suit, my feet mirroring hers. It had been that way between us forever, or so it seemed. Sometimes I forgot where I ended and Caroline began, despite our differences.

'So,' she said. 'Spill the beans. How's Ellie?'

'Not good. I don't get it. When we last talked, she seemed so happy.'

Caroline sipped from her glass, her expression thoughtful. 'Wasn't she back working part-time as a store assistant?'

'Yes. Her website was doing well, too.' A while ago, with my help, Ellie had set up an online shop for her custom-made handbags and wallets. Her sewing abilities had always astounded me. By her teenage years she was creating gorgeous bags and purses, each one a masterpiece, her embroidery exquisite in its detail. Once I'd shown her the basics, she'd surprised me with how well she handled running her own business.

'Any idea what caused it this time?' Caroline asked.

'She's not talking. The usual, I suppose. I doubt she'll ever get over Alyson's death.' The knotted rope, the two overdoses – they all led back to the car crash.

Caroline stood up, breaking the tension. 'Feck, I forgot the chocolate. Back in a minute.' She headed towards the kitchen.

I leaned back in my chair and closed my eyes, my mind flitting over the events of seven years ago. Our parents had given Ellie a course of driving lessons for her eighteenth birthday. She'd needed three attempts to pass her test, becoming sick with nerves before each one. After she managed to get through, Dad bought her a used Nissan, along with the insurance and tax. I worried every time she drove it, but kept my fears to myself. Had she known, Ellie would have misinterpreted my concern as further proof she was a failure.

Back then I'd been waiting for the results of my final accountancy exams. The day I got the notification that I'd passed, I felt as though the world had knelt at my feet, begging me to conquer it. I saw myself being promoted at work, painting in my spare time and maybe even earning money from my art one day. Life was sweet. Until Dad's mobile rang just before ten o'clock that night.

Ellie had been involved in a serious accident while driving. She'd lost control of her car, ploughed off the road and into a tree. A broken collar-bone and three shattered ribs were the result, but what concerned her doctors more was the extent of her head injuries; a fractured skull, inter-cranial bleeding, damage to her front temporal lobe. The latter, thank God, had been slight. Her neurologist explained the likely effects of her brain injury, how any change would be permanent but not extensive.

And change she did. The effects were subtle, but noticeable. Always shy and lacking in confidence, Ellie withdrew even further into herself. Her behaviour turned erratic, impulsive at times. She also became evasive, prone to distort the truth. On a day-to-day level she coped fine, but bigger issues tended to derail her. As for the car crash, she swore she'd swerved to avoid an oncoming vehicle, the driver of which had rounded a bend too fast and on the wrong side of the road. No witnesses came forward to disprove her story, but her manner told me she was lying. Whatever took place that night, Ellie hadn't driven since. I doubted she ever would.

She'd fared better than her passenger, though. When she awoke from her coma, Dad faced the grim job of breaking the news that Alyson Hart, Ellie's best friend, had died in the crash.

Caroline breezed back in, tossing a slab of dark chocolate onto my lap. She settled into her armchair again, breaking a chunk off her own bar. 'So what will happen next with Ellie?'

I released a long slow breath. 'We'll have to wait until she's allowed to leave Southmead. When she does, I'm hoping she'll be more forthcoming.'

'You'll think she'll open up to you? Given enough time?'

'Yes.' Ellie had operated that way after the last two suicide attempts. Stony silence at first, followed by a deluge of words. We'd talked for hours, Ellie's insecurities pouring forth along with her pain. I'd listened, and I'd tried to help her, but clearly my efforts hadn't been sufficient.

I sucked in a breath. 'I suppose Alyson's death might not be the reason she tried to kill herself. Maybe things went wrong with this guy she's been dating.' Too late, I realised I'd not told Caroline that particular detail.

Surprise flickered across her face. 'Ellie was seeing someone?'

'She didn't tell me much when we spoke on the phone. Just that she'd met a guy. That they'd become an item.'

'How long had that been going on?'

'A couple of months. She clammed up when I probed too hard. I admit I was concerned. What with how she is.'

'Ah, feck. You were worried it might end badly.'

'Yes.' I exhaled the tension I'd been holding. 'She'd never cope with getting dumped.'

'Has your mother met this guy? He wasn't at the hospital, then?'

'No, to both. Mum doesn't realise Ellie's been dating someone. You know how interfering she can be. Ellie didn't mention anything to her, and asked me not to.'

'Will you tell her?'

'It depends. On whether I can get Ellie to talk, I mean. Maybe this guy had nothing to do with her suicide attempt.'

'He's not exactly playing the concerned boyfriend, though, is he?' Caroline drained her wine. 'I suspect you're right. He must have broken up with her, and she couldn't cope with the rejection.'

My protective instincts arose full-force. If that was how it happened, I wanted to kill the bastard with the nearest blunt instrument.

A brittle laugh escaped my friend. 'And you wonder why I stick two fingers up to monogamy. Who needs that shit?'

My eyes strayed to the photo on the windowsill. Richie, his dark hair in a ponytail, his smile radiating from the silver frame with the force of a thousand suns. *I do*, I thought.

I'd almost had it, too. Until I ruined everything.

Caroline must have noticed the direction of my gaze. 'You can't avoid him forever.'

I didn't trust myself to speak.

'You do realise he's never got over you?'

'Don't.' Impossible to deal with that comment.

Caroline seemed to sense my withdrawal. 'You look exhausted, lovey. Forget any daft notions about driving home, especially after half a bottle of wine. You're staying here tonight.'

***

Later in bed at Caroline's, Ellie's pale face haunted me. Despite my fatigue, I couldn't relax. Instead, I lay against my pillows, my shoulders tight with tension. Had I really been in Spain that same morning, a brush between my fingers, lost in painting another seascape? When I'd return to Andalucía, and my art, was anyone's guess. Both Ellie and Mum needed me, and I'd not let them down. I wouldn't book my flight back until I was convinced my sister wasn't suicidal anymore.

I remembered I needed to arrange with Mum about visiting Ellie in the morning. With that in mind, I sent her a text.

Within seconds, my phone rang, her name flashing on the screen. 'Lydia,' she said when I answered. 'Are you okay?'

'Yeah, I'm fine. Just peachy.' Irritation edged into my voice. What did she expect? No, I *wasn't* fine; Ellie had almost killed herself yet again. If Mum hadn't come round when she did ... and with that thought my anger faded. She'd saved my sister's life, the same as both previous times Ellie had attempted suicide. Mum and I might be fellow control freaks who often grew prickly around each other, but I'd never doubted her love for me. Or for Ellie.

'I've no idea how to help Eleanor anymore,' she said, despair in every syllable.

I already had a plan for that. 'I'm going to take her to the cottage.'

Memories of Devon washed over me. Our favourite walk along the cliff top. The steps to the tiny beach. Seagulls screeching as they whirled above our heads. If anywhere could heal my sister, it would be our family holiday cottage.

'That's a great idea,' Mum said. 'With any luck, she'll confide in you why she got so unhappy again.'

'Yes. Although whether she tells me the whole story is another matter.' No disagreement from my mother on that front. Both of us were familiar with Ellie's tendency to skirt around uncomfortable truths, to lie outright on occasions. Not that she was dishonest by nature - lying was the coping mechanism she'd adopted over the last seven years. Used whenever she believed, wrongly of course, that her family might think the worst of her.

'I wish you'd move back to the UK, Lydia. It's not right, you being so far away. Not with Eleanor the way she is.'

My mother was on a roll. 'You can't tell me you wouldn't be better off here. Your former boss would snap you up in an instant if you asked for your job back.'

'Not going to happen.' I took a deep breath, pinching the bridge of my nose, while reminding myself Mum didn't mean to be overbearing. I'd had a gutful over the years of her attempts to control me, though. Besides, I'd established a life for myself in Spain. My villa, all pink tiles and whitewashed walls, its tiny courtyard fringed with almond trees. The annexe containing the art gallery I'd worked so hard to set up. My burgeoning career as a painter.

'I'll talk to you tomorrow.' Cutting my mother short, I ended the call. I still struggled to sleep, though. Somehow I had to coax Ellie to reveal what had prompted her latest suicide attempt. Unless my sister got to grips with her mental health issues, chances were one day she'd succeed in killing herself. She'd struggled with depression for years. Her self-esteem, along with her confidence, had always been patchy, but since the car crash both had been non-existent. Her first suicide attempt came just two months afterwards.

'I killed my best friend,' she had sobbed against my shoulder. 'I deserve to die. Can't you understand that?'

Back then I'd grasped the depth of her despair, sure, but it hurt on multiple levels. The accident wrenched a chasm between us; we'd been close once and I missed the easy affection we used to share. Six years her elder, I'd always been fiercely protective where Ellie was concerned. When she'd been at school, I'd loved playing the supportive older sibling, aware she'd never attain the same level of academic success I'd achieved. In the evenings I'd tutor her with her maths and correct her homework, happy to help. No matter that she'd failed most of her exams, I'd always told myself. As her big sister, I'd be there whenever she needed me. Hadn't I promised Dad I'd look out for her?

And I would. Whatever it took. I'd set her world to rights. The alternative was unthinkable.

'I won't let you down, Els,' I whispered into the darkness.

CHAPTER 2

It took several days before her doctors judged Ellie fit to be released, and only then because I promised to look after her. She left Southmead medicated, pale and withdrawn. But at least she was talking, even if sporadically and only to me. Our mother looked every bit as haggard as her daughter. I'd noticed her hands trembling earlier, the way she stumbled as we left the ward. She was in no state to care for Ellie.

Hence my decision to do so myself. My sister would stay with me that night, and tomorrow we'd drive to Devon. We'd stroll along the cliff path, eat fish and chips in the local pub and at some point she'd tell me why she'd tried to kill herself. One way or another, I'd prise the truth from her. Failure was not an option.

'I'll call you tonight,' I promised Mum after I dropped her off at our family home in Sneyd Park. In the back of the rental car, Ellie remained silent, closed off.

'Want to sit up front with me?' I asked, but she shook her head. I decided not to press the issue. Given the accident, I judged it a miracle she'd even ride in a car.

It didn't take long before we arrived in Kingswood, at the house I'd bought six years ago, persuaded by my rising salary as an accountant to purchase a property. I pushed my key into the lock, safe in the knowledge that Amelia would be at work. She'd been my lodger well before Andalucía became more than a distant fantasy, and I was happy for her to stay, despite the higher rents I could command if I let the house in its entirety. It suited me to know my room was still available whenever I returned to Bristol.

Ellie looked lost, standing in the hallway, her expression blank. I squeezed my arm around her shoulders. 'Let's get your stuff upstairs, then we'll eat. We'll leave first thing tomorrow.' I'd allow her no choice in the matter. The fewer decisions she needed to make, the better. I judged it best not to discuss her suicide attempt that night. She was still too raw, too bruised, and the timing wasn't right.

That evening, over the steak supper I'd cooked, Ellie seemed less withdrawn, which gave me a measure of comfort. Once we finished eating, she began - her voice hesitant - to ask me questions. I sensed her desperation to keep any probing into her own life at bay. No problem. I could respect that. For the time being.

'How's the art gallery going?' she enquired.

I shrugged. Our father had left Mum, and his two daughters, financially secure after his fatal heart attack four years ago. Before he died I'd been unsure whether I possessed enough talent to make painting my primary occupation. The inheritance money offered me the choice, although I continued to dither. Two years later, spurred on by my failed relationship with Richie Maston, I quit accountancy for life under the fierce Andalucían sun. My legacy from Dad, which I'd invested with care, subsidised my life in Spain, as did Amelia's rent, meaning I didn't need to make a profit from my art to stay afloat. So far I had no regrets, despite Mum's wish for me to return.

'Ticking over. There are dozens of retired ex-pats in Andalucía, all keen to depict the local landscape.' I laughed. 'I'm not likely to run out of stock anytime soon. And I'm painting lots myself.'

'Do you think ...' Ellie paused. 'That you'll ever come back?' The hope in her voice hung in the air between us.

When I didn't reply, she continued her probing. 'It was because of Richie Maston, wasn't it? Why you moved to Spain, I mean?'

'Not something I want to discuss.' My tone had been too abrupt, and she flinched. Ellie had hit a sore spot, though. My engagement to Caroline's brother hadn't ended well. Not the only reason I'd gone to Spain, but the main one.

'He was part of it,' I admitted. 'But I also wanted to paint and try life in a different country. Besides, I'd had a bellyful of figures. All that time spent poring over balance sheets, when what

I yearned to do was earn my living as an artist. I'm not there yet. But I'm getting closer.'

She smiled, her lips unmatched by her eyes, and I sensed she'd endured all the small talk she could manage for one evening. 'You look shattered,' I said. 'Why don't you get an early night?'

'Good idea. I'll see you in the morning.'

Once I was alone, Richie Maston refused to quit my thoughts. Two years had passed since I'd last seen him, our parting filled with hurt on both sides. I'd known Richie since I turned eleven, but back then he was simply Caroline's older sibling. After university he emigrated to Australia, but returned to live in the UK when his father's health declined. One day I went to visit Caroline and Richie was there, and blow me if he hadn't turned into a rock god, minus the musical career. In my eyes, anyway. His dark hair, soft smile and oh-so-blue eyes reeled me in like a fish on a hook, the attraction on my side instant. On his too, it seemed. He called the next day to ask me for a date.

Things moved with lightning speed after that. We'd discussed marriage, the number of children we'd have, growing old together. For the first few months of our relationship, I couldn't have been happier.

After a while, though, events from my past conspired to destroy our bliss. The man I adored told me he loved me, but we no longer had a future together. Caroline took the news well, despite her disappointment. From what she said, I deduced Richie hadn't told her why he'd broken off our engagement, and I didn't either, too ashamed of the way I'd acted.

Tears stung my eyes, and I realised the wound was still raw.

***

The August sunshine penetrated my bedroom curtains early the following morning. As I showered, dressed and cooked breakfast, hope crept into my mood. Ellie's latest suicide attempt seemed different to the previous two. This time she'd reached out to Mum before swallowing the pills, something she'd not done before. A cry for help, then, rather than a genuine desire for oblivion.

In addition, she'd recovered faster this time. Everything considered, I judged I had good reasons for my optimism. Later that day we'd drive to Devon, and I'd do my best to heal my damaged sister.

We set off at eleven. The journey didn't take long, not on a weekday morning with sparse traffic. By the time we arrived on the south coast, so had one o'clock, and the sun beat fiercely on my skin once I exited the car. Ellie remained in the passenger seat. She'd not spoken a word on the way, but I wasn't bothered. Wasn't it enough to have her alive and in my care, instead of catatonic in a psychiatric ward?

I walked round to open her door. 'Come on, Els. In you go. I'll fix lunch for us.' She stood up, moving like an automaton to the boot of the car to retrieve her suitcase. While she did, I leaned against the bonnet, the wind whipping my hair around my face. Above me, seagulls circled, the harshness of their squawks familiar and welcome. In front of me was the Hunter family cottage.

Its size always reminded me of an inflated dolls' house. Two bedrooms and a bathroom were squeezed under the roof, the middle of which bowed more each year. Underneath were tucked a living room, kitchen and pantry. A sheen of lichen slicked green over the tiles around the chimney. The paint on the windowsills was recent - its soft blue a reminder of the nearby sea and a contrast to the bare oak door. Tiny gardens bordered by low fences sat behind and in front, with rose bushes straggling over the wooden posts. Off to one side stood a small woodshed.

To my sister and me, the cottage had always represented safety, fun, good times - the perfect place in which she could recuperate. The location was hard to find, its remoteness offering total privacy. Dad had bought the place after my birth once he'd persuaded Mum his investment banker salary could afford it, pointing out it would be fantastic for family holidays. And he'd been right. After his death, Mum had kept it and I didn't need to ask why. She loved the cottage as much as Ellie and I did.

By the time we'd unpacked and settled in, it was after two o'clock. Ellie continued her silence over a late lunch, a simple affair of salad, cheese and fruit. I'd packed enough food to see us through today, but we'd need to visit Torquay tomorrow to pick up more. Once we'd finished eating, I donned my bossy-older-sister mantle. 'Come on. We're going for a walk.'

Ellie complied without a word. After we left the cottage, we headed towards the cliff top, our destination the beach below. We proceeded in silence along the narrow path that led there, our arms entwined. Brambles scratched my face, tangled in my jeans, the wind lashing my hair again. The smell of the sea grew stronger once we approached the stone stile at the end of the track. On the other side of it, grass extended to the cliff edge, a sign warning walkers not to venture too close. In front of us, steps led to a tiny inlet - its rocky shoreline and pebble beach little incentive for holidaymakers to descend their stony steepness. Few tourists ever came that way. The route was unmarked, difficult to find and too short to interest potential ramblers. Most preferred the longer marked trail that meandered east from Torquay. The beach became our private haven back when we were children, and I hoped its tranquillity might encourage her to open up to me.

Once at the bottom, we sat on our favourite rock, a flat-topped monstrosity big enough to allow us to stretch our legs out in front of us. The sound of the tide washing against the pebbles was soft in my ears, a rhythmic *one-two* interspersed by the noise of the gulls overhead. Sheltered as we were by the cliff, the wind was a gentle breeze, no more, against my skin. In that moment nobody but us existed.

I wrapped my arm around Ellie, bringing her head to rest against mine. She seemed so frail, a dandelion clock that might blow away in the next puff of wind.

'Talk to me,' I whispered into her hair. 'What was so terrible you couldn't pick up the phone and tell me?'

A sob shook her body. 'You'll think me such a fool.'

'I won't judge you, Els.' I steeled myself - we couldn't discuss her suicide attempt without mentioning the car crash. 'Was it because of Alyson's death?'

She shook her head. I pulled her tighter, feeling her shoulders heave as she cried.

'What, then?'

She didn't reply at first. Just as I was weighing up how far to push her, her voice sounded out, so faint I struggled to hear it. 'I met a man. The one I told you about.'

So that was the reason. Caroline had been right, it seemed. The guy had decided to split up with her. Unable to deal with the rejection, she'd tried to kill herself. My poor Ellie.

'Tell me what happened.' I kept my tone soft, gentle. My sister was a frightened filly who might bolt if pressed too hard. 'You didn't say much when we spoke on the phone. Not that I didn't try to squeeze information out of you.' I laughed, but the sound rang hollow. 'Where did you meet him?'

She pulled away, fumbling in her sleeve for a tissue. Her eyes were red with crying, her nose pink and wet. 'Online.'

'On a dating website?'

She nodded. Surprise hit me. I wouldn't have pegged Ellie as having enough confidence to tackle internet dating. But then, I reflected, establishing contact that way might be easier for someone so nervous. Their relationship had clearly progressed beyond the keyboard and into the real world, however.

'I believed he was The One,' she whispered. 'His name was Steven. He talked about us living together, marriage if everything worked out. How was I to know?' Fresh sobs choked her, her anguish slicing my heart. Anger filled me at the dickhead who had made false promises to her. Had this Steven guy been in front of me, I'd have punched him, right on his lying mouth. The bastard's game plan wasn't hard to fathom; he'd been acting out the age-old story, one for which I'd fallen myself, long ago. Ellie, unused to the wiles of predatory males, must have tumbled into the same trap.

'He already had a wife, didn't he?' I murmured into her hair. 'Oh, Els. I'm so sorry you've had to suffer this crap.'

To my surprise, she shook her head. 'He wasn't married. Or if he was, I never knew. No girlfriend on the side, either.'

'Did he cheat on you? A one-night stand, perhaps?'

Another shake. 'No.'

'What, then?' But she was lost to me, drowning in her grief. Useless for me to press her further while she remained so raw, so wounded.

We stayed that way for hours, until the breeze turned chilly against my skin. The sun was starting to set, painting the horizon a delicate orange. My body had stiffened after sitting in one position for so long and I winced as I eased myself away from Ellie.

'Why don't we go to The Royal Oak for a drink?' I said. 'Remember how Dad used to love their beer garden?'

Her expression clouded, and my heart hurt for her. *Nice one, Lyddie*, I chided myself. I'd been tactless in mentioning our father, given her distress. Her grief over his death had been part of the reason for her second suicide attempt. No wonder she was crying again.

I was wrong though.

'He'd have been so ashamed of me.' I could hardly make out her words through her sobs. 'Furious, too.'

I was stunned. Always a besotted father, fiercely protective of Ellie after the car crash, Dad would not have been angry with her under any circumstances that I could imagine. 'Why, Els?'

'The money he left me. It's all gone.'

I couldn't think what she meant. Not all of it, surely? After the solicitor distributed Dad's estate, Ellie had bought a flat in St George, on my advice. Once the purchase went through, she'd been left with just over fifty thousand pounds, not a bad situation for a twenty-one-year-old to find herself in. She'd stuck the money in a savings account and still had most of it left. Or so I'd believed.

'Gone?' I queried. 'I don't understand.'

Her only response was a shiver. Shocked, I sat immobile, unable to speak for a while.

'Where? How?' I managed at last.

She raised her face, shame in her expression. 'Steven took it,' she said. 'Steven Simmons, the guy I've been dating.'

CHAPTER 3

Whatever I'd expected Ellie to say, it wasn't that. I stared at her in disbelief, unsure what she was telling me. 'You mean he stole it?'

'Yes. No. It's hard to explain.' I sensed she was close to breaking point. To have any hope of extracting the whole story, I needed to handle her with sensitivity. I schooled my face into a neutral expression and said nothing, waiting for her to continue.

'I gave him the money.' I was lost again. Why would she do that?

The wind blowing in off the sea grew stronger, causing me to shiver. I stood up, flexing my stiff legs. 'Let's go home.' I reached out a hand to help her. 'It's getting late, and we can talk better there.'

She didn't reply, just nodded. Together we walked back to the cottage.

'Come,' I said once we were inside, gesturing towards the sofa. She followed me without a word, and we sat next to each other on the worn hessian. Ellie seemed unable to look at me, the waves of shame pouring from her almost tangible. *I gave him the money.* A smidgen of suspicion crept into my mind. Might this Steven Simmons be a professional con artist?

'Tell me more about this guy,' I said.

She wiped away fresh tears. 'I was so lonely. Every night I watched television on my own. Outside of work, I never saw anyone except Mum. You only came back every few months.' I winced with guilt, even though I doubted she'd intended that comment as a rebuke. And her lack of friends had long been a concern of mine.

'I used to walk down the street and I'd see couples holding hands and I'd wonder whether I'd ever enjoy such happiness,' Ellie continued. 'I got bitter; I needed that for myself.' She swallowed a convulsive sob.

'You wanted a relationship.'

She nodded. 'Yes. But I didn't have a clue how to find one. Until I considered the internet.' She glanced at me, firing love for my damaged sister through my heart. She was so pretty, even with her blotchy cheeks and pink nose. When those eyes weren't red and swollen with tears, they were lovely - large and whisky-brown - and I'd have killed for skin as clear and soft as Ellie's. She didn't realise that men would fight for a chance to be with her.

'So you tried a dating website ...' I prompted.

'Yes. Soulmate Search, it was called. You needed to pay a lot for membership, and I liked that, because I wanted a guy who was serious about finding a partner. I decided I'd just look at first, maybe check out a few profiles. I didn't tell anyone, not even Mum.'

'You were embarrassed about joining?'

'Yes. Because I couldn't meet a man the usual way. Parties, mutual friends, that kind of thing.' She smiled, but her expression remained sad. 'I didn't even put up a profile picture. Too frightened someone might recognise me.'

'Did you get much response?'

'Loads of messages in the first week, but I didn't reply to any. They all seemed too pushy, asking to see my photo, saying they wanted to meet up straightaway, and it scared me. I almost deleted my profile.'

'But you didn't?'

'No. Right when I'd decided to quit the whole thing, I got a message. It was different to the others.'

'How so?'

'He seemed so sweet, not pushy at all. Like me, he didn't have an online picture.'

I bet, I thought sourly. Not if what I suspected was true. One less means of identifying the bastard. 'What did he say?'

'That he'd read my profile and decided I sounded lovely, someone he could relate to. He liked the fact our interests were so similar - books, poetry, plays. How he'd been hurt in his last relationship and had taken a while to recover. He said he was now ready to move on and find his soulmate. Steven was older than me - thirty - but I didn't mind that. What's five years, anyway? He suggested we swap messages for a while, and when I felt comfortable with the idea, we could meet for coffee.'

The fact our interests were so similar. Had my sister met a man who tailored his approach based on whatever gullible female caught his attention? Perhaps I was jumping to conclusions. Wouldn't any prospective date highlight areas of mutual interest?

'We chatted online most days after that,' Ellie continued. 'He seemed so kind, so caring. I told him about Dad dying, and he said his own father passed away when he was nine. How he missed him, always would.'

The suspicion I'd harboured earlier grew in strength. A neat ploy, one designed to show common ground and build sympathy. No doubt interspersed with a few well-chosen questions about Ellie's inheritance.

'Steven understood about my mental health problems too,' Ellie said. 'He told me his aunt had suffered from head trauma, like me, as well as depression. He was always so easy to talk to, no matter what we discussed. When he suggested meeting up, I agreed, even though I was nervous. And when I met him - oh, God.' More tears.

'I don't know why he didn't upload a photo,' she said once she'd stopped crying. 'But I'm glad he didn't. Less competition for me. So handsome, he was.'

That made sense. Any con artist would be more George Clooney than Willem Dafoe.

'His eyes were the most amazing shade of blue,' Ellie continued. 'His hair was long and dark, almost black, and so soft I wanted to run my fingers through it the second we met. And his smile - I swear it could outshine Las Vegas. I was hooked from the first time I saw him.'

'What about his personality?'

'He seemed confident, more so than I'd expected. Not in a cocky way, though. Just sure of himself, which appealed to me. Like he was strong, someone I could lean on. We ordered coffee, and we chatted, and I felt so lucky to have found such a wonderful man. I was amazed that he seemed to like me too.'

'So you started dating him?'

'Yes. And he was so gentle, so considerate. He never pressured me, not once.' Embarrassment flushed her cheeks. 'About - well, you know.'

'So the two of you didn't ...?'

'No. I wanted to, but was too scared. He said it was natural for me to be nervous, how he understood my hesitation.'

Too right he did. Because it wasn't sex the bastard was after, was it?

I squeezed her close. 'You don't have to tell me. Not if it's too painful.' At least Ellie hadn't slept with this man. To the best of my knowledge she was still a virgin. Unusual at twenty-five, but not unknown. Before the car crash, she'd been too shy to date. Afterwards she'd been too damaged.

She shook her head. 'There's not much to say on that score. We agreed to wait until we knew each other better.'

'And he was okay with that?'

'Yes. We seemed so in tune. He told me he loved me, how he hoped we'd always be together. And I believed him. How stupid is that?'

'Did you tell him you loved him too?'

Ellie nodded. 'I still do, in spite of everything.' More sobs. 'I keep going over it in my head. Hoping there must be a rational explanation. That he'll call me soon. Except I know he won't.' Her body shook with anguish.

Anger flared inside me. No wonder my fragile sister had attempted suicide. She'd done so well in recent years: finding part-time work, running her online shop and starting to date. The world had begun to knit together for her at last.

Then, without warning, her fairy-tale romance had crumbled to dust. The humiliation must have been so crushing that death seemed the only solution.

'He was so charismatic,' Ellie said. 'He'd look at me with those blue eyes, and that smile, and I'd melt. I began to fantasise about the life we'd have together.'

Just like I'd done with Gary McIlroy.

Don't go there, I warned myself. 'So when did it all go wrong?'

She gulped back a sob. 'We went to Cornwall one weekend - a holiday cottage close to St Ives. The place had two bedrooms, and he insisted I take the big one at the front while he slept in the back. All the while I expected him to hassle me about sex, and dreading it, because I still wasn't ready. Steven was the perfect gentleman though. That was when I realised I loved him.'

'Did he ask for money that weekend?'

'Not in so many words. He told me he was building a holiday complex nearby. His business was in property developing, or so he said. I guess that was all lies too. We went to where his company was planning to start work. The plot was fenced off, with a sign warning the public to keep out. I had no reason to suspect the site wasn't his.'

'Of course you didn't.'

'He told me he was concerned the complex might not go ahead. Mentioned he'd incurred huge expenses already, that the project was likely to exceed its budget. He seemed so worried, and I believed him.'

'That's when he hinted he needed money?'

'Yes. He told me he was cutting costs by employing labourers off the books. Illegal immigrants who needed to keep a low profile, he said. How everything would be fine if he could get his hands on some cash to pay them, then the building work could start. But he couldn't use the money in his bank account as then he'd have to account for it. And he didn't have any spare funds of his own after pumping every penny he possessed into the company.'

'So you offered to lend him money.'

She nodded. 'He seemed taken aback. Almost offended. Told me he couldn't take my savings, that it wouldn't be right. The more I insisted, the more he refused.'

Of course he did. The man sounded a professional at his game.

'In the end he said yes. He asked for ten thousand pounds, swore he'd repay me as soon as possible. I told him I'd give him the cash straight after I'd been to my bank.'

Clever, I thought. No trail leading from Ellie's finances to his, not like with an online transfer. 'He asked you for more money afterwards?'

'Yes. Every week, saying he needed to pay his workers. He explained that most of the costs on a construction project came at the start, but how he'd soon be able to sell units off-plan and repay me with interest. He promised to take me to the Caribbean to thank me for being so supportive.' She sobbed against my shoulder. The ache in my heart bordered on painful.

'How did you discover the truth?'

'He dumped me after I gave him the last chunk of cash,' Ellie said. 'I lost fifty thousand pounds, all my savings.' She pulled away, fishing in her bag for a tissue.

'I'm guessing you never saw him again?'

She shook her head. 'He didn't call, or text, and when I tried to get in touch, he never replied. Wouldn't answer any of my messages. I persuaded myself he'd lost his phone or forgotten to charge it. After three days I was beside myself with worry. I pictured him dead, or unconscious in hospital. I couldn't even contact him via the dating website. He'd deleted his profile.'

'What about going to where he lived?'

'I didn't know the address. How stupid is that? He told me he owned a flat in Clifton, but he always came to my place, because of me not driving.'

Another manipulative tactic - to mention living in the poshest part of Bristol. His ploy was clearly to paint a picture of a successful businessman, albeit one with short-term financial problems. I hated the prick.

Ellie drew in a long breath. 'Eventually I realised I'd been suckered. And it hurt like hell.'

My poor sister. I'd remembered a television documentary I'd once watched about con artists. The programme highlighted how men like Steven Simmons sought out women to use as cash machines by playing on their insecurities. Some victims that were interviewed had lost as much as half a million pounds. All of them appeared bewildered, as though unable to understand what had happened. Most said they still loved their ex. At the time, I'd found their gullibility an embarrassment to my gender. Right then, with my beloved sister a victim, the only emotion I felt was empathy. Hadn't I also been hoodwinked by a man, albeit in different circumstances? Who was I to judge?

All the women included in the documentary said they were reluctant to involve the law. I wondered if Ellie had ever contemplated such a course of action. Probably not. Too damaged, too raw, she decided on suicide instead.

I needed to ask though. 'Did you consider going to the police? What he did was fraud, Els. This guy should be in prison.'

'No.' Emotion choked her voice. 'Hadn't I been humiliated enough? I couldn't bear the idea of telling some police officer how gullible I'd been. The shame of it, Lyddie. Mum would be so disappointed. Dad too, if he were alive. That's why ...' She swallowed, and I realised what was coming. 'I didn't want to live anymore. Everything hurt too much.'

Silence filled the room for a minute.

'You won't tell Mum? Please, Lyddie. She must never know.'

I agreed. Our mother lacked a filter on her tongue, and I didn't trust her not to wound Ellie further. 'I won't say a word.'

'It's all right for you,' Ellie burst out. 'Fifty thousand pounds wouldn't wipe you out the way it has me. You're smart with your finances, whereas I'm not. I don't have a clue about stock market investments and all that stuff.'

She was right. Financial skills were my forte, not hers, but that could be changed. What was that saying about teaching a man to fish, thus feeding him for a lifetime?

'I've lost everything. With no hope of getting it back.' Her shoulders hunched in defeat.

Manipulation wasn't Ellie's style. She wouldn't realise her words sounded like a plea for money. Nevertheless I almost offered.

'I'll help you,' I said. 'We'll go through your finances, see where you can cut costs, make changes. I'll get you through this, I promise.'

Ellie stood up, her mouth tight. She looked exhausted. 'I'm going to bed.'

After she'd gone I poured myself a whisky, allowing its smoky taste to soothe my soul. My preference in alcohol might be unusual for a thirty-something woman, but I had Dad to thank for that. He'd first introduced me to the delights of a decent single malt on my eighteenth birthday; my first few sips made me shudder and I'd endured them out of sheer stubbornness. In time I learned to love the fiery taste. Dad and I often set the world to rights over shots of Lagavulin. God, how I missed him.

Glass in hand, I sat on the sofa and mulled over what Ellie had said about Steven Simmons. She'd been foolish, I didn't deny that, too besotted to realise that her gallant knight's armour was dirty and corroded. How could I blame her, though? It wasn't her fault, given her brain injury and mental health issues. The bastard had tricked a vulnerable woman into handing over her savings, and if what I suspected was true, he'd have conned other victims as well.

Anger burned inside me at how Steven Simmons had walked away without a twinge of conscience. His behaviour was all kinds of wrong – criminal, in fact. I loathed him, and not just because he'd driven my sister to attempt suicide.

Impossible to deny that my own pain was helping to fuel my fury. Hadn't I also been a victim of a con artist? Oh, I'd not lost any money to Gary McIlroy. The bastard stole my heart instead, and with it, my self-respect. We dated for six months, during which time I plummeted headlong into love. Gary possessed a faulty memory, though. So bad he forgot to tell me he had a wife. My world shattered into fragments so small I didn't think I'd ever piece them together again. Throughout one long, dark night I considered suicide. Some instinct of self-preservation saved me, after which I locked my emotions in a metaphorical cage and threw away the key.

And then Richie returned to Bristol, and the bars around my heart melted. Gary had ruined me where other men were concerned, though. As my love for Richie grew, so did my insecurity. I knew he wasn't married, thanks to my friendship with Caroline, but I still couldn't accept he was mine. Everywhere I looked, women slimmer and prettier than me posed a threat. I interrogated him about where he was going, his friends, his work colleagues. One evening he caught me snooping through his phone, and our relationship ended that night.

'I love you, Lyddie,' he told me, anguish in his eyes. 'But if you don't trust me, we can't be together.'

So, thanks to the damage inflicted by Gary McIlroy, I lost Richie. In the light of Ellie's revelations, all the hurt came crashing back. My sister and I had both been conned, just in different ways. The only difference was that Ellie's heartbreak came with a fifty-thousand-pound price tag. In both cases, the bastard concerned got off scot-free. Not how it should be, in my opinion.

Caroline often said I had a downer on men. She was right - the rotten, cheating ones, anyway. An idea was gathering force in my brain. One that involved revenge, retribution, justice.

CHAPTER 4

I didn't sleep much that night. Instead, I lay in bed, rehashing what Ellie had told me, fury blazing in my belly. I thought of one of the women interviewed on the documentary I'd watched. Wasn't she conned by a guy she met on a dating website? A premium-price site provided an obvious hunting ground to prey on lonely well-heeled women. It made sense for swindlers to source their victims online; that way such men could hide behind any mask they chose.

And now one of them had hurt my sister. My father's voice came into my head. Once we'd been warned by Ellie's doctors of the effect the temporal lobe damage might have, he'd taken me aside, his expression serious.

'Promise me you'll look out for her,' he'd said.

'Haven't I always?'

'Yes. And I love you for that. Now, though ...' He'd shaken his head. 'She'll need you more than ever.'

'I'll be there for her,' I'd said. 'I swear.'

Guilt shot through me as I recalled our conversation. No matter how well Ellie had appeared, I shouldn't have left her to cope alone. I was back in Bristol again though, and it was time to keep the commitment I'd made. My sister needed me, and I'd look out for her the way I'd promised. If that included administering vengeance to her ex, that was fine with me.

When the red numbers on my bedside clock showed the time as 3am and I'd still not fallen asleep, I gave up the attempt. Instead, I swung my feet out of bed, making for my laptop sitting on the desk under the window. Once online, I searched for the dating website Ellie had used. Soulmate Search, wasn't it?

She was right; it appeared a cut above the meat-market mentality of the freebie sites. I didn't think I'd find Steven Simmons on it, though. Hadn't she told me he'd deleted his profile? He must have shifted his focus to a different site. With that in mind, I typed 'premium dating websites' into Google.

The top result was called Premier Love Matches. I clicked the link and scanned the homepage. Similar in style to Soulmate Search, it touted itself as offering 'a quality service for the discerning seeker after love' and required a sizable set-up fee and monthly charge. Members had to complete a questionnaire together with a personality profile, both designed to persuade them they stood the best possible chance of finding love among Premier's clientele. The site also allowed searching and filtering of profiles before joining. That made sense - few people would sign up unless they could view the goods on offer.

I drew in a deep breath, preparing to look for the bastard who had shattered my sister's heart.

I kept my parameters wide, figuring that if he was still in the South West, he'd prefer a different poaching ground for his next target. I chose a radius of forty miles around Bristol, searching for a dark-haired male between twenty-eight and thirty-five. A few seconds after I clicked the 'search' button, dozens of results filled my screen.

Most of them I dismissed at once. All those with a profile picture, for example; Ellie had said this man operated without one. That left seven possibilities. I clicked on the top one and skimmed though it. It didn't take long to discount the guy. An insurance broker, widowed with one son, his interests lay in football and camping. Not how a con artist would portray himself. I also discarded the next four after reading them. Two of them claimed to be divorced and one had a profile so badly written it could only attract a dictionary. And the last guy stated he preferred casual relationships. None of them appeared to be my target.

The next one seemed a possibility despite living in Bristol, which didn't fit with Steven Simmons shifting his game further afield.

He called himself Scott, user name Scotty123, but I didn't expect Ellie's ex to have kept the same name. The bastard would already have morphed into his new persona. This guy listed his profession as middle management, but the rest of his profile was sparse, citing his interests as art, music, travel and sport. A wide enough net to capture most women.

The final line caught my eye. Scotty123 mentioned being ready to move on after a failed relationship, how what he wanted was to find Ms Right. His profile ended with '*why don't we meet over coffee?*'

Weren't those similar words to the ones that hooked Ellie? Many profiles used near-identical wording, though. I clicked on the final one, that of Looking For Love.

This guy appeared a far better prospect. He gave his name as Liam and his age as thirty, the same as Steven Simmons. Tall, almost black hair, blue eyes. He listed his location as Charlcombe, not far from Bath, within easy distance of Bristol. What caught my eye was his occupation; he'd ticked 'construction and property development'. While I understood Ellie's ex would use a new name each time, I thought his method unlikely to change. Easier that way, fewer lies to remember. As for his spiel, it was well-written, designed to portray Mr Nice Guy who wanted to find his princess and make her his wife. As proven by the answer to the 'seeking' question. He had ticked 'marriage', not 'long-term relationship' or 'casual fun'.

As with Scotty123, the final line of his profile snagged my attention.

'*I got my heart broken in my last relationship,*' he wrote, '*but I'm now ready to move on and find my soulmate! Could it be you? Let's talk over coffee!*'

Soulmate, that was it, not Ms Right - the word Ellie said Steven Simmons used on his profile. It had stuck in my mind, given the name of the site she'd joined. His other wording was similar, too. From what I could see, this guy Liam was the best match to my sister's con man.

I hesitated, unsure whether I should take this any further. The clues I'd found on Liam's profile were tenuous, easy to explain.

Lots of men worked in construction and property development. And didn't most people on dating websites claim to be searching for their true love? Wasn't an invitation to coffee a common ice-breaker? None of it meant anything by itself.

And yet it might mean everything if Looking For Love was the bastard who'd hurt my sister. If he was, I planned to take him down, and hard. Two could play his game.

Only one way to find out.

I took it.

Within half an hour, I had completed my profile, paid my first month's membership and was live on the site. Not as myself but as Lynnette Connor, user name Lynnie Loves Art, with my other details more or less truthful. Aged thirty-one, curvaceous build, blonde hair, brown eyes, occupation that of manager in an accountancy firm. Well, the last part had been true once, and should flag me as sufficiently well off. As for my pitch, I kept it brief, describing myself as hoping for a serious relationship that would lead to marriage. I debated over whether to email Looking For Love but didn't. Let him assume the role of predator, I decided. If I had found Steven Simmons, he would be in touch, and soon.

One thing concerned me a little, and that was the picture I uploaded. This man had been to Ellie's home - the odds were good he'd seen my sister's family photos. I'd have to risk him recognising me if we met, although those photos had been taken when Dad was still alive; I'd weighed less then and my hair had been shorter. With any luck, it would be okay. Chances were the prick been too engrossed in fleecing Ellie to notice a few old snapshots.

Once I put the first part of my plan into practice, I felt tiredness steal over me. It was after 5am by then. I fell asleep making plans for when we left the cottage.

I'd also need to decide what, if anything, to tell Ellie. Caution warned me to keep quiet for the time being, especially as she still fancied herself in love with Steven Simmons.

***

Over the next couple of days, I concentrated on my sister. Ellie remained withdrawn but small improvements signalled her recovery. Her appetite increased, she seemed more forthcoming when we talked and the shroud of pain that cloaked her didn't seem so thick. We walked each day along the cliff top, the wind in our hair and the shrieks of the gulls in our ears, and I allowed myself to hope that Ellie might mend.

Every night I logged onto Premier Love Matches, only to be disappointed. No messages from Looking For Love, but dozens from other hopeful guys. A thirty-one-year-old accountant seemed quite the catch, although I guessed my blonde hair, dark eyes and curves were more of a draw than my occupation. I sent a polite reply to each one, saying I didn't think we had enough in common to justify a meeting. With each passing day, my urge to contact Looking For Love grew but I told myself to stay patient.

I also joined another site. Not the dating kind though. Instead, I created a profile on a site called Love Rats Exposed.

My rationale was that Steven Simmons must have conned other women besides Ellie. It wouldn't hurt to check whether any had told their stories online. I wanted to understand more about how Ellie had been duped. Know thy enemy, as the saying went. I called myself Sad Sister, keeping my profile information brief and not making any posts. Instead, I browsed those already there.

No shortage existed of women eager to recount their stories. Most of them, like Ellie, were too ashamed to contact the police. Many possessed scant evidence to warrant pursuing prosecution anyway. The majority of these men operated under the radar, avoiding paper trails of their activities, the sad tales on Love Rats Exposed their victims' only recourse.

One woman described her experience with a man she met while on holiday in Tunisia. He had been a waiter at her hotel, younger than her by ten years, all soulful eyes and practised patter. Once married to her and in the UK, he disappeared back to Tunisia after two weeks, leaving her broken-hearted and several thousand pounds worse off. She'd given him her life savings to fund his college education. I snorted. More likely the money had vanished on hookers and drugs.

Another victim told of the man she married having a wife and two children in Scotland.

'*I believed all his lies about why he needed to be away from home three weeks out of four*,' she posted. The bastard ended up serving time in prison for bigamy, a fact that had done little to assuage her grief.

Two other postings caught my eye. One woman based in Swindon, calling herself Broken And Betrayed, described being conned by a man called Rick Montgomery. She explained how she met him via a dating website, and had been touched by his description of himself as ready to find his soulmate. Same method of operation as with Ellie, with a similar result: Broken and Betrayed lost all her savings, convinced that Rick Montgomery was sincere about his building firm needing short-term cash. By the time she'd realised the truth, he was long gone and so was her money.

'I want to make sure no other woman falls for his lies,' one of her vitriol-filled posts stated. 'Although if you're reading this, it's probably too late.' She followed up with a detailed description of her ex, along with his mobile number and email address.

Interesting, I thought. Swindon was a mere forty miles away from Bristol. The guy who had fleeced Broken and Betrayed might well be Steven Simmons - the physical description was certainly close, as was his method of operation. I filed the thought in my head and continued reading. Another story from a poster called Sophie's Mum, real name Anna, grabbed my attention.

Anna hadn't been the victim of a love rat, but her daughter had. She spoke with feeling about Sophie, who fell prey to a man calling himself Michael Hammond, whom she met on a premium dating website. At first, all went well, although her mother became concerned over Sophie's reluctance to introduce her new boyfriend to her parents. She'd claimed he was shy, then cited his need to travel for work most weeks.

That fitted the profile, I thought. Meeting his victim's parents wouldn't have featured in his game plan. Far better to stay anonymous, unmet by friends and family.

I read on. By the time Sophie realised she had been duped, she'd lost her life savings. In total he'd fleeced her of forty thousand pounds. The man's method was what snagged my attention. Michael Hammond had persuaded her to part with cash so he could pay construction workers at the holiday complex he was developing. The similarity was too strong to ignore. Could Michael Hammond be Steven Simmons? As well as Rick Montgomery?

Sophie lived in Melksham, a town within easy driving distance of Bristol. It was possible.

Anna said she was encouraging her daughter to go to the police, despite the lack of hard evidence. She'd also noticed similarities between her daughter's story and that of Broken and Betrayed, convinced the same man had struck twice. Sophie was resistant though. Like Ellie, she was too ashamed.

Two more potential victims within a close radius of Bristol. I was onto something, of that I was sure. Rick Montgomery, Michael Hammond and Steven Simmons might well be the same guy, claiming to need funds for struggling businesses and who requested cash to avoid creating a paper trail.

Every night from then on I visited Love Rats Exposed, familiarising myself with how these men operated. A definite pattern emerged. Chameleon-like, they adapted their strategy to fit their latest target, capable of making any lie sound believable.

'*He seemed so genuine*,' one woman wailed. '*Every day he'd tell me how much he loved me, how precious I was. How was I to know it was all an act?*'

I'd know, I told myself. Hadn't I been inoculated against deceit through dating Gary McIlroy? My bullshit radar was on full alert, ready to detect any love rat that dared cross my path. More specifically, Steven Simmons. Forearmed with Ellie's description of him, I felt confident I could spot the bastard with ease should we ever meet.

The posts on Love Rats Exposed also revealed darker tactics. Many women told how, without realising it, they'd been isolated from their friends and family. Purposely turned against them in several cases, so that when they were left bereft, their support structure had crumbled. Some, like Ellie, had attempted suicide. Without anyone to back them up, no wonder they'd been so reluctant to inform the police. Fresh guilt sliced through me for deserting my sister when she was so vulnerable, and my desire for revenge edged higher. One way or another I would con the con artist, force a dose of his own medicine down his scheming throat.

***

One night, after Ellie went to bed early, I stayed downstairs, nursing my third glass of whisky, my mood dark. I'd been rereading the posts on Love Rats Exposed, convinced that Sophie, Ellie and Broken and Betrayed had met the same man. On scanning through the latter's posts, I noticed something I'd seen before but forgotten - she'd posted her ex's mobile number to warn other women. Fuelled by alcohol, angry and in the mood for vengeance, I grabbed my phone. My fingers stabbed like knives at the screen as I composed a text.

You fucker, I typed. *You hurt my sister, and that's pissed me off big time. Watch your step. Because I'm coming for you*. Before I could stop myself, I pressed 'send.' Then I added the number into my contacts, labelling it 'Steven Simmons, Ellie's Bastard Ex'. That done, I switched off my phone and went to bed.

The next morning a dull ache throbbed behind my eyes, accompanied by a mouth that felt full of feathers. Fuck, had I overdone the whisky the night before, but I'd been so goddamn mad. In a rush of post-alcohol regret, my drunken text came back to haunt me. Clearly the Lagavulin had overridden my common sense, but it was too late to worry about it. Besides, the chances were good that Rick Montgomery, a.k.a. Steven Simmons, would never even read the text, not if he changed mobile numbers or phones after each scam.

Satisfied all was well in my world, I drifted back to sleep.

When I awoke two hours later, I went downstairs and into the kitchen, downing a pint of water with a couple of aspirins. Then I switched on my phone, to find its notification light winking at me. *Mum*, I thought, *or Caroline*. When I pulled up my messages, however, I saw Steven Simmons, if it was indeed him, had sent me a reply.

Pleased to meet you. You're Lucy's sister, I presume.

The cocky bastard. Cool, too, in his refusal to rise to my bait. I thought quickly. Lucy, I assumed, must be Broken and Betrayed's real name. The last thing I wanted was for her to suffer any repercussions from my drunken text. I typed out a message as footsteps sounded on the stairs.

Wrong. Not Lucy. I'm related to another of your victims.

The second I sent the text, Ellie walked in, rubbing sleep from her eyes. In one swift movement, I shoved my phone into my pocket. She didn't need to know I'd swapped messages with the man I suspected of being her ex.

'Want some breakfast?' I asked, my smile bright.

That morning we walked to the nearby village with no particular aim other than to kill time. Ellie seemed more animated, which cheered me. My mobile was in my jacket pocket, nestling against my hip. After we'd browsed the souvenir shops for a while, I felt it vibrate.

'You fancy a coffee?' I asked Ellie.

'Sure. How about that new place on the high street?'

Once inside, with Ellie ordering our cappuccinos, I made my way to the toilet, intent on checking my messages. Steven Simmons had sent a reply.

Interesting. So many women. So many possibilities.

My jaw tightened with fury. Before I could stop myself, I typed out a response. *You think you're so clever. But I'm onto you, dickhead.*

Ellie must have noticed the disquiet in my face when I returned. 'Something wrong?'

I shook my head, a false smile on my lips. 'Nope. Everything's fine.'

I didn't get a reply to my text until that afternoon. Ellie and I were back at the cottage, a thunderstorm preventing us from taking our usual cliff-top walk. Rain poured down in torrents, the sky pierced by stabs of lightning. Ellie was curled up in the window seat, absorbed in a romance novel. I pretended to read a Stephen King paperback, but my mind was on the latest message I'd received.

That sounds like a threat. Is it, my unknown friend?

Outside the cottage, the skies continued to rumble and flash. My fingers clenched my mobile, my anger equally stormy.

I composed a reply. *You bet your arse it is. One way or another, I'll send you to prison.* Next I pressed 'send'.

And waited. Then waited some more. No response.

***

We'd been at the cottage for a week by the time Ellie made her announcement. The two of us were at the beach, sprawled on our usual rock, the incoming tide tickling our toes. Beside me, Ellie shifted her bottom on the hard granite, poking at a strand of seaweed with her foot.

'Something bothering you?' I asked.

She shook her head. 'No. But I want to go back to Bristol sometime soon.'

'You sure?' I wasn't convinced she was ready.

'Yes. It's done me good, being here with you. I need to return to some sort of routine, though.'

'Will you be okay? At home by yourself?' I hated to think of her alone in her flat, brooding.

Her response was a shrug. 'To be honest, I don't have a clue how to restart my life.'

I risked another question, although I dreaded the answer. 'You're not still feeling like you want to die, are you?'

She shook her head. 'No.' Her eyes refused to meet mine, however.

I decided to keep close tabs on her. 'I'll be there for you. Whatever you need.'

'The thing is ...' She dropped her gaze. 'I'd love to do more with my online shop, but Steven wiped me out savings-wise. Without Dad's money, or the wages from my job, I'll struggle to get by, let alone expand my business.'

'Remember what I said? About helping you? We'll sort through your finances together, I promise.'

Ellie bit her lip. 'That's great, but I was hoping you could lend me some funds.'

Teach a man to fish, I reminded myself. Much as I wanted to ease her problems, I didn't consider a cash injection the best solution.

'This way is better,' I told her. 'We'll set up a spreadsheet, prepare some financial forecasts. See how best to grow your business.' I made a promise to myself. If the figures stacked up, and Ellie seemed capable of handling more sales, I'd give her the money at a later date.

'Easy for you to say,' she retorted. 'You understand that stuff. I don't.'

'I'll help you,' I repeated.

A nugget of optimism grew in my belly. My sister was holding up better than I'd dared hope, and I couldn't deny I was itching to get back to Bristol. I'd still not received any response to my last text to Steven Simmons, but I'd promised myself a month to track him down. If I hadn't found the prick by then, I'd either change tactics or give up the hunt.

All that changed when I logged onto Premier Love Matches that night. Looking For Love had finally contacted me.

CHAPTER 5

He didn't say much in that first message. Just a brief paragraph, saying he liked my profile, how he'd love to meet for coffee or a drink sometime. I hesitated before replying. Should I abandon my pursuit of Steven Simmons? Persuade my sister she should go to the police? Then I remembered her insistence that the law wasn't an option. The shame of it, she'd said. Hadn't the women from the Love Rats Exposed website been similarly reluctant?

Something hardened inside me. This bastard deserved to be punished, and I, Lyddie Hunter, was the one to mete out justice. Meaning I needed to discover if Looking For Love was Steven Simmons.

'A drink sounds great,' I replied. Then I switched off my laptop and went to bed.

An enthusiastic response from Liam greeted me the next day. Throughout the morning we chatted online, and I agreed to go for a beer with him on Wednesday, at the Watershed bar near the Harbourside. I spun him a tale about how it was close to where I lived. That should snag any con man's interest. Flats near Millennium Square didn't come cheap, either to rent or to buy. I finished by asking Liam for a photo of himself.

'Don't get me wrong. Looks aren't important to me,' I wrote. *'But I'd like to put a face to the name.'*

Ten minutes later, Liam replied. As I'd expected, he blew off my suggestion, saying he hated having his picture taken.

'I'll wear jeans and a green polo shirt,' he wrote back. *'And I'll wait for you outside. See you Wednesday evening.'* He ended by giving me his mobile number. I checked it against the one I had

labelled 'Steven Simmons, Ellie's Bastard Ex' in my phone. They didn't match, but that didn't mean Liam and Steven weren't the same guy. He probably used several different phones and numbers.

That got me thinking. I checked my watch; by then it was half past eleven. Plenty of time for me to drive to the local shopping centre before lunch.

'Going to get some extra groceries,' I told Ellie. 'I won't be long.'

Ten minutes later, I had parked the car and was walking towards my destination, one of those 'cash converter' shops, which bought goods from those in need of quick funds and then sold them on. I wanted a second mobile phone, one I could pay for without a credit card and for which I wouldn't have to provide a home address. I found what I was after straightaway. A decent model Samsung with a pay-as-you-go SIM, one I'd top up via vouchers and which couldn't be traced back to my real identity.

Once back at the cottage, I texted Liam my new mobile number. Thank goodness Ellie seemed keen to get back to Bristol. I'd use that to my advantage. I was all set for Wednesday.

***

The next morning, Ellie reiterated her determination to return home, that very day.

'Sure,' I told her. 'If you pack up your stuff, we can get going right away.'

If my eagerness to leave the cottage surprised her, she didn't comment. On the drive back to Bristol, she was quiet, but I didn't expect much else. After I kissed her goodbye, she gripped my hands, looking straight into my eyes. 'I'll be okay,' she said. 'You don't need to worry about me.'

I wasn't convinced. 'No?'

She shook her head. 'I'll get by. Somehow.'

I frowned, the pain in her expression piercing me. 'You deserve better.'

Her smile was strained, not reaching her eyes. 'It'll have to do. I can't manage more, not now.'

Before I could quiz her again about whether she was still suicidal, she squeezed my hands, then let them drop. 'What about *your* plans? Will you be going back to Spain soon?'

'No.' Relief registered in her face. 'I think I'll hang around for a while, spend time with Mum and Caroline. You too, of course.' My reason was halfway true. Besides, I couldn't tell her the real story. 'Can I stop by later? Do my big-sister thing and check up on you?'

She smiled, then nodded, but tension was evident around her mouth, and I promised myself I'd keep a close eye on her while I remained in the UK.

Maybe that wasn't enough. On an impulse, I spoke. 'You shouldn't be by yourself right now. Come and stay at my place. For a few days, at least.'

She hesitated. 'You wouldn't mind?'

'Need you ask?'

'Then yes. If that's okay.'

***

Ellie proved an easy house guest. 'I promise I won't be a nuisance,' she told me once she'd unpacked her stuff. 'You'll hardly know I'm here.'

She was right. I rarely saw her; she spent most of her time in her room. When she did emerge, she seemed cheerful enough, and I relaxed a little. With any luck, the worst was over.

Each night I checked in with Premier Love Matches and Love Rats Exposed, my anticipation building about meeting Liam. We continued to swap messages online and a few texts as well, the tone of his keener with each one. I responded in kind while I waited for our date, my mind ruminating on what I'd do if he turned out to be Ellie's ex.

Wednesday evening eventually arrived, and I dressed with care, choosing white linen trousers and a pink strappy top, along with flat sandals and a clutch bag. I also gave consideration to what jewellery might portray me as a wealthy woman. In the end I selected a gold bangle bought for me by Mum on my eighteenth birthday. As I fastened it around my wrist, pain stabbed me at the memory of a different bracelet, given to me by my father. Dad had presented me with it after I passed my accountancy exams, the same night Ellie crashed her car.

'I'm proud of my clever daughter,' he'd told me. 'I bought this for you, darling.'

So beautiful, the bracelet had been. A thick circle of gold engraved with roses, lilies and forget-me-nots. A bittersweet reminder of my father's love, yet mislaid years ago. I'd never forgiven myself for such carelessness.

With an effort, I dragged myself back to getting ready. Dad's gift might be lost, but I still had Mum's. I teamed the bangle with diamond earrings, a present to myself for my thirtieth birthday. Before leaving, I surveyed myself in the mirror, hoping Liam would approve. Caroline often told me how attractive I was, as had Richie when we dated. I shoved my ex-boyfriend from my thoughts, staring at the way my hair tumbled around my face, the soft brown of my eyes. Pretty enough, but ...

In my mind there was always that *but.*

I stared at the hint of an extra chin. Did my cheeks look chubby? The few extra kilos I carried had been an issue for years, my body the one area in which I lacked confidence. I reminded myself Ellie's ex was more interested in my bank balance than my dress size. Besides, I could hardly shed a stone in the next half hour. As I walked downstairs, Ellie came out of the kitchen.

'You look lovely,' she said. 'Going somewhere special?'

'Only to Caroline's.' I hated lying, but it was for the best. 'See you later.'

My hands shook as I drove towards the Harbourside. I parked up and walked in the direction of the Watershed, as nervous as I'd ever been before a date. I prayed I could carry this off. I arrived at eight, the time we'd arranged, but by five past Liam hadn't shown. Irritation prickled within me.

While I waited, I wondered how the evening would pan out. If this guy was Ellie's ex, he'd need to bait the hook. A few well-chosen compliments, a sprinkling of subtle flattery, spread out over several weeks and designed to make me fall in love with him. Then he'd begin his attack on my bank balance, most likely using the same tactics he'd employed with Ellie. Meanwhile I'd see how things played out and gauge how best to deliver the prick's comeuppance.

The evening closed around me, the air cool after the heat of the day. At ten after the hour I spotted a man coming towards me. As he drew closer, I took in his appearance. Six feet and more of muscle was heading my way, along with hair that verged on black. The guy wore jeans and a green polo shirt. When he stopped in front of me, I noticed his blue eyes. Yup, this was Liam all right.

'Lynnie,' he said. His voice hovered between bass and tenor, its rich timbre loaded with confidence. He didn't apologise for his lateness, and my annoyance grew. 'Liam Tate. It's good to meet you.'

I forced a smile. 'Likewise.'

He gestured towards the door. 'Shall we?'

I followed him inside, upstairs to the bar. Around us the noise of the other customers was a low hum.

'What can I get you?' he asked. 'My treat. I insist.'

Smooth, I thought, once I had regained my composure. 'A pint of the guest beer, please.'

I studied him while he ordered our drinks. The woman who served him was clearly taken with his charm. A few lines radiated from around his eyes when he laughed at something she said, and his grin revealed white, straight teeth. His clothes looked expensive, the cut of his jeans screaming top quality. I made a bet with myself that I'd spot a Ralph Lauren logo on his polo shirt when he turned my way. I wasn't wrong.

He steered a path to a table at the back, our drinks in his hands.

'It's good to meet you,' he said, once we'd sat down. 'I'd almost given up hope of finding anyone online.'

'Me too. I don't normally do this sort of thing. Internet dating, that is.'

'So what persuaded you to give it a go?' His voice was pure honey, his smile warm and soft. God, he was a charmer all right. The curve of his mouth posed a temptation to any straight woman still breathing. Except me. I brought to mind Ellie's pallor in her hospital bed, the betrayal that led her to swallow a bottle of pills, and my resolve hardened.

I looked him square in the eyes. 'My sister joined a dating website. And met a man. Thought it was time to try it myself.'

He sipped his beer. 'I'm glad you did.' A clouded expression settled over his face. 'I'll be honest with you. My last relationship didn't end well.'

I adopted a suitably sympathetic tone. 'I'm sorry to hear that. What happened?'

'The bitch cheated on me.' For a second, darkness snaked into his eyes. A sense of unease needled up my spine.

Liam waved a contemptuous hand in the air, his former ebullience restored. 'Water under the bridge. Tell me more about yourself.'

We conversed further over our drinks, the usual insubstantial chit-chat that marked most first dates. I touched on my employment, professing a lack of love for my accountancy role. 'Not my dream job,' I declared, my tone dismissive. 'It pays great, though.' Was it me or did his interest perk up?

'You mentioned you live near here?' he queried. 'Wow. Property in the city centre doesn't come cheap.'

I shrugged, the epitome of nonchalance. 'Like I said, I earn good money. And my father left me well off when he died.' Another seed planted. A few minutes later I let slip that I drove an almost new mid-range Audi. It was the rental car I'd collected at the airport, but he wasn't to know that.

Over the next hour, I drew him out, enquiring about the construction firm he professed to own, as well as his past relationships.

His replies were nebulous, giving a smidgen of information but he'd switch the conversation if I probed too hard - a deft flick of the subject, steering our discussion into safer waters. His evasiveness intrigued me. I wasn't certain, but it seemed possible that Liam Tate and Steven Simmons were the same man. He wasn't what I'd describe as sweet, like my sister had done, but we'd always viewed the world through different lenses. Liam certainly possessed a fraudster's charm by the bucket-load.

'You live in Charlcombe, right?' I asked.

He nodded. 'I was stupid enough to buy a house that's a total money pit. The place needs renovating from top to bottom – new roof, plumbing, the works. Right now it's uninhabitable, so I'm staying in rented accommodation until everything's completed.' He flashed a few pictures from his phone my way. The house he showed me was huge and, once finished, would be stunning. My bullshit radar kicked off at once. He'd probably culled the photos from an estate agent's website. If my intuition was correct, Liam must be paving the way for a future scam. The quasi-mansion he claimed to own was needed to convince me he was a man of means, although temporarily short of funds. Before long he'd mention he needed cash for the restoration work, a twist on his usual ploy. My suspicion grew stronger that seated opposite me was the man who'd conned Ellie.

When the time came to leave, he pressed my hand. 'I've enjoyed meeting you, Lynnie. I hope we can do this again sometime.'

'I'd love that,' I said, pasting a flattered smile on my lips.

'Do you enjoy French food? There's a new restaurant in Bristol I've been meaning to try.'

'How about one evening next week?'

'Fine by me. I'll call you to arrange a date,' Liam said. 'Sorry, but would you excuse me? All that beer has gone straight to my bladder.' Without waiting for a reply, he strode off in the direction of the toilets. I waited.

From the depths of my handbag, my mobile pinged. When I fished it out, I saw I had a message from Steven Simmons.

Hey there, stranger. Missed me?

Like a hole in the head, I typed. *I hoped you'd died a slow painful death and left the world a better place.*

Within seconds a reply came. *Not nice. And I thought we were friends.*

Fuck you.

I'd love to, darling. Assuming you're female, that is, and my instinct tells me you are.

Too angry to respond, I threw my mobile back in my bag. A minute later it pinged again.

Been checking my lady friends who have this number. Those ones who have sisters. You're connected to one of four possibilities.

My earlier worry resurfaced; might my drunken text result in Broken and Betrayed getting hassled by this man? And if he'd used the same mobile number with Ellie, the prick might pester her as well.

Wrong, I typed. *Think again, fucker. Leave it enigmatic,* I told myself. Buy time to consider my next move.

Oh, I will, believe me. I'm getting ever closer to discovering who you are. And when I do, we can meet in person. Won't that be fun?

Goosebumps prickled my skin. I didn't bother replying. Why gratify the fucker with a response?

Look at the facts, I told myself. If Liam Tate was also Steven Simmons, Rick Montgomery and Michael Hammond, he could have no idea I was behind the anonymous texts. I'd given him the pay-as-you go mobile number before our date, yet I'd been using my regular phone for the weird text exchanges. I was safe. Right?

A couple of minutes later, I watched Liam stride back through the bar. He'd been gone an awfully long time. Had he been messaging me while he was in the toilets? Despite my best efforts, worry coiled around me, my conviction I'd found Ellie's ex growing stronger.

***

Back home after our date, I checked my Premier Love Matches account to peruse Liam's profile for any clues I'd missed. When I did, I saw Scotty123 had sent me an email.

Like Liam, he didn't say much in his initial message. Just that his name was Scott, that he had read my profile and liked what he saw. How he was shy when it came to dating but that his goal was a long-term relationship, preferably marriage.

'I'm intrigued by your user name,' he ended. *'I'm guessing you enjoy art - me too! Have you checked out the exhibition of watercolours at the city museum? If not, could we go together sometime? Or at least have coffee somewhere?'*

Coffee, I decided, not the exhibition. I'd love to see it, but it suited my purpose better to sit opposite this man, study his reactions while we talked - something best done over a cappuccino or espresso. While there, I would make sure Scott knew I was a woman of means, suss out whether he might be Ellie's ex instead of Looking For Love. I'd not yet ruled him out on that score, despite Liam seeming the more likely candidate. With that in mind, I composed a reply.

'Coffee sounds great! How about Jumping Beans at the Harbourside? I have an apartment close by,' I typed. *'Are you free Saturday lunchtime?'* Before I could think twice, I clicked the 'send' button. All I could do next was play a waiting game until he replied. He didn't, not that day.

Instead, Steven Simmons got in touch again. I awoke the next morning to another text.

Hello, friend. How is your lovely sister?

I composed a reply. *Doing much better now you're out of her life.*

His response came within a minute. *Been thinking about that message you sent. About me doing jail time.*

My fingers flew across my screen. *I meant every word. Get used to the idea of going to prison, fucker.*

'You want some breakfast?' Ellie called up the stairs.

'Sure. I'll be down in a minute,' I shouted back. In my hand, my mobile vibrated.

Another threat. Not a good idea, my friend.

The arrogant prick. *Oh, yeah? And why is that?*

'Scrambled eggs okay for you?' Ellie asked, still from the hallway below.

'Whatever you're having.' I held my breath, willing my phone to ping. And it did.

The last person who threatened me ended up regretting it. Followed by: *Got to go. I'll be in touch, don't worry.*

Over breakfast, I pondered the texts. They rattled me, especially the penultimate one, but I reminded myself that Steven Simmons had no idea who I was. Nevertheless, the man was both ruthless and unscrupulous. No way could I afford to underestimate him.

Later that morning, I logged onto Premier Love Matches again. Scotty123 hadn't let me down. A message beckoned from my inbox.

Can't wait to meet a fellow art enthusiast! Is one o'clock on Saturday good for you?

I typed a quick response. *Perfect. How will I know you? Can you send me a photo?*

Ten minutes later he replied, with a picture. The focus was blurry, sure, and it wasn't a close-up, but I judged it better than nothing. From the little I could see, he looked like many women's dream guy – the quintessential tall, handsome male. An apology came with it. '*Sorry I have nothing better to send over! I'll wear jeans and a blue shirt. Can't wait to have coffee with you.*' He added his mobile number as well.

Game on, it seemed. Either Scott was a lonely man searching for love, or else he was the bastard who'd fleeced my sister. I planned to decide which one when we met. The fact he'd sent me a photo indicated the former, however, as did his location. Besides, I was growing ever more convinced that I'd found my target in Liam Tate.

***

Saturday arrived, and I dressed for Scott with the same care I had for Liam. Outside my window the sun shone hot and strong, meaning cool clothing was in order. Different top and trousers, identical jewellery, same air of understated wealth. After leaving the house, I drove to the Harbourside and parked under Millennium Square, then walked the short distance to Jumping Beans.

A guy dressed in tight jeans and a blue shirt was waiting for me outside the entrance. An uncertain smile played around his lips as I drew near, one that grew once I stopped in front of him.

'Scott?' I queried, fighting to keep the tremble from my tone.

'Lynnette,' he said. 'Scott Champion. Pleased to meet you.'

Wow, with a cherry on top. The man before me could have starred as the love interest in a Hollywood movie. Blue eyes appraised me from a chiselled face, his nose perfectly balanced with the full lips below. His hair was mid-brown, thick and cut into short spikes, touches of blond showing in the sunlight. A grin quirked one side of his mouth, which nestled amongst cultivated stubble. And, oh my God, that dimple. As though an invisible finger had drilled into his right cheek. When he shook my hand I was the only woman in the world, or so it seemed. Scott was sex on a stick, his allure hot and potent. I doubted I'd found the guy who'd conned my sister, though. Something about him didn't fit.

From somewhere I found my voice. 'My friends call me Lynnie.'

He cleared his throat. 'It's good to meet you. Shall we ..?' He gestured towards the door.

Once inside, he seemed hesitant, his eyes roaming the crowded space. 'There's a table free over there,' he said.

'I'll get the coffees. How do you take yours?'

After I'd paid for our drinks, I led the way to our table, Scott following close behind. Around us the café hummed with the buzz of conversations and piped music, and I wished everyone else a million miles away. My cappuccino provided much-needed caffeine while I fished for something to say. In the end Scott spoke first.

'So,' he said, his gaze on his espresso. 'Have you been on many dates through Premier Love Matches?'

'This is the second. You?'

He glanced at me, a faint smile on his lips. 'The first. Like I mentioned in my message, I'm a bit shy. I've only had a few relationships, to be honest.'

A bit shy. I realised what didn't fit about this guy. He appeared nervous, not the confident man Ellie had portrayed. His looks didn't gel with her description either, his hair being too light, too short - his height and eye colour matched, but nothing else. I didn't think the guy opposite me was Steven Simmons.

'So you're into art,' he continued. 'Me too. Are you an artist yourself, or just an admirer?'

'I paint. Landscapes, seascapes, all in watercolour. What's more, I own a small gallery. I run it as a sideline to my job.' I'd already decided the fewer lies I told, the better.

'Wow. I'm impressed.'

'What about you?'

'I dabble in acrylics. Still life, the odd abstract.' He frowned. 'I'm not very good, I'm afraid.'

'What do you do for a living?' I remembered his profile said he was in management.

'I run a Toyota dealership, near to where I live. Not the most exciting of jobs, but it pays the bills. You're an accountant, right?'

'Yes. I'd rather be a full-time painter, though.'

'Me too.' I watched his lips as he spoke and all I could think of was kissing them. Everything about this man called to me with a megaphone. I'd always been a sucker for blue eyes - *hello, Gary McIlroy!* - and Scott's stellar looks, combined with his shyness, packed a powerful punch. After Gary, I found cocky, arrogant men a turnoff. Give me a guy unsure of himself, and I was hooked.

Scott grew in confidence as our conversation progressed, and I found myself enjoying our date. I mentioned Dad's death, the fact I had a sister, whom I renamed Emma in case the man opposite me *was* Steven Simmons. We discussed travel, films, our mutual love of Italian food, and by the time Scott said he needed to go, two hours had flown by.

Once we were outside the coffee shop, words hovered on my tongue, ones I couldn't bring myself to voice. As Lyddie Hunter, I considered myself a confident woman. In my role as Lynnie Connor this man made me nervous.

Say it, I urged myself. *Tell him you'd love a second date.*

I remained mute.

'So,' Scott said, his gaze fixed on his shoes. 'I've enjoyed this. Meeting you, I mean.'

'Me too.' My voice was barely a whisper.

A pause, during which time neither of us spoke. My embarrassment doubled, then tripled.

He cleared his throat. 'Can we ... er ... do this again sometime? Maybe take in that art exhibition I mentioned?'

Thank God. I smiled at him. 'I'd like that.'

Relief crept into his expression. 'That's ... um, that's great. I'll call you. Soon.' He leaned in, his lips brushing my cheek. Desire shot up my spine. Then he stepped away and the moment passed.

On the drive home, excitement raced through me. I'd been lucky enough to meet an insanely handsome man, one who shared my love of art and travel. Who wasn't brash or arrogant, but refreshingly normal. Was it wrong of me to hope that, besides snaring Steven Simmons, I might find Mr Right at last?

That evening, I sent Scott a text, saying how much I'd enjoyed our afternoon together. He replied at once, saying he'd also had a wonderful time. How he'd phone me in the next few days. Things were looking up.

***

'It's time I went home,' Ellie informed me over breakfast the next morning. 'Thanks for taking care of me, but you've done enough. I'll be fine. Really.'

I eyed her critically. 'You're sure?'

'Totally. Could you give me a lift back to my place sometime?'

'Of course. How about after lunch?' I'd miss her, but maybe she was right. Perhaps she was ready to return home.

I dropped Ellie off at her flat that afternoon. To fill the void left by her departure, I turned to my art. My brushes and paints were in Spain, but I unearthed an ancient sketchpad and box of pencils from a cupboard in my bedroom. Drawing had been my first love, and my fingers flew over the paper, every line an attempt to capture Scott's essence. Portraits weren't my forte, and my efforts failed to depict the delights of that dimple, the sweetness of that smile. God, I had it bad for him, and so soon too. Our next date couldn't come quickly enough.

To my relief, he called me that evening. We chatted, then I made my move. What did I have to lose?

'About that watercolour exhibition. Do you fancy seeing it next weekend?' I held my breath.

'I'd love to,' he replied. I punched the air in triumph.

After the call ended, a note of caution crept into my happiness. I couldn't overlook the fact we'd started with a lie. To Scott, I was Lynnie Connor, accountant and life-long resident of Bristol. He'd have to discover the truth at some point, along with the reason for my ruse, if we were to forge a meaningful relationship. Would he walk away if I confessed what I'd done? Most men wouldn't want a liar for a partner, and I couldn't blame them. Hadn't I been burned that way myself?

Caroline might know what to do. That meant telling her what I'd planned for Steven Simmons, however, and I wasn't ready for that. First I needed to decide if Liam Tate was my target.

CHAPTER 6

That same evening Liam also called me to arrange our second date. We settled on Le Bistrot d'Yves, a restaurant he'd long wanted to try, on Monday of the week after next. It was the earliest evening we could both manage. Part of me chafed at the delay, but at least I'd get a decent meal out of meeting him - besides, scamming Liam might prove fun. I relished the idea of taking the bastard down a peg or several, my disquiet over the texts I'd received while he was in the Watershed toilets gone. Boldness would bag me my prize, not cowardice. For the time being, my former confidence had been restored.

I'd play things by ear, I decided, perhaps record our conversations on my phone. I'd draw him out, drop further hints that I was a wealthy woman. All the while, I'd be considering how best to trap him. At some point he'd spin me a sob story about his construction company needing funds, or his house repair costs escalating. How he hated to ask, but could I lend him some money to tide him over? Followed by a promise to pay me back straightaway. If I recorded everything, then confirmed it as lies – although I wasn't sure how I'd do the latter part - would that be enough evidence to involve the law? Maybe not, but it was a start. Ellie might refuse to go to the police, as had most of the women on Love Rats Exposed, but I, Lyddie Hunter, was a different animal.

I reminded myself I'd need proof of where he lived, if the cops were to pay him a visit. That might prove more of a challenge, given his penchant for lying about his address. Maybe I'd follow him after one of our dates. I could work out the details later.

In the meantime I needed a new place to live. My house in Kingswood didn't portray the image of wealth I required to trap a con man. Moreover, after living on my own in Spain for two years, sharing with Amelia was proving claustrophobic. I'd already mentioned to both Liam and Scott that I lived at the Harbourside. Time to give shape to that illusion.

I switched on my laptop and typed 'short-term serviced apartments in Bristol' into Google. I was searching for an apartment block at the Harbourside, one that didn't have any signage indicating it housed serviced accommodation rather than regular flats. No reception area staffed by management, that kind of thing - just a normal entrance lobby.

I struck lucky. I found a company that owned six properties in a block close to Millennium Square. I scanned through the photos. The flats looked impressive, justifying their steep rates, and I relished the chance to spend some time alone, as well as fool Liam Tate. Within twenty minutes, I'd booked and paid for my first fortnight, and received key codes to the block and apartment. My intention was to extend my tenancy week by week as required. I'd move my things shortly before I invited Liam there and buy food, flowers, candles, etc., to make the place appear lived in. The hook had been baited.

***

Excitement buzzed through me on Sunday afternoon while I waited outside Bristol's main museum, which also housed a small art gallery. The current exhibition was 'West Country Landscapes in Watercolour', and even if I hadn't been meeting Scott I'd have wanted to see it. We'd chatted on the phone most days and his soft voice always sent delight throbbing through me. We discussed paintings, styles, techniques, and I told him about the challenges of running an art gallery. Thank God I didn't have to bend the truth there, although it tore at my heart I couldn't reveal Spain was the location, not Bristol. Every time we spoke it pained me more and more that we'd begun with a lie, or several of them.

This time my outfit was chosen not to flaunt my money but to look nice for Scott. I'd opted for a dress in a soft shade of blue, halter-necked and flowing to my knees, matched with strappy sandals - perfect for a hot summer's day. My make-up was minimal and I wore my hair loose but clipped back on one side. A long look in the mirror before I left home reassured me I'd done well, even if I thought so myself.

'Wow. You scrub up great,' Amelia told me as I descended the stairs.

I laughed. 'Angling for a reduction on your rent?' I remembered the serviced apartment at the Harbourside, prompting another lie. 'By the way, I'll be out of your way soon. I'm going to stay with Mum for a while.'

She believed me. Why wouldn't she? Guilt stabbed me but I told myself it was a white lie, nothing serious.

Inside the museum entrance hall I sucked in a deep breath. Was it the heat making my palms sweat, or was I nervous? I glanced at the time on my phone. One minute to two o'clock. At the exact second the numbers changed to 14.00 the doors opened and Scott Champion walked through them. A huge grin lit up his face when he saw me.

'Hello, Lynnie,' he said, and damn me if that voice didn't send tingles shooting up my spine, despite the weirdness of being called Lynnie instead of Lyddie. His eyes roamed over my dress, my hair, my face. 'You look lovely.'

Heat rose into my cheeks. My mouth was dry, but I was glad I could even speak. 'Thank you.'

'It's the truth.' The words were accompanied by a shy smile, and I was a goner.

I sucked in another deep breath and managed to find my voice. 'The exhibition's this way.'

We walked in silence towards the swing doors. Once inside, I stared around the room in awe. Paintings covered the walls - a mass of colour depicting the local countryside. Art and a gorgeous man - could the afternoon get any better?

It took an hour to view every painting, an animated discussion running between us all the while based on composition and technique. 'I must try landscapes someday,' Scott declared after we exited the hall. 'I need a change of direction, something other than cranking out pictures of fruit. Or weird abstracts.'

I laughed. 'I'd love to see your work.'

He grimaced. 'I'm not sure it's worthy of inspection. Listen, would you like to grab a coffee?'

As if I could say no. 'I'd love to. There's a good place not far from here.'

We walked outside, heading towards the Triangle. The sun had retreated behind a swathe of clouds, rendering the afternoon cooler than before. On the way we passed an amusement arcade, all flashing lights and loud music, and Scott paused. His gaze was fixed on one of those skill-crane machines, its glass case filled with soft toys and kids' baubles. He reached into his wallet, extracted a pound coin and pressed it in the slot.

'Let me win something for you,' he said, that endearing smile back on his face. All I could do was nod.

Scott manipulated the grabber with ease, and within a minute its claws had fastened on a child's bracelet, hauling it to the release chute. He pulled the circle of plastic beads – small gold spheres strung on elastic - free from its packaging and bounced them on his palm.

'Hold out your wrist,' he instructed. As he fastened the cheap trinket around my arm, his fingers brushed my skin, causing a shiver of desire to barrel through my body. Scott glanced at me, his expression concerned. 'You're cold. Let's go get that coffee, shall we?'

Once inside, we both ordered cappuccinos. After we got seated, I sensed a change of mood steal over Scott. He looked sad, and I had no idea why. I searched his face for clues, but then he spoke. 'My sister would love to see those paintings.'

He'd mentioned his family circumstances when we'd spoken on the phone. Both his parents had died in a car crash five years ago. Scott had a younger sister called Darcy, aged twenty-seven, to whom he was close, doubly so after the pile-up that left them orphaned. He'd seemed reluctant to discuss her, which puzzled me. Scott appeared to care for Darcy the way I did for Ellie, so why the reticence?

'Perhaps you should have invited her along,' I said, keeping my tone light. 'I wouldn't have minded.' I cursed myself the minute the words sailed out of my mouth. Would he decide I was too pushy, hinting at meeting his family on our second date?

He smiled but his eyes stayed sad. 'Thank you for that. You're a good person, Lynnie.'

Shame at the lies I'd told, my false name an unwelcome reminder, stole over me. Before I could torture myself further, he continued, 'She's not well, you see.' Tension tightened his lips and I ached at the pain in his blue eyes. My hand reached out to cover his. 'Tell me about her,' I said.

He shook his head. 'It's hard to talk about.'

I kept quiet, figuring he needed space. The café's customers milled around us, their voices loud, grating on my nerves. Once again I wished everyone else gone so only Scott and I remained. I suppressed the urge to stroke my fingers over the skin of his hand. Too much, too soon.

Instead, I touched the bracelet around my wrist. Cheap and gaudy the trinket might be, but he'd staked his claim on me with its plastic beads. For a second, the loss of Dad's gift stabbed through me, the memory of the flowers etched onto its gold ever poignant.

'She's sick,' Scott said. 'Really sick.'

I paused a second, reluctant to probe deeper. 'That's tough.'

'Like I told you, Darcy's the only family I have left.'

'You obviously love her very much.'

He nodded. 'Are you close to your sister? Her name's Emma, right?

'Yes.' Another fib returning to poke me in the eye. 'She's also been ill, although she's getting better now. At least I hope so.'

'Then you'll understand how I feel. I can't lose her, Lynnie.'

'I get that.'

'I'm sorry. I didn't mean to shove my problems onto you.' His eyes wouldn't meet mine.

'It's fine.' I vowed I would get the rest of the story about Darcy before long.

I sensed our time together was at an end, at least for then. I stood up, reaching for my handbag. 'Shall we go?'

His expression relaxed into a smile. 'Can I walk you home? You're down at the Harbourside, right?'

Damn the lies I'd told. My rented Audi was in Trenchard Street car park, a few hundred metres away, but I couldn't risk him knowing that. Nobody would drive the short distance from Millennium Square to the museum unless they had mobility issues. I thought through my options.

'That would be lovely, but I want to browse the shops on the Triangle before they close,' I said.

Uncertainty stole across his handsome features. 'Would you like to go for a walk sometime? With me, I mean?' He shook his head. 'I'm such an idiot. Who else would I be referring to?'

That endearing modesty again. 'I'd love to.'

We made arrangements for the following Tuesday, the evening after I next planned to see Liam Tate. Scott suggested a stroll around the Harbourside if the weather stayed fine, to which I readily agreed. Outside the museum, he leaned in, his lips grazing my cheek, this time closer to my mouth. Desire pulsed through me.

'I'll call you,' he said. 'Soon.'

I watched until he disappeared into the Trenchard Street car park, my eyes nailed to his back. Our third date couldn't come quickly enough.

***

After I got home, the first thing I did was call Caroline.

'Hey, stranger,' she answered. 'Long time no see. You planning to honour me with a visit soon?'

'Yeah, now you mention it, I am.' I needed to talk to her about Scott. 'Are you free this evening? There's something I want to run past you.'

'Tonight's fine. Are you okay, lovey? Is this about Ellie?'

'No.' I drew in a breath, knowing how Caroline would react. My friend was well aware of how deeply I craved a steady relationship. 'I've met someone.'

Her squeal of delight was loud enough to reach Australia. 'I'm so pleased for you.' Her voice rose high with excitement. 'I can't wait to hear all about him. Bring wine, and I'll cook for us.'

I laughed. I hadn't realised how much I missed Caroline. 'See you later, you daft bat.'

After we ended the call, I sat back, glad we'd talked. I'd tell her about Scott, about the lies I'd told, and she'd know what to do. She always did.

On the coffee table, my mobile pinged. A text, no doubt from Caroline, even though we'd spoken seconds before. With a grin on my face, I grabbed my phone. My smile faded the second I realised who'd messaged me.

You don't want to piss me off, friend. There are ways to track down mobile phone users.

Oh, God. Dear God. I'd made that first drunken text from my regular phone, meaning my real name and address were registered to that number. Might this man be a hacker, skilled enough to access my details? Amelia could be at risk if this prick got my Kingswood address and targeted it on the assumption she was me. My lodger was often away for work, but I couldn't afford to be complacent about her safety.

I fired off a reply, yet another lie. *I'm one step ahead of you, fucker. This is a crappy old pay-as-you-go mobile I stole from my sister, who's forgotten she ever owned it. You think I'd be stupid enough to use my own phone?* Except I had been, of course.

Another ping from my mobile. *You're cleverer than I thought. I'm enjoying our little game, friend. Let's talk again soon.*

I didn't reply, my earlier happiness having soured. The unwelcome texts from Rick-The-Dick Montgomery reminded me I'd not logged onto Love Rats Exposed for a while. I grabbed my laptop, navigating to the website and scanning the recent threads. Broken and Betrayed had posted some more, convincing me further she and Sophie had fallen prey to the same swindler as Ellie. A guy who sounded a lot like Liam Tate.

So far I'd only browsed the forum. Time to change that. Chances were I could glean useful details from these women.

I began a thread called 'Sad Sister Seeks Information' and recounted Ellie's story. I told of my distress at her attempted suicide, my fear she'd fallen victim to a serial con artist. I tagged both Broken and Betrayed and Anna, saying that from what I had read of their posts I suspected the same guy was responsible.

'This man is ruining women's lives,' I ended. 'And I'm going to ensure he gets his comeuppance.' Satisfied, I closed my laptop.

I fixed myself a whisky while I mulled over the messages on my phone. One thing continued to reassure me. If Liam Tate, Rick Montgomery and Steven Simmons were the same guy, he could have no idea I was behind the texts. To Liam, I was a potential mark, nothing else. For the purposes of dating him I was using the pay-as-you-go Samsung, not my main phone, meaning he'd never connect Lynnie Connor with his anonymous texter.

I drained my glass, satisfied I was safe.

An hour or two later, I checked back with Love Rats Exposed, gratified to see several responses to my post.

Sophiesmum: *'I understand what you're going through, Sad Sister. My daughter's lost all her confidence, says she'll never trust a man again, rarely leaves her flat. She's still refusing to go to the police, despite me telling her I'll support her all the way. What did you mean about giving this guy his comeuppance?'*

BrokenAndBetrayed: *'I think you're right, SS. This Steven Simmons sounds like the jerk who called himself Rick Montgomery.'*

Hurtingbad: *'Such a tragic story. How's your sister doing these days? She should sign up here, then she'd realise she's not alone.'*

HeartbrokenHelen: *'So sorry to read your post. Men are bastards, aren't they?'*

Hurtingbad: '*You're not wrong there, Helen. What are you going to do, SS?*'

I clicked on 'reply to thread.' *'Ellie won't go to the police. So I intend to. First I have to get evidence though.'* I waited, refreshing the screen every few seconds. Within a minute Anna had posted.

Sophiesmum: '*Good luck with that. If it's the same guy, he always asks for cash. He takes care not to leave a paper trail.*'

While I considered my reply, more responses appeared.

HeartbrokenHelen: *'Hey, SS! Yeah, you should totally do that. Stick it to him, I say.'*

BrokenAndBetrayed: *'But how will the police find him? After he fleeced me, he disappeared. Do you have an address for him?'*

I began to type.

'I don't have his address, but I'm pretty sure I've tracked him down. Found the bastard through Premier Love Matches. I've already been on a date with him. He doesn't know who I am, of course. You ask what I'm planning? To play him at his own game.'

Within a minute, I got a reply from Broken and Betrayed. *'You've found him? What name is he using these days?'*

'I don't want to say until I'm sure it's him,' I replied. *'I'll post again when I'm certain. He'll ask me for money soon, and when he does, I'll be ready. Just not in the way he's expecting.'*

'Good on you, girl,' Heartbroken Helen posted. *'You've got guts, I'll give you that.'*

'There's an upside to all this,' I typed. *'I met an amazing guy while I was searching for the bastard who conned Ellie. We've had two dates already. With another planned.'* I paused before clicking the 'post' button, worried they might resent my happiness.

I was wrong, it seemed. *'So pleased for you!'* Heartbroken Helen replied. *'I hope it turns out better than it did for your sister. You going to tell us the name of this one?'*

'Scott,' I typed. *'We've arranged to go for a walk on Tuesday.'*

The thread went quiet for a while. I was beginning to think I'd pissed the rest of them off with my good news. Then Sophie's mum Anna replied. *'I'm delighted for you, Sad Sister. Keep us posted, won't you?'*

I would. Of that I was sure.

***

That evening I tried to park close to Caroline's house but failed to find anywhere. In the end I squeezed into a space two streets away, cursing as I wrestled with the steering wheel. As I locked the car, a bottle of wine in one hand, I glanced towards the end of the street. A man stood on the pavement, hands in pockets, his face masked by a hoodie. His gaze appeared to be directed my way.

Just some guy hanging around, I decided. After I'd walked halfway towards Caroline's, I looked back to where he'd been. The man was strolling behind me at a distance of about a hundred metres. As my eyes fixed on him, he stopped, extracting a mobile from one pocket. Turning his back on me, he pressed the phone to his ear, apparently having a conversation.

Weird, I thought. Well, if some nutter was following me, for whatever reason, he'd picked the wrong time and place. The evening was still light, and I was a minute's walk from my destination, in a well-populated area. With a shrug, I carried on. Once I arrived at Caroline's, I took a quick look over my shoulder. The man had stopped on a street corner, his phone clamped to his ear, his identity still concealed by his hoodie. A second after he caught me staring at him, he turned down a side road and disappeared from view.

Dismissing him from my mind, I rang Caroline's doorbell. I pictured her face when I told her about Scott. If her squeal of delight earlier was an indicator, she'd be ecstatic.

The door opened, and Caroline pulled me into a fierce hug. 'Hey, you,' she said. 'Great to see you, so it is. Come on in.'

I followed her into the hallway, the smell of garlic growing ever stronger in my nostrils as we approached the kitchen. Pans and utensils lay strewn over every surface.

'Take a seat. I've done us a pasta bake. Here, let me have that.' She grabbed the wine, twisted off the cap and poured liberal measures into two glasses. While she busied herself serving up the food, I considered my options. Caroline and I were close, always had been, and I disliked keeping secrets from her. I'd tell her about Scott, sure, but Liam Tate was another matter. Impossible to reveal my plans for him without mentioning Ellie and the missing money - and she'd sworn me to secrecy. But how could I broach having lied to Scott without disclosing the reason?

I remembered Ellie had only made me promise not to tell Mum. Perhaps I could discuss this with Caroline after all.

She placed a bowl of steaming pasta before me. 'So,' she said, taking the seat opposite me. 'Spill the beans, girl. You've met a guy? When, where, how? Tell me everything.'

So I told her. I described Scott's blue eyes, the warmth in them when he gazed at me. That dimple, sexy beyond words. I talked about the strands of gold in his otherwise brown hair, the lilt of his voice, how charming he was when he got nervous. All the while I was aware of the inane grin pasted across my face. The way my fingers toyed with the child's bracelet he'd won for me, still fastened around my wrist.

'You've got it bad,' Caroline said when I paused to draw breath. She laughed. 'Good to see. I want you to be happy, lovey. I'd hoped ...' Richie's name hovered between us, the atmosphere tight with tension.

She cleared her throat. 'But anyway. So you met this guy on a dating website? Does that mean you're intending to stay in England?'

She'd raised a valid point. Would I consider returning to the UK to be with Scott? But how could we progress our relationship if he believed I was an accountant based in Bristol, rather than an artist living in Spain? The enormity of my lies threatened to suffocate me. For a brief moment I wished I'd never started this insane quest. But then I'd never have met Scott. God, was this ever a mess.

'Lyddie?' Caroline's voice punctured my thoughts. Her forehead was crinkled with concern. 'What's wrong? Is there something you're not saying?'

She knew me too well. I took a gulp of wine, needing the alcoholic hit. Then I told her the rest. About Ellie being conned, how I planned to get revenge on the man who'd almost killed my sister. How I believed I'd found the culprit in Liam Tate. I didn't mention the texts I'd been swapping with him, too ashamed of my drunken stupidity in firing off the first one. When I finished, I didn't dare look at Caroline.

'Holy shit,' my friend said at last. When I glanced up, alarm was written across her face. 'You're playing a dangerous game, girl. This man is an expert at extorting money. Ruthless. Cold. Calculating. Who knows what else he's capable of? I've known you for twenty years, Lyddie, and you're as straight as they come. No lies, no bullshit. Until now, that is. You reckon you can beat a con man at his own game?'

She had a point. But then I remembered Ellie's suicide attempt, the pain I'd endured because of Gary McIlroy.

'I don't know,' I admitted. 'But I have to try.'

'Why not persuade Ellie to involve the police?'

'She won't. I've tried. None of his other victims will either.'

'His other victims?' I realised I'd omitted something from my explanation. I outlined what I'd discovered on Love Rats Exposed.

'He's conned at least two other women from that site,' I finished. 'They're too ashamed to tell the police. One of them might, if her mum can persuade her, but even if she does, it's unlikely he'll get caught. Like you said, he's an expert at his game. That's why I need to do this, don't you see?'

Caroline looked unconvinced. 'I still say you're playing with fire. Fecking crazy, this is.'

Silence, awkward and tense, settled around us. She was right, but my obsession still clung to me. *One more date with Liam Tate*, I told myself. Then I'd decide whether or not to drop the whole thing.

Unwelcome as crap at a christening, the memory of the texts returned. *You don't want to piss me off, friend... The last person who threatened me ended up regretting it...*

'So you met this guy Scott while you were hunting for the man who conned Ellie?' Caroline said at last. 'At first you thought he might be her ex, is that right?'

'Yes. He's not, though. Different hair, he doesn't work in construction, and he's too unsure of himself. No way is he a con man.' An absurd idea. Scott's shyness was beyond endearing.

'So he thinks you're ... what name did you say you gave him?'

'Lynnie Connor.' Caroline had recognised my dilemma.

'And that you're an accountant who lives at the Harbourside?'

'Yes.' I squirmed in my seat. My sins had returned to bite me on the butt, and I had nobody to blame but myself.

Caroline's mouth tightened into a frown. 'Tell the poor guy the truth. You have to, if this relationship is to go anywhere. He needs to know the real you. Sooner rather than later.'

'I know.' Misery threatened to swamp me.

'The longer you leave it, the worse it will be.'

'What do I say, though?'

'You tell him what you've told me - about Ellie, about wanting justice for her. How you dreamed up this hare-brained scheme without thinking it through - don't look at me like that, you know I'm right - and now you want to set the record straight.'

'He'll hate me, Caroline. He won't want to see me anymore.' My greatest fear made real. The thought of happiness with Scott being snatched from me hurt like hell. After two dates he'd burrowed under my skin, and I never wanted him to leave.

She blew out a breath. 'There's a chance that'll happen, yeah. A good chance, if you ask me.'

'I'll talk to him. Soon.' Panic washed over me, but Caroline was right.

'Feck, Lyddie. What if Scott discovers you're also dating this Liam guy? If he does, you're screwed. And not in a good way.'

Oh God. I'd not thought of that. What the hell was I playing at?

My brain felt as though someone had forced it through an emotional wringer. 'Shame I'm driving tonight. I'd kill for a single malt.'

CHAPTER 7

After my visit to Caroline, I headed back to Kingswood and went straight to bed, my brain unable to decide my next move. My friend was right. I was playing a dangerous game, one that might destroy my chance of happiness with Scott. I procrastinated, telling myself I'd see how my evenings with him and Liam panned out and make a decision then.

I lay in the dark, my thoughts a mess. The display on my alarm clock read 2am. As I tried in vain to doze off, my mobile pinged, causing me to jump.

Hey there, friend. I'm right behind you. Getting ever closer. xxx

I stabbed at the 'off' button. The fucker didn't mean that literally, did he?

The memory of the hooded man I'd seen earlier tormented my brain, despite my best efforts. I'd not spotted anyone hanging around after I'd left Caroline's house, thank God. Nevertheless, I didn't sleep at all that night.

***

Exhausted, I spent the first part of Monday morning moving my things to the Harbourside flat. It came fully furnished so all I had to do was transport my personal possessions there and make the place appear lived in. Several potted plants worked wonders, as did replacing the bland prints on the walls with my own paintings. A few throws on the sofas, plenty of cookery books in the kitchen, and it looked great, although still somewhat sparse. Everything was ready for Liam's visit.

On impulse, I picked up my mobile and called Ellie. She'd seemed okay the last time we'd spoken, but I still preferred to keep tabs on her in person. Besides, she ought to know where I lived, should her mood ever take a downturn and she ended up needing a bolt-hole.

'How about lunch?' I suggested. 'My treat.' We arranged I'd pick her up from her flat at one o'clock.

Ellie looked better than I'd dared hope after I collected her from St George. We chatted about her sewing projects, about Mum, and she appeared animated, almost happy. After I pulled into my parking space at the Harbourside, she glanced around, confusion in her face. 'I thought we were going to a restaurant?'

'Not today.' I switched off the engine and got out of the car. 'Come with me.'

Ellie was silent as we walked into the entrance lobby, which boasted a profusion of potted ferns and a riot of marble. She didn't speak a word while we rode the lift towards my apartment. No comment after I unlocked the door and ushered her inside. Instead, her eyes roamed around, taking in the leather sofas, the sleek coffee table, the rest of the furnishings.

'What is this place?' she asked. 'And why are your paintings on the walls?'

'This is my new home. For now, anyway.'

Her face clouded. 'I don't understand.'

A slight distortion of the truth seemed in order. 'I needed somewhere to stay while I'm in Bristol. My house is too cramped, what with Amelia always inviting her friends to stop over, and I didn't want to impose on either you or Mum. Or Caroline. So I rented this apartment.'

She frowned. 'Must be costing you a bomb.'

I laughed. 'It's only short-term. Besides, I can afford it. Come on, I'll make you lunch.'

Ellie was silent as I fixed us soup and sandwiches, her gaze hovering over the high-spec appliances, the granite work surfaces. Was that envy in her expression? She made no comment, however.

'Are you all right?' I asked.

Another frown. 'I guess. It's just that I've been missing Dad a lot lately.'

'Me too.' So that was why her mood had nosedived. She must have noticed the ornament on the kitchen windowsill. Black onyx, carved into an infinity symbol, it had been a gift from our father one Christmas. Ellie owned an identical one.

For the rest of our time together, she remained withdrawn, and her abrupt mood swing concerned me. Meanwhile, I had a date lined up with the very man who might have conned her.

***

That evening Liam was waiting for me by the door of Le Bistrot d'Yves, and I noticed his eyes flicker over my Audi as I parked up. I'd done my best to project wealth, having treated myself to a designer-label dress at the weekend. If I said so myself, I looked good, the cut flattering my curves and giving the illusion of a waist. My confidence was high. Tonight was the night I'd decide whether Liam Tate was also Steven Simmons, Rick Montgomery and Michael Hammond.

My thoughts went to the text I'd received that morning. *I'm still watching you, friend. Every day I'm getting closer to finding out who you are.* A shiver ran through me, despite the warm evening.

I forced my attention onto the man standing before me. He leaned in to peck me on the cheek. 'You look lovely, Lynnie.'

'Thank you.' I smiled a fake grin, then led the way into the restaurant. I'd read good reviews about this place, and at first glance they didn't appear wrong. The ambiance was intimate, cosy, upmarket. The silverware was heavy, the wine glasses top quality. Waiters sporting bow ties milled around bearing trays of covered dishes. Everything screamed expensive, opulent, chic. An impression confirmed once I saw the prices on the menu.

After we ordered - coq au vin for me, veal for Liam - I pulled my mobile from my bag. 'I'll just switch this to silent,' I said, flashing a smile his way. 'So we're not disturbed.' In reality, my fingers found the recording option and turned it on. It wouldn't hurt to get into the habit of capturing our conversations on audio for when he revealed the fraudster behind his Mr Nice Guy mask.

Despite the circumstances, our date had its plus points. My chicken was delicious, the wine sublime. Liam was way too cocky for my tastes, but if I had to fake-date him, things could have been worse. Most of the time we talked about travel, with him professing to love Asia and regaling me with stories of his trips to Thailand. At times I almost forgot why I was there. Liam couldn't compete with Scott though. I remembered the latter's shy smile, that dimple, and grinned to myself.

'Can I ask you something?' Liam's words pulled me from my reverie. 'Have you dated anyone else? From Premier Love Matches, I mean?'

I wasn't sure how to respond. Honesty held no appeal. I didn't care to discuss Scott with this man, and besides, what would I gain? If Liam was my quarry, wasn't it better he believed me solely interested in him?

'No,' I said. 'Not since meeting you.'

'It's a sore subject, you see.'

I didn't follow. 'What is?'

'Remember I told you my ex cheated on me?'

I nodded.

'I know we've only met twice, Lynnie, but I don't want you seeing other men.'

Whoa! Was this guy for real? Like he'd said, we were only two dates removed from strangers. I almost told him to go to hell, but didn't - because of his expression. That darkness I'd glimpsed before sat in his eyes again, only blacker. More intense.

Apprehension drained the saliva from my mouth. I swallowed hard, then remembered my aim, which was to convince Liam I was interested in a relationship. However hard it might be, I needed to overlook his controlling behaviour. 'Fine. If you'll do the same.'

'Of course.' All smiles, he reached over and squeezed my hand. 'Shall we get the dessert menu?'

It was while we were eating our next course I got another clue that Liam might be Ellie's ex.

'It's done me good to come here tonight,' he said. 'I've been a bit down recently.'

'How so?'

He exhaled a long breath. 'The house renovations are bleeding me dry. And business isn't great either. Construction's an expensive game, cash flow is always erratic, and to be honest, I'm worried sick.'

'I'm sorry to hear that,' I replied, acting sympathetic. 'You're concerned about money, right?'

'Yes. I've no problem in landing the contracts. It's funding them that's the difficulty.' He ran his fingers through his hair, the motion jerky. Worry sat in the creases around his eyes, and a defeated air hung over him, in contrast to his former upbeat tone. I had to hand it to him; this man was an expert faker of emotions.

'Will it get better?' I asked. 'If you can ride out the worst of it?'

He paused before answering. 'Maybe. Some extra capital would work wonders, though. It wouldn't have to be a huge amount, just enough so I could pay my office staff and settle a few overdue accounts.'

I wasn't certain how to respond, but found I didn't need to. Liam flashed me a quick smile. 'Listen to me, burdening you with my problems. Forget I said anything. I don't want to ruin a wonderful evening.'

'You haven't.' I remembered my phone, recording our conversation, and how my next step would be to bag another date with him. Once he'd sown the seeds, I didn't think he'd wait long before making a more tangible move.

After the bill arrived, he stopped me when I took my credit card from my purse. 'This one's on me.'

'I can't let you do that. Let me pay my share. Please.' The total came to a shade under one hundred and fifty pounds, the most expensive meal I'd ever eaten.

'My treat. I insist.'

'But what you said earlier ... about your finances, I mean.' I floundered, stymied in my search for words that didn't sound tactless.

He waved a dismissive hand. 'Mum gave me cash for my birthday a while ago. I've been saving it for a special occasion.' He took out his wallet, removed a wad of notes and counted them, slapping down a cool one hundred and eighty pounds for the bill and the tip.

A slick touch, I decided, to drop hints about his business problems and then demonstrate his generosity in the face of those issues. The fact he'd not used a credit card wasn't lost on me either. Hadn't Sophie's mum Anna indicated this man dealt in cash whenever possible?

Outside the restaurant, I leaned against the Audi, smiling at Liam. The time had come to wow him with my new flat at the Harbourside. 'I'd love to cook for you sometime. Do you like braised beef?'

We made arrangements accordingly. 'See you Wednesday,' I told him.

***

Satisfied with the way the evening had gone, I drove back to the Harbourside. The underground car park was deserted at that time of night, the silence magnifying the clicking sound as I locked the Audi's doors. As I made towards the stairwell, I noticed someone watching me. He - his height and build betrayed his gender - was positioned at the top of the driveway leading to the parking area, his gaze fixed on me. A hoodie, along with the half-light up there, concealed his face.

'Hey!' My anger, and with it my fear, ricocheted off the walls. 'Who the hell are you? What do you want?'

Useless, of course. The moment the man spotted me staring at him, he took off. I sprinted up the slope, but by the time I'd got to where he had been, he'd disappeared.

I leaned against the nearest wall, my breath coming in harsh gasps. *Relax*, I reassured myself. *You're fine*. Probably just some bum, hoping to snatch my handbag, but he hadn't succeeded, had he? I'd been safe enough, the parking area itself brightly lit and monitored by security cameras. The bastard would have been minus a brain to have ventured any closer.

Then I remembered. The night I'd gone to Caroline's, the man I'd thought might be following me. Also wearing a hoodie. About the same height and build, too.

Liam's words came back to me. *I don't want you seeing other men.* Was he spying on me? It would have been easy enough to keep a hoodie in his car, ready to transform himself into Mr Creepy whenever he chose. Might he have tailed me on my way home from Le Bistrot d'Yves? Had that been him stalking me when I visited Caroline?

God, the darkness in his eyes when he'd mentioned his cheating ex. I couldn't discount the possibility that, besides being a con artist, Ellie's former boyfriend might border on being psychopathic.

For several minutes I propped myself against the wall while my breathing returned to normal. I considered the possibilities. Could Broken and Betrayed's ex have tracked me down, despite my conviction he'd never find me? If he and Liam Tate were the same guy, then maybe, but I still considered it highly improbable.

Or perhaps Liam *was* following me, driven by his jealousy issues, but unaware I was the anonymous texter who'd threatened him with prison. That seemed a more likely explanation.

Quit being so paranoid, I admonished myself. Weirdos abounded in any city after dark, and life in my sleepy Spanish coastal town had most likely rendered me complacent. The guy had probably been some random bum. So long as caution was my watchword, I'd be fine.

So why did fear continue to haunt me?

***

In the sanctuary of my apartment, I checked the sound quality of my recording. It was faint, but Liam's mentions of his money worries were audible, which was all I needed. For the time being, anyhow. I saved the file on my laptop and logged onto Love Rats Exposed.

'Sad Sister here, reporting back after my date,' I typed. *'I'm pretty sure I've found who I'm after. He's using the name Liam Tate now. Whatever it takes, I swear I'll nail this bastard. I'll keep you posted.'*

Brave words, belied by the anxiety that was growing inside me. Caroline was right - I was playing a dangerous game. I mulled over my options. First I'd cook for Liam at the Harbourside flat, see whether he dropped any further hints about a financial bail-out. Depending on how that went, next I'd come clean to Ellie, tell her what I'd done and urge her to go to the police along with the evidence on my phone. If I exerted some gentle persuasion, surely she'd see sense?

As for Scott, first I would wrap up the situation with Liam and then tell him the truth. Dread gripped my gut at the prospect of unveiling my deceit, but it needed to be done. All I could do was pray ridding Ellie's life of one man wouldn't wreck my chance of happiness with another.

A solitary bright light burned on my horizon. Tomorrow evening I had a date with Scott.

***

And what a night it turned out to be. We met at seven o'clock outside the Arnolfini for our walk, the air still warm after the heat of the day. Scott seemed more confident when he greeted me, although I glimpsed an occasional flash of the shyness I found so charming. Especially when he caught sight of the bracelet of gold beads around my wrist. He didn't comment, but his soft smile spoke for him. As we strolled past the M Shed towards the SS *Great Britain*, we laughed and chatted, and I never wanted our time together to end.

Once we arrived on the other side of the harbour, we stopped to gaze at the boats bobbing on the water, the night air cooler by then. Neither of us spoke for a while, the evening perfect without words.

Then, emboldened, I decided to chance my luck. The suggestion left my mouth before I could rein in my impulse.

'Would you like coffee at my place? It's only a five-minute walk from here.' Heat flushed my cheeks. Had I been too pushy?

He nodded. 'Great idea. I'd love that.'

Relief flooded through me. I'd been afraid he'd say no, despite how well we'd been getting along. A prickle of nervousness stirred in my gut, though. Might Scott want, or expect, sex? However much I liked him, our relationship was too new for me to take that next step. We barely knew each other, I'd not slept with a man since Richie, and ... oh God. Lynnie Connor, my alter ego, would have jumped into bed with Scott Champion in a nanosecond, her initial nervousness around this man long gone. Lyddie Hunter was a different matter. Since I'd put on weight, I had lost confidence in the bedroom, insecure about my cellulite and stretch marks.

His next words diffused my anxiety. 'I can't stay long, I'm afraid. I need an early night.'

'Are you going somewhere tomorrow?'

His expression clouded. 'I'll tell you about it over coffee.'

We set off in the direction of my flat. To my surprise, Scott reached for my hand once we'd gone a few paces, his fingers warm against my own as we walked towards Millennium Square. My heart thrilled at his skin touching mine, the sensation electric and filled with promise. I wrapped myself up in the cosy silence, happy beyond words. Without warning, Scott stopped abruptly, a frown on his face.

'What's up?' I asked.

He didn't answer at once, his gaze directed somewhere behind us. Then: 'I think we're being followed.'

My mouth turned desert-dry. 'Are you sure? Where?'

Scott gestured in the direction of the city centre. 'Over there. He took off once he caught me staring at him.'

'What did he look like?

'Just some guy, dressed in jeans and a hoodie. I didn't get a chance to see more.' He shook his head. 'Sorry, I didn't mean to scare you.'

'It takes more than that to rattle me. Probably just some dope-head.' My voice sounded more confident than I felt. We continued the rest of the way in silence.

Once inside my apartment, I busied myself with coffee, kettle and mugs while Scott leaned against the door jamb to the kitchen. 'Nice place you have here,' he said.

'Isn't it great? I only moved in recently, which is why it looks a little bare.'

He moved closer to the wall on which I'd hung some of my early work. 'Wow. Are these yours? You're really talented.'

My cheeks flushed with pleasure. 'Thank you.'

He smiled. 'You must come to my house soon. It's not as smart as this, but I like it. You can check out my crappy paintings while you're there.' He gave a self-deprecating laugh.

A visit to Scott's. I approved of the idea. A lot.

We settled on one of the sofas in the living area, facing each other. 'So where are you off to tomorrow that needs an early start?' I probed.

Again that clouded expression. He sipped his coffee, clearly considering his answer. When he spoke, his voice shook a little. 'I need to collect Darcy, my sister. From hospital.'

Then he said the words that made my soul ache for him. 'She has cancer. An aggressive form of leukaemia.'

No wonder he looked so bereft. Concern squeezed my heart. I set my coffee mug on the floor, moving closer. We stared at each other, tension crackling through the atmosphere. Then I reached out my hand, took one of his and wrapped my fingers around it. Ah, skin on skin again. Perfect.

'I'm sorry.' Such inadequate words, yet I hoped my tone conveyed my feelings.

'We thought we had it beaten. She'd been in remission for two years. Then ...' He shook his head. 'Seems we were wrong.'

'Will she ...' I stopped, aware I couldn't ask Scott whether his sister would live or die. He understood what I meant though.

'Maybe she'll pull through,' he said. 'Darcy's young, and the survival rates for leukaemia are better than many other forms of cancer. I can't deny I'm scared though. She's not in a good way. Who the hell is when undergoing chemotherapy? She's just completed another round of treatment, and looks like shit.'

'I wish I could help.' Anything to wipe that haunted expression off his face.

He shrugged. 'All I can do is hope. If I lost Darcy, my whole world would collapse.'

Selfish it might be, but I had to ask. 'Is now a good time for you to be dating? With your sister so ill?'

'Probably not.' He sighed. 'It's been hard, though. Watching her hair fall out, seeing her so drained, so pale. Apart from my art, I've precious little in my life. I don't care about my job - it's a means to pay the bills, nothing more. I just wanted ...' His expression grew troubled, and I yearned to lean in and kiss him. 'Some hope for a better future, I guess. Which is why I joined Premier Love Matches.'

'I understand.'

Scott got to his feet. 'I should go.' A hint of nervousness crossed his face. 'Listen, do you fancy coming round to my place sometime next week? This weekend is out of the question, what with making sure Darcy's all right.'

That sounded a great idea. As well as spending more time with him, I'd get to see his paintings. 'I'd love to.'

We edged closer to each other. Sex might be off the menu, but other things might prove possible. Much as I yearned for our first kiss, I was worried. Was my breath still fresh? Should I have gargled first?

Then Scott pulled me to him, our mouths met, and my brain melted.

***

Liam was late again on Wednesday evening. Only by five minutes, but such rudeness annoyed me. Scott had always been on time, his punctuality added to the list of things I liked about him. While I waited, I went into the bedroom to check my appearance.

Wariness hung in my expression as I stared in the mirror. I knew full well that, had I been cooking for Scott, I'd have appeared far more radiant. God, that kiss ...

The piercing sound of the buzzer made me jump. Liam had arrived.

When I opened the door, I spied a bouquet of yellow roses in his right hand before he enveloped me in a hug, his cologne heavy in my nostrils. Despite my best efforts, I tensed, my body rigid in his arms. He drew back but didn't say anything. Instead he thrust the flowers at me. 'These are for you. You look lovely, by the way.'

I buried my nose in the roses, inhaling their heady scent. 'Thank you. They're beautiful.' I busied myself with finding a vase, gesturing towards the dining area. 'Make yourself comfortable. The food will soon be ready.'

Liam plumped himself on one of the fat sofas, his gaze roaming the room. He whistled under his breath. 'Wow. This apartment is stunning. You've not lived here long, I take it?'

So he'd noticed the lack of personal possessions. 'I only moved in recently.'

'Do you own this place? Or rent it?' He shook his head, the movement accompanied by a laugh. 'You don't have to answer that. It's none of my business.'

'I bought it. A couple of months back.' My bullshit radar was on full alert again. So the prick was probing into my finances, was he? Yeah, he was Steven Simmons all right. As well as Rick Montgomery and Michael Hammond.

I found it damn hard to put on a convincing act that night. My anger over Ellie burned hot while we ate. I listened while Liam talked about himself, making comments where appropriate, careful to preserve the façade of Lynnie Connor.

We'd finished the beef and started on dessert by the time I decided to raise the stakes. So far Liam hadn't mentioned his business, which didn't gel with how I'd expected him to play things. Unbeknown to him, I had activated the recording function on my phone before I served up our first course.

'So how's work?' I injected concern into my tone. 'When we went for that French meal, you seemed so down about everything.'

A frown. 'Sorry about that. I'd had a rough day.'

'Want to share?'

He shook his head. 'I shouldn't dump my issues on you.'

I leaned forward, the epitome of a supportive girlfriend. 'I'm interested. Really.'

'Like I said, money's always a problem. I've just completed a new development site and need to sell the houses as soon as possible. Several creditors are threatening me with court action and have frozen my accounts in the meantime. I'm behind with paying the men's wages as well. That's how it goes in construction … cash flow's often erratic.' His mouth tightened. 'I should be used to it, but it stresses me out big time.'

'Can you talk to your bank? Get an overdraft, perhaps?'

A snort of derision. 'That ship sailed a long time ago.'

'Sounds like you need an injection of cash. And soon.' I kept my voice concerned, watching him all the while.

He grimaced. 'Don't I know it, especially with the house renovation costs escalating. Wish I had a hotline to the money genie, that's for sure.' His eyes roamed the apartment for a second time, no doubt assessing its understated luxury. I could almost hear the cash registers singing *ka-ching!* in his head.

Liam ate the last bite of his cheesecake. 'Can we talk about something else? Please?'

'Of course.' The certainty inside me grew. He'd planted the seed, and had started to water it. The bastard would attempt to harvest his crop soon. *Bring it on*, I told myself, as I prepared our coffees.

The evening ended with his hands seeking my breasts, his lips clamped to mine once we'd moved to the sofa. Had he given me enough warning, I'd have dodged his mouth before it landed on my own, but he didn't grant me that luxury. Liam was no match for Scott, not even close. I endured the kiss while removing his fingers from inside my bra.

'It's too soon,' I said after I pulled away.

His eyes narrowed. 'Are you seeing someone else? Is that why you're so goddamn standoffish?'

'No!' The denial flew from my mouth, followed by guilt at my deception. 'I told you that already.'

'I won't be lied to, Lynnie. If you can't keep your legs shut around other men, I deserve to know.'

'Don't be so bloody crude.' I shot off the sofa, putting distance between us. 'There's no-one else, I swear.'

We stared at each other, anger written large in my face, suspicion dominant in his. Then he gave me a weak smile.

'Sorry. I didn't mean to offend you.' He grabbed his jacket, his expression contrite. 'I should get going, I guess.'

Before he left, I promised to see him again in a couple of nights' time, just to get rid of him. Once I'd shut the door, I wiped my hand across my mouth. Yuk. I'd just kissed the bastard who had swindled Ellie, who'd creeped me out with those weird texts, maybe even by stalking me. What the hell was I playing at?

I reminded myself what was at stake. Justice for my sister.

CHAPTER 8

Ellie remained a concern. She'd sounded stressed the last time we'd spoken on the phone. Mum and I were in contact with her every day, our worry being she might still be suicidal, yet burying her feelings. She operated as though it were a sin to appear anything other than perfect in front of her family. Whether she'd always been so devious, I couldn't recall. I'd known the damaged version of Ellie for so long I barely remembered how she'd once been.

The morning after my date with Liam, I drove to my sister's flat in St George. When she opened the door, her appearance did little to reassure me. The shadows under her eyes had returned and an air of worry clung to her, evident in the frown she wore. Something wasn't right, and I prayed this time she'd confide in me, rather than seek solace in a bottle of pills.

'Lyddie,' she said. 'You should have called. The place is a mess.'

'Doesn't matter.'

She stood aside to let me pass. The air in the hallway was stale, a faint odour of old cooking increasing the closer I got to the kitchen. Papers and files lay strewn across the dining-table. From the glimpse I got, most were bank statements, the rest being invoices. Some had 'overdue – please pay at once' red-stamped on them. Ellie pushed past me, sweeping everything into her arms before I had a chance to speak, and exited the room. When she returned, I pulled her into a hug.

'I'm here for you,' I said.

She shoved me away, her eyes not meeting mine. 'For now, sure.'

It wasn't her style to sound so resentful. 'What do you mean?'

'You'll be off to Spain before long.'

So that was why she was hurting. 'I might be moving back to Bristol,' I said. Perhaps I was being premature, but so what? Before Ellie could respond, I pressed her into one of the chairs around the table, sitting opposite her. 'I've met a man, Els.'

Her tired expression lifted. 'Who? How? Where?'

Encouraged, I told her about Scott, leaving out any mention of searching for Steven Simmons, merely saying we'd met through a dating website. When I finished, she squeezed my hand. 'I'm pleased for you.'

A positive sign. Part of me felt guilty for parading my happiness in front of her, but my aim was to reassure her I'd be around for a while. Maybe for good.

Silence fell over the kitchen. I knew I should go, but I couldn't ignore the frown that had crept back on Ellie's face.

'What's wrong, Els? I know you're upset about something.' I remembered the red-stamped invoices. 'Are you concerned about money?'

Her lips tightened, but she shook her head.

'Steven Simmons, then?'

I watched the shutters slam shut over her brown irises, saw her expression morph into neutrality. 'I'm fine, Lyddie. Nothing for you to worry about. I've not been sleeping well, that's all.'

I knew better than to argue. Ellie was lying and I intended to discover why.

***

On Friday evening I'd arranged to meet Liam at an upmarket wine bar, all brushed steel and black marble, in Clifton. My expectations were high he'd continue his pursuit of my money, and when he did, my phone would record every word. Loathing filled me while I waited, my urge to be with Scott fierce. The game with Liam had to end soon, and with any luck I might bring matters to a head on this date. I hated Lynnie Connor, mistress of deceit. I yearned to be Lyddie Hunter again, a woman who wanted only one man in her life, and it wasn't the snake with whom I'd be drinking wine once he arrived.

As usual, Liam was late. He struck me as uptight the minute he walked through the door. I noticed his sullen expression as he yanked his chair out. He sat down without greeting me, his eyes averted.

'Is something wrong?' I asked.

When he'd didn't reply I tried again. 'I realise it's a sore subject, but are things at work still bad? With your cash flow problems, I mean?'

His tone was curt when he replied. 'Crisis averted, as they say. I sold two of the houses on the development site, subject to the contracts being signed. With that in place, the bank agreed to extend my overdraft. My men have all been paid, along with the most urgent bills.'

'That's great.' I'd not expected that, and my brain scrambled to catch up. No sob story, no hints that he might need my help. It didn't fit with tapping me up for money, a contradiction that rendered me unsure and floundering. I still couldn't fathom the reason for his foul mood.

'Not that you give a fuck,' he continued.

Alarm edged into my voice. 'What do you mean?'

'I saw you earlier today.' Darkness glowered in his eyes. 'At that Italian place on Park Street, holding hands with some guy. So much for you not dating other men.' Contempt filled his tone.

'You followed me?' My visit to Caroline's, the parking lot under my apartment. The man Scott spotted the other night. Our impromptu lunch at Bella Pasta. Liam, guilty every time.

'Don't make *me* out to be the bad guy in this.' Fury sat in every line of his face. 'You're nothing but a goddamn slut.' His voice was growing louder with every word, and people were staring.

'For God's sake, Liam, stop shouting.' My cheeks flushed with embarrassment.

'Couldn't keep your legs together, could you? Just my luck to date two cheating whores in a row.' He shoved the table away as he stood up, causing the wine list to fall to the floor. 'Fuck you, bitch. We're through.'

***

Back in the Harbourside apartment, I plumped myself onto the nearest sofa, my legs tucked under me, thoughts whirring through my head. One thing was obvious: Liam Tate wasn't Steven Simmons. However hard I tried, I couldn't reconcile the fact he'd ended our relationship with him being a con artist. A misogynist, no doubt, one with entrenched jealousy issues, but not Ellie's ex. Whoever had conned my sister had been cool, focused, self-controlled, and that wasn't Liam Tate, not in a million years. Especially seeing as he'd said his money worries were solved. In my haste to obtain justice for Ellie, I had targeted the wrong man.

It was hardly surprising I'd not yet found Steven Simmons. I'd taken a gamble in the hope of finding Ellie's former boyfriend via a dating website. Several catered to a more upmarket crowd, and I'd only joined one. Moreover, I had no reason to assume her ex was still in the area. Chances were he'd taken off to another part of the country to try his luck elsewhere. I was back at square one with finding the bastard.

My mood wasn't total despondency, though. Hadn't I met Scott through my search?

My mobile pinged in my handbag, causing my heart to pound, my pulse to skyrocket. *Get a grip, Lyddie*, I told myself. With shaking fingers, I pulled out my phone.

A text message. *Hello, friend. Long time no talk.*

I forced myself not to respond. He'd soon tire of goading me if I ignored him, surely?

Another ping arrived after ten minutes. *Aw, have I upset you? You're not my friend anymore?*

My brain composed a retort, but I resisted the temptation. Instead I dug my nails into my palms, my hands clenched into tight fists.

A third ping followed. *Remember what I told you. You don't want to piss me off. I'm not always Mr Nice Guy.*

After my phone beeped a fourth time I hurried to the drinks cabinet and poured myself a whisky, even though scotch had landed me in this mess in the first place. Once seated again, I took a gulp, the Lagavulin burning in my stomach. Fuelled by the courage it provided, I read the latest message.

What, no more threats about the police? You're no fun these days.

I wouldn't reply. No way in hell.

I know lots about you, friend. More than you think.

I shot bolt upright, whisky spilling from my glass onto the sofa. Shit. Had I been right? Was this man a hacker? Had he uncovered my name, my address?

Screw not replying. *OK, fucker. So what's my name?*

You've got me there, I admit. But I'm working on it, trust me. My shortlist of possibilities is down to two.

A bluff on his part. My details couldn't have been hacked, because if he'd possessed the skills, he'd have done so already. Even so, his words scared me.

A final ping.

And when I find you, and I will, you're dead, bitch.

I switched off my phone and proceeded to get very drunk.

***

Saturday morning brought with it the inevitable hangover, sorted with copious amounts of water and some painkillers. To distract my attention from my lingering headache, I trawled the profiles on Premier Love Matches, not finding any likely candidates for Steven Simmons. My enthusiasm for finding Ellie's ex had waned. Caroline had been right - it was a hare-brained scheme. If I was honest, the text messages, especially the last one, frightened me. I tried to reassure myself. Hadn't he admitted he didn't know my name? That crack about killing me was his attempt at rattling my cage. Or so I hoped.

I considered my options. Even if I found the bastard who conned Ellie, could I ever trap him? Wouldn't I be better off hoping one of his other victims, such as Anna's daughter Sophie, might involve the police instead? With that in mind, I abandoned Premier Love Matches and logged onto Love Rats Exposed.

A few posts had appeared on the thread I'd started. *'Any news?'* Sophie's mum had posted. *'You said you thought you'd found the bastard - did you?'*

'*Update, please!*' Broken and Betrayed had posted, to which Heartbroken Helen had added, *'Yes, keep us in the loop! What's going on?'*

'I was wrong,' I typed, sour disappointment in every word. *'That guy Liam, the one I believed conned my sister? Turns out he didn't.'*

Within minutes I had a response. *'Shame! I've been rooting for you, girl. You're not still dating him, are you?'* Heartbroken Helen asked.

I was quick to reassure her. *'Nope. He's a control freak, with major jealousy issues. Turns out he's been stalking me.'*

A slew of replies ensued. From Sophie's mum: *'Stay safe, SS. Get the police involved if you have to.'*

'*Buy yourself a rape alarm. Don't take any chances with a guy like that.*' From Broken and Betrayed.

'I agree. He sounds dangerous.' From Heartbroken Helen.

I typed suitable responses, ensuring everyone I'd be careful. Then I logged off. I'd catch up with any new replies later.

I considered texting Scott but decided against it. I didn't want to crowd him, what with things with Darcy being so difficult. He'd told me he would call on Sunday evening, and I needed to give him space.

On a whim, I drove over to Caroline's. It was almost midday, and I was sure she'd be home after her morning yoga class. Besides, I could drop in on Ellie afterwards.

After I'd parked the car, I glanced around, scanning for a man in a hoodie. No sign of Liam, but I couldn't shake the sensation I was being watched. The scene at the wine bar still had me rattled. Worry clung to me that a guy with such anger issues might be the vengeful sort, intent on payback. I did another three-sixty-degree survey of my surroundings. Two teenage girls, an elderly man, but nobody else. I'd been imagining things. Hadn't I?

Caroline greeted me at the door, still in her workout gear. To my surprise, she seemed reluctant to let me in. Eventually she stood aside, and I walked past her into the living room, instantly realising why I should have texted first.

Richie occupied one of the armchairs. God, he looked handsome, but then he always did, at least to me. He stood up as I entered, his expression unfathomable, and our eyes met. I drank in his height, the blue irises that had always melted me, the neat goatee he'd grown since our last encounter. Was it my imagination, or was his dark hair longer? He'd lost weight too, and replaced it with muscle. A pang of regret squeezed my heart before I pinned a smile on my face.

'Richie,' I said, my voice higher than normal, my breath tightening in my chest. 'How are you?'

He shrugged. 'Not so bad. You?'

'The same.' An awkward pause descended before Caroline saved the day. 'I'll make us all coffee,' she announced.

'Actually I was about to ...' Richie got to his feet, but too late - she'd disappeared into the kitchen. He sat back, defeated, in the armchair. I took the seat opposite, self-consciousness needling me. Would he notice I'd put on weight? Why hadn't I worn something classier than jeans and a T-shirt? Richie wasn't looking my way though. If the tension in the room was an accurate measure, he must feel as awkward as I did.

Despite my feelings for Scott, Richie would always own a piece of my heart. I doubted it was mutual. By now he'd have found himself a girlfriend who didn't constantly accuse him of cheating. Besides, hadn't I moved on myself, with Scott and me becoming an item? It was time to lay the past to rest.

Caroline breezed in, bearing a tray of mugs, her gaze flitting between her brother and me. Richie took a gulp of his coffee, then set the mug on the windowsill. 'I should get going,' he announced. He gave his sister a hug, then turned to me. 'Good to see you, Lyddie.' Then he was gone.

I let out a long breath. 'That was awkward.'

'You two were bound to meet up sooner or later. Best to get it out of the way.' Always the practical one, my friend.

She settled herself opposite me. 'So how's it going with Mr Wonderful?'

The mention of Scott brought a smile to my mouth. 'Great, thanks. You want every last detail?'

'Need you ask?'

'That'll be a yes, then.' I described our last date, including what he'd told me about Darcy. 'He's so caring,' I finished. 'I think I've struck lucky at last.'

Caroline grinned. 'He sounds like a keeper, all right.' Her lips pursed a little. 'What about the other bloke? The one you thought conned Ellie?'

'Turned out I was wrong. He dumped me. In public.'

'Ouch. That's good, though. It means it's all systems go with this Scott guy. Have you told him the truth yet?

'No. But I will.' First I needed to work out what to say.

Caroline set down her coffee and fixed me with a stare I knew only too well. 'Listen, lovey. You've found yourself a decent guy, and I'm happy for you, so I am. But you need to quit this obsession with finding Ellie's ex. Either persuade her to involve the police, or let it go.'

'You're right.' The part of me that loved Ellie was stubborn, though. Devious too, as evidenced by my reply. I hadn't actually promised I'd follow Caroline's advice, had I?

After I left her house, I glanced around again, scanning my surroundings. I didn't spot anything suspicious at first. Then a movement in my peripheral vision alerted me. A man, tall and well-built, a hoodie pulled over his head, was striding away into the distance. He turned a corner and disappeared from view before I could register much about him. Maybe it had been Liam, maybe not. Broken and Betrayed was right - I shouldn't take chances, not with a guy who might well be unbalanced. I made myself a promise. The next time I spotted Mr Creepy, I'd swing into action against him. No more of this Ms Passive nonsense.

CHAPTER 9

Excitement tingled through me on Tuesday evening as I exited the shower. Scott and I had spoken on the phone on Sunday, ending with us planning a takeaway at his place. When I'd enquired about Darcy, his voice took on a strained tone.

'I'll tell you when I see you,' he said.

That night my heart hummed with happiness as I made myself look pretty for our date. My jeans were new, bought that morning, teamed with a mint-green top that skimmed my hips and concealed my thighs. Never one for much make-up, I contented myself with mascara, eye-liner and lip gloss, grateful for the soft caramel of my skin - a legacy from the Spanish sun. A squirt of perfume, some chunky earrings, and I was almost ready. All I needed was the bracelet of gold beads Scott had won for me. With a smile, I slipped it over my wrist.

Scott lived in Southville, on the other side of the city, his house at the end of a Victorian terrace. After I parked my car behind his Toyota, I glanced around, searching for any sign of Liam, but saw nothing to alarm me. Reassured, I stared at the house, observing the fresh paintwork, the window boxes of flowers. Before I could lift the cast-iron knocker, he opened the door and a flutter of happiness hit me.

He didn't speak. Instead, he pulled me inside, his lips seeking mine. In my belly the tremors swelled into a storm. God, this man could kiss.

When he drew back, he smiled. Out popped that damn dimple, and I was a lost cause. 'Can't believe I've had to wait since Friday lunchtime to do that,' he said.

I laughed. 'Something smells good. And I don't mean just you.'

Scott led me towards the rear of the house, into a dining area separated from the kitchen by a breakfast bar. A number of cartons sat on the counter, smears of curry staining their tops orange. 'Chicken balti with pilau rice,' he announced. 'Plus some side dishes. I hope you approve.'

I did, opening my mouth to tell him so, then shut it, my attention diverted by the wall in front of me. I turned, taking in the other three. The most incredible artwork I'd ever seen covered each one.

Out of the corner of my eye, I saw Scott watching me as I stared at the riot of colour. Still life scenes, depicting the standard subjects: fruits, vegetables, baskets of bread, vases of flowers, all in exquisite detail. Were I to reach out a hand, I could pluck an apple off the wall and bite into the succulent flesh he'd painted. The same with the oranges, the cantaloupe melons, the bunch of purple grapes. I'd always admired photorealism and the paintings before me were exquisite examples.

The world stilled around us. All that remained were these phenomenal works of art and the man who'd created them. Scott had been way too modest about his talent.

Behind me, I heard him clear his throat. 'Those are my early efforts.' His voice was hesitant, unsure. Holy crap. That promised well for his later stuff.

'These are incredible. I'd love to see more of your work.'

God help me, but he blushed. Right when I'd thought he couldn't get any more endearing.

'Come with me,' he said.

In the living room, another explosion of colour met my eyes, but God, what a difference. These paintings were abstracts, all of them fantastic. Mandelbrot swirls, most of them, drawing my attention toward the centre of each while also directing it outside their frames. Scott liked to slather his acrylic paint thickly on the canvas when not painting still lifes, I noted. An invitation to dive into every painting, roll in its gooey sensuality and die of bliss. Such an incredible talent this man possessed.

'Have you ever had any exhibited?' I asked.

He shook his head, that shy expression back in place. 'Not many people have seen them, to be honest. You're one of the few.'

I leaned forward, my eyes on the signature across the corner of the closest canvas. Scott Champion - the name executed with a flourish - along with the year he'd painted it. In my brain I hatched plans. The sale of my villa in Spain, my return to Bristol, the opening of a new gallery in my home city, one in which I'd stock his art. Manager of a car dealership be damned - this man should paint full-time. Then I remembered. To make any of that happen, I needed to come clean to Scott about deceiving him. I turned to him, a forced smile on my lips. 'Let's go eat. I'm famished.'

The food proved to be as delicious as it smelled. While we ate, I glanced around. To one side of the table sat several letters addressed to Scott, all unopened - circulars, by the look of them. A spider plant straggled across the windowsill. Next to it stood a plastic air freshener, its base furry with dust. Everything was so normal, so cosy, and I smiled with relief. I'd been beyond lucky to meet this man. I reminded myself not to judge all guys by the rotten ones. Gary McIlroy had been a bastard, sure, as was Steven Simmons. Scott was different, though. I'd found myself a man worth keeping, and I didn't intend to let him go.

Time to broach the subject of his sister. 'How's Darcy?'

His expression clouded. 'She's not doing so great. I'm worried sick, to be honest.'

My heart hurt for him. 'Will she need more chemo?'

He nodded. 'Yes. And the little minx is refusing to have it.'

Shock hit me. Okay, so chemotherapy was tough going, but surely a leukaemia sufferer would endure the side effects if it meant getting well?

'What's her reasoning?' I asked.

'She says she hasn't the strength to go through the treatment again. "That hell", as she describes it. That there's no point, given that the disease came back anyway.' He scrubbed his hand over his jaw, the movement jerky, his eyes haunted. 'She's looking into alternative options.'

'Isn't chemotherapy the best way to treat cancer?'

'Yes. But Darcy's always been into strange stuff. Crystals, chakras, meditation. She reckons she can heal herself through such crap.' His voice rose high with stress. 'She's being ridiculous. I don't say that, of course. But I think it.'

'She wants to try complementary therapies to replace the chemo?' I'd long been convinced of the benefits of natural remedies, but with an enemy such as cancer, the best course of action must be to pull out the big guns, right? That meant conventional treatment. Perhaps I was being unfair, though. Impossible to know how I'd react in similar circumstances. I shouldn't judge Darcy.

'Yes. I've tried to talk with her, but it's a thankless task.' He let out a long exhalation, his eyes closed. 'I'd like you to meet her sometime.'

Delight flared within me. I hadn't expected that so soon in our relationship. Because that was what we were forging - a real connection rather than casual dating. Why else would he introduce me to his sister?

'Lynnie?' Scott sounded hurt. I realised how he must have interpreted my lack of response.

'I'd love that,' I said, with a smile.

We polished off the rest of the food in a comfortable silence, allowing me to savour my happiness. At last I sat back, certain I might burst if I ate any more. 'That was delicious.'

He laughed. 'I'll fix us some coffee. Make yourself at home in the living room.'

While I waited, I surveyed more of his fantastic artwork. Scott appeared after a few minutes, bearing two steaming mugs. He handed me one before sitting beside me on the sofa. 'I've really enjoyed tonight,' he said.

'So have I.'

He sucked in a deep breath. 'Maybe it's too soon to discuss this. But we always have a good time together. At least that's my opinion.'

'Mine too.'

His gaze slid away. 'I don't find talking about emotional stuff easy. But what we have feels right. Like we're meant to be.'

My happiness bubbled higher.

'I want us to be a couple,' he said. 'To make it work with you.'

I didn't reply, but my inane grin spoke for me. He leaned over, took my hand. 'Is that a yes?'

'Need you ask?'

I suppressed the voice in my brain reminding me I had lied to this man. *Not now*, I told myself. Later, when I'd worked out what to say. I sipped my coffee, the atmosphere between us relaxed, like that between old friends.

'I want to tell you,' he continued. 'About my last relationship and how it ended. Like I said, I got hurt.'

'I'm sorry to hear that.' This woman must have been a fool.

'I'm over it now. Although the break-up hit me hard.'

'You loved her?'

He shook his head. 'We weren't together long enough for that. Just a couple of months, but I could easily have fallen for her. Partly due to her pretty face, but also because she seemed so fragile. A combination guaranteed to bring out my protective instincts.' He laughed. 'I told myself I'd shield her from everything bad in the world.'

'What went wrong?'

He swallowed. 'She dumped me. After telling me I was a useless boyfriend, how she wished she'd never met me. She only wanted me for one thing, you see.'

I was puzzled. 'What do you mean?'

'She was a gold digger. All she was after was money.' His voice shook a little.

Scott drained his coffee, setting the mug on the floor. 'Her business was in trouble. She sold stuff online, but wasn't getting enough sales, so she opened a shop in the Galleries. Her rent was astronomical, way beyond what she could afford. She'd run up debts with her website designer, her suppliers and her landlord but couldn't pay them. When she asked me for a loan, it was more of a demand. I refused - I didn't have any cash to spare - so she turned nasty. Broke off our relationship.' He shrugged. 'It's water under the bridge now. This all happened six months ago. When I met you, though, all the hurt resurfaced.'

'You can relax. I've no intention of asking you for money.'

'Thank God. I can put Ellie behind me at last.'

The name caught me on the hop. The facts didn't fit, however. Ellie sold stuff online, but she'd never rented a shop in the Galleries. What's more, Steven Simmons had been her first boyfriend. As far as I knew, she'd not dated anyone before him.

I had to be sure, though. 'Did you meet her through a dating website?'

'Yes. Not Premier, though. Soulmate Search, it was called.'

A finger of fear slid up my spine. Please God, no. 'That's a coincidence,' I managed. 'I know an Ellie who used that site. Wouldn't it be weird if it was the same person?' My laugh sounded forced.

'What's your friend's surname? My ex was called Ellie Hunter.'

My world shattered, along with the happiness I'd felt earlier. Unaware of the devastation he'd caused, Scott collected our mugs off the floor. 'I'll make a fresh pot of coffee,' he announced, disappearing into the kitchen. All the while I struggled to breathe. This couldn't be happening. Scott hadn't just said he'd dated my sister, had he? Who, it seemed, had lied to me. About her business, her past boyfriends, maybe more.

As for Scott, he deserved the truth. I still had to figure out a way to reveal my real identity. This, though? I had to tell him.

When he returned bearing fresh coffees, I dived in before my courage could call quits on me. 'Looks like we know the same Ellie Hunter.'

Surprise spread through his expression. He handed me a mug then sat beside me. 'Wow. I never expected that. Small world, hey?' He smiled, but it didn't reach his eyes.

'Ellie isn't my friend,' I said. 'She's my sister.'

Disbelief morphed into shock in Scott's face. 'Tell me you're joking.'

'Nope.'

'There must be some mistake.'

'What did your ex-girlfriend look like?'

He exhaled a long breath. 'The Ellie I knew was about five feet six, I guess. Slim, pale blonde hair, big brown eyes. She said she was twenty-five years old. Come to think of it, she mentioned having an older sister, but I can't remember her name.'

'So far, that all fits.'

'What line of business is she in? Is it custom-made bags and purses?'

Every last shred of hope drained from me. 'Yes.' I pulled my wallet from my handbag - she'd designed both - and flipped it open to show him the photo tucked inside. Ellie and me, taken just before my departure to live in Spain.

Scott paled. 'Oh, my God. That's her.'

He took my hand and gave it a squeeze, concern in his eyes. 'This is weird, all right. But does it matter? Okay, so it would be awkward to meet Ellie again, but I can handle that. What about you? Would it be a problem?'

I considered for a second. The answer was yes. Unless ...

'I hate to ask you something so personal,' I said. 'But how far did your relationship progress?'

He understood my meaning straightaway. 'We never did have sex.'

Thank God. That made a huge difference. 'She didn't want to?'

He shook his head. 'She seemed uptight in so many ways. I never got the full story, but it was obvious some tragedy in her past had damaged her.'

'You're not wrong there. One day I'll tell you what happened.'

'You haven't answered my question.' His expression remained anxious. 'Does it bother you I once dated Ellie?'

'If I'm honest, yes. We're all adults, though. And things never got serious between you two.'

'Thank God. Because I want to keep seeing you, Lynnie.'

'I want that too.' I stood up. Much as I hated our evening to end, I needed time to consider what Scott had said. Before long, I'd thrash this out with Ellie. I was determined to drag the truth from her.

CHAPTER 10

Thank God Scott hadn't asked me many questions. I'd left in a hurry, not giving him the chance to say much other than that he'd call me. An icy sweat broke out on my body when I considered how close I'd come to being unmasked. What if he'd wanted to know why my surname was different to Ellie's, given that neither of us had ever married? Or if he had remembered my sister was supposedly called Emma, not Ellie?

Too wired to sleep, I opened my laptop. I pulled up the Companies House website, so familiar from my accountancy career, and searched for Ellie Hunter Designs Limited, the business I'd formed for her before I left for Spain. I was looking for her last set of filed accounts.

The figures didn't make good reading. They were for the period ended eighteen months ago, the first year Ellie had been trading. Although they gave the bare minimum of information required, it was obvious the business had been insolvent at that stage. Not to a huge extent, but bad enough. I'd bet money that, in the months that followed, the deficit had increased, especially if Ellie had rented a shop somewhere expensive like the Galleries. My sister's business was in a financial hole, something she'd kept a secret from me.

I fired off a text to Ellie, saying I wanted us to meet up, that I'd be at her flat by eleven the next day.

I didn't sleep much that night.

***

By the time I awoke, Ellie had replied to my text, confirming she'd be at home at eleven, how she was looking forward to seeing me.

She wouldn't if she knew the reason for my visit. I reminded myself I couldn't barge in and play the bossy older sister, not if I wanted honesty from her. Any high-handed behaviour from me and she'd retreat into more lies, meaning I'd accomplish nothing.

When Ellie opened the door, she looked far better than the last time I'd seen her. Her hair was pulled back in a neat ponytail and a hint of blusher brightened her cheeks. She didn't look as harassed, either; the tension around her eyes was absent.

'It's good to see you,' she said. 'Do you want a coffee?'

'Please.' I'd need a caffeine boost to get through this without sparking an argument. While Ellie busied herself in the kitchen, I glanced around the living room. Everywhere was clean, a whiff of lemons in the air, and the carpet bore the marks of a recent vacuuming. Housework wasn't the hallmark of the depressed. Along with my sister's improved appearance, it boded well for her mental health. I doubted our ensuing discussion would, however. I reminded myself to proceed with caution.

Ellie returned bearing our coffees. She placed a steaming mug in my hand, then sat beside me on the sofa. 'So what's up? Your text sounded urgent.' Worry stole over her face. 'Is Mum all right?'

'She's fine.' My tone was curt. 'It's you I'm here to discuss.' Damn, I was sounding like a bossy older sister already.

'Me?' Surprise drove Ellie's voice higher than normal. 'Look, I understand you've been worried. But I'm okay. Not great, but getting there.'

'It's about Ellie Hunter Designs. Why didn't you tell me your company was insolvent?'

Ellie shook her head. 'I don't understand. What makes you think my business is in trouble?'

'I saw your accounts. The ones at Companies House.'

Anger crossed my sister's face. 'You've been spying on me? Why?'

'Don't be so melodramatic.' I reined in my irritation. 'They're public documents. Anyone can access them.'

'I know that. More to the point, why did *you*?'

'A friend of mine told me your business was struggling. That you'd overextended yourself.'

'What? Who said that?'

'Scott Champion, the guy you dated several months ago.' The memory of his pained expression as he told me about her demands for money honed my anger. 'He's a decent bloke. One who deserved better than the shitty treatment you dished out.'

My sister stared at me. A myriad of emotions passed over her face, none of which I could decipher. The thought occurred to me that she was preparing to lie. Again.

'I have no idea what you're talking about,' she said. 'Wait - isn't your new guy called Scott?'

'Yep. Seems I'm going out with your ex, although I only found out last night.'

Ellie shook her head. 'I don't know anyone called Scott Champion. As for dating someone with that name, that's ridiculous. I've only ever had a relationship with one man, and that was Steven Simmons.'

I fought against my anger. 'For someone whom you've never met, Scott sure knows a lot about you.'

She paled. 'What do you mean?'

'His description of you was spot on. What's more, he knew you design purses and handbags. Oh, and he also identified you from the picture in my wallet.'

She shook her head. 'I've no idea who this guy is, I swear. There must be some mistake.'

'So two Ellie Hunters live in Bristol, both of whom make custom bags and wallets, and who look identical?' I eyeballed her straight on. 'This is how you operate when life get tough, isn't it? You hide behind a smokescreen of untruths, so Mum and I never discover what's really going on.' I blew out a breath. 'It's got to stop, Els. We can't help you if you lie to us.'

'I've not been lying!' Her voice could shatter glass, it rose so high.

'Your business isn't insolvent?'

'No. Well, at one time, yes. But that's the norm, isn't it? To lose money in the first year of trading, I mean. My accountant's been great in helping me get back on track. Everything's fine now.'

'What about the shop you rented? The one that failed?'

'You're mistaken. I've never opened a shop.'

'You're lying again. You leased a unit in the Galleries but it proved too expensive and dragged the business under. That's why you tried to use Scott like a cash machine. Then you dumped him when he refused.' My tone was harsh, any intentions of going easy on Ellie having long vanished.

'That's nonsense. My business is all done online. I've never rented a shop in the Galleries or anywhere else.'

'What about when I was last here? You couldn't wait to clear that pile of invoices and bank statements off the table. So I wouldn't see the figures on them. You were worried about the business's finances, weren't you?'

'Not in the way you think. I was sorting everything to send to my accountant, that was all. If I seemed in a mood, that's because financial stuff bores the pants off me.'

More lies. While I considered my next move, Ellie spoke again. 'Let me talk to this Scott guy. If he meets me, he'll confirm we've never dated, and this will all blow over.'

'No.' My voice was crisp, incisive. Hadn't Scott suffered enough? Despite his protestations, I'd sensed he was still raw over the hurt Ellie had inflicted, and I wouldn't expose him to her manipulations again. She'd swear night was day if it suited her.

In that moment, a thought, terrible yet compelling, burst into my brain. An idea I rejected at first, reluctant to accept my sister could be so devious. The longer I considered the possibility, the more it made sense.

'Steven Simmons never existed, did he?' My words cracked through the air like a whip.

A strangled gasp issued from her throat. 'Of course he did! He took all my money, then tossed me aside like I was garbage ...' Sobs, harsh and hacking, burst from Ellie. She was a damn fine actor; I had to give her that. The part of me that loved her flinched at seeing her that way. The other side, the one that acknowledged Ellie lied when it suited her, strengthened its resolve.

'Your business failed,' I said. 'It drained all your reserves, left you penniless. You were ashamed, desperate, unwilling to admit the truth. So you invented a cover story.'

She shook her head, the strangled sobs continuing. I made no move to comfort her.

'No wonder you didn't want to involve the police. They'd have nothing to investigate.'

'That's not true! I couldn't bear anyone knowing what a fool I'd been.'

'You may as well admit it. You lied, Ellie.'

'I'm not lying, I swear!'

My patience snapped. 'Do you have the slightest idea of what Mum and I suffered when you tried to kill yourself again? All you had to do was to reach out, accept you needed help. But you didn't. Instead you deceived your own family, and in the worst possible way.' I strode towards the door, leaving her still crying on the sofa. Where this left our relationship, I wasn't sure, but I couldn't be around my sister right then. Her duplicity had cut too deep.

***

After I returned to the Harbourside apartment, I paced my bedroom, my mind awhirl. Part of me knew why Ellie had lied. Always keen to hide her insecurities, she must have been knocked for six after the failure of her business. I understood her reasons, but her behaviour still shocked me. Someday I'd forgive her deceit, and we'd move past it, but at present I was too angry. I had lied to Scott, and for what? Some twisted notion of revenge on a man who'd never even existed.

One thing was obvious. I needn't waste any more effort hunting for Steven Simmons. He'd been a figment of Ellie's imagination, nothing more. Oh, a real life con artist was at work all right, one who'd swindled money from Broken and Betrayed, as well as Anna's daughter Sophie. A prick who'd harassed me by text, but not someone with any links to my sister. The two issues were completely separate. In a way, I was grateful. I had been losing enthusiasm for finding the bastard anyway.

I wouldn't tell Mum any of this, not considering her likely reaction. She didn't need to know the extent to which her daughter had lied. If Ellie had any sense, she'd keep quiet too.

Without warning, loneliness engulfed me. I yearned for Scott to wrap his arms around me, kiss away Ellie's treachery. That meant no more procrastination. However much I dreaded the prospect, the time had come to reveal my true identity. Scenarios filled my head, ones in which he rejected me, called me awful names. I prayed they weren't a forewarning. If, please God, he forgave me, Ellie would have no choice but to accept us as a couple. At least Scott had never slept with her. I only felt a little weird about dating my sister's ex, and those feelings would pass, given time.

In an effort to soothe myself, I turned to my art. I'd bought brushes, paints and a pad after I moved into the Harbourside flat, my urge to create as strong as my need to breathe. My efforts to capture Scott in watercolours were as unsuccessful as my attempts in pencil. The man I was growing so fond of proved elusive, his essence indefinable through art alone. Only the real thing would do.

My bones aching with longing, I sent him a text. *Any chance we could meet? Tonight?*

Within a minute, my mobile pinged. *Was going to ask the same thing. Your place this time?*

Fine by me. Is seven o'clock OK?

You're on. Followed by a row of kisses. My heart did a somersault. Ridiculous, but I'd fallen hard for him.

Another ping from my phone. I picked it up, expecting an additional text from Scott, but the message was from Ellie. *Can I come over? You've got it all wrong, I swear.*

I snorted. My fingers tapped out a reply. *No. Scott's coming here tonight. I don't want to see you anyway.* With that, I switched off my mobile. I wasn't in the mood for my sister after the pain of her deception.

CHAPTER 11

The rest of the day crawled by, anticipation at seeing Scott spiking me first with longing, then dread. In my head I rehearsed the words I'd say to restore his faith in me. None of them sounded convincing.

My buzzer rang on the dot of seven o'clock. When I opened the door, Scott stood before me, all blue-eyed and dimpled, and I drank him in, aware tonight might be our last date. I prayed that wouldn't be the case.

He quirked his mouth in a shy smile, his eyes raking over my body. 'Hello, gorgeous.'

I stood aside to let him pass. Once I closed the door, I had no idea who moved first, but we ended up in each other's arms, our mouths hot and hungry. I could live off such kisses, of that I was certain.

I pulled away with a grin that bordered on embarrassed. 'Hello to you too.'

Scott laughed. He followed me into the kitchen, moving behind me to nuzzle the back of my neck as I opened a bottle of red wine and poured two glasses. Despite the kiss, nerves rendered my palms clammy, terror burning fierce in my belly. We'd have a few drinks first, I decided, and then I'd tell him. Everything would be all right. The alternative was unthinkable.

We sat side by side on the sofa, sipping our wine, while he filled me in about Darcy.

'She's doing better than I expected,' he said. 'I'm still worried sick, though. She's got more energy than after the first round of chemo, but that's because she's obsessed with the idea of curing herself without drugs. Yeah, right. As if that's likely.'

I was intrigued. 'Does she have a particular type of treatment in mind?'

His jaw tightened with anger. 'She's still checking out alternative therapy centres, believing the bogus success rates quoted on their websites. Most of it is New Age crap, and a lot of it sounds downright dangerous. Take fasting, for example. How the hell can it do Darcy any good to starve herself and just drink juices if she's sick? She needs food to build up her strength, damn it.' He was almost shouting, worry in every line of his face.

Scott shook his head. 'I don't know what to say to her anymore, Lynnie.'

I decided not to mention my firm belief in complementary medicine. Part of me had been sceptical at first, but that changed over time. I'd tried aromatherapy for relaxation, flower remedies for stress, herbal tablets for period pain, and been impressed with the results. Perhaps Darcy wasn't as deluded as Scott believed.

We finished our glasses of wine, it being obvious he didn't want to discuss the subject any further. The moment was edging closer when I'd have to reveal my deception.

'Coffee?' I suggested.

He flashed me his megawatt smile. 'Great idea.'

Unable to maintain eye contact, I escaped to the kitchen. As I fussed with the percolator, he came up behind me again, one hand resting on my hip, his breath fanning my neck. The musk of his aftershave wafted into my nostrils, and my bones melted with desire.

I couldn't put it off any longer. 'I have something to tell you.'

His arms slid around my waist, pulling me close. 'You sound upset. Is everything all right?'

'Not really.' Tears stung my eyes.

'Never mind the coffee. Come and sit down.' He led me back towards the sofa, concern in his expression. 'Talk to me. Please.'

My voice shaking with nerves, I plunged straight in. 'My name isn't Lynnie Connor. It's Lyddie Hunter.'

Confusion washed over Scott's face. 'Lyddie? As in short for Lydia?'

'Yes.'

'I don't understand. I noticed you and Ellie had different last names, and I wasn't sure of the reason, but why lie about your first name? Or your surname, come to that?'

I swallowed hard. 'It's complicated.' Then I told him everything. Ellie's recent suicide attempt, the burning rage that spurred me to seek justice for her. The fact I'd dated Liam Tate, how Steven Simmons had never been real, just another of my sister's lies. Scott didn't interrupt, not once. At last I drew to a close, my hands trembling in my lap. 'So now you know,' I finished.

Oh God. It was like waiting for a firing squad to shoot. I couldn't look at him, so great was my apprehension. *Say something*, I pleaded in my head. *Anything. Just save me from my misery.*

Scott released a long, slow breath. 'This has come as a shock,' he said. 'I'd thought ... I'd hoped ...' I glanced at him then, but his face was inscrutable. His hand rubbed over his jaw the way it did when he got tense.

'I'm sorry,' I whispered.

'You have to understand, Lynnie. Excuse me, I mean Lyddie. God, this is so weird. What I'm trying to say is ... I'm an honest kind of guy. What you see is what you get. So finding out you've lied ... well, it's hit me hard. Especially after what happened with Ellie.'

'I realise you're hurt. Please ...'

'I hoped we had a shot at something special. But now ...' He shook his head. 'How can I ever trust you again?'

'You have to believe me.' A tremor ran through my voice. 'If I could change things I would.'

'This Liam guy. Should I be worried about him?'

'God, no. I only dated him because of Ellie. He meant nothing to me.' I ran out of breath, falling silent. It wasn't the right time to broach my suspicion that Liam had been stalking me.

No response for a few seconds. Then Scott spoke again. 'Are you hiding any other secrets?'

I nodded. 'There's more.' I explained the Harbourside flat was a temporary rental, how I lived in Spain but had returned for

Ellie's sake. 'I'm not even an accountant anymore,' I finished. 'I went to Andalucía to paint. I run an art gallery there, not here.'

To my relief, a faint smile curved his mouth. Hope flickered within me.

'I can't pretend I wouldn't rather date an artist than a bean-counter,' he said. 'Although the fact you live abroad might be a problem.'

The tension in my gut loosened a little. Scott was disappointed, but not as angry as I'd feared. Might he be prepared to give me - *us* - a second chance?

At that moment, the doorbell buzzed. I cursed under my breath as I went to answer it. Whoever had come calling, their timing was lousy.

When I yanked open the latch, Ellie stood in the entrance. Anger ignited in me. I stepped into the hallway and pulled the door partly closed.

'What game are you playing now?' My words dripped with bile. 'I told you Scott was coming over tonight.'

'That's why I'm here.' Her expression was nervous, yet determined. 'I've been so upset, Lyddie. You were so mad at me earlier, but you must understand I never lied to you. About my business, about Steven Simmons, about him taking my money.' She chewed her lip, her eyes anxious. 'I hoped if he met me, your boyfriend would realise he'd made a mistake. That he'd dated some other woman, not me.'

That wasn't an encounter I had the strength for, not after my recent revelations to Scott. I shook my head. 'Not going to happen. You need to leave. Right now.'

I'd not reckoned on my sister's determination. Before I could stop her, Ellie pushed past me into the apartment.

My anger boiled over as I followed close behind. 'What the hell do you think you're doing? You can't force your way in here like this ...' A strangled cry from Ellie interrupted my protest. She'd halted in the middle of the living area, her back to me. I positioned myself between Scott and my sister, unsure what was going on. She was staring at him as though he was her worst nightmare made real.

'Hello, Ellie.' Scott got up from the sofa, his body language awkward. 'This is, um, a surprise. How are you?'

She didn't respond, her expression one of horror. Her face was paper-pale, her eyes wide with shock.

'Ellie?' I prompted, my anger replaced by concern. 'Els? Talk to me.'

'It's him,' she whispered. 'Oh, my God. Get him out of here, Lyddie. Please.'

Her next words sucker-punched me. 'That's Steven Simmons. The guy who stole my money.'

I stared at her in disbelief. 'That's ridiculous. Impossible.'

'Ellie?' Scott's voice sounded agitated. 'I don't understand. You know my name is Scott Champion. Not whatever other one you just said.'

Ellie took a step backward. She'd grown even paler. 'Liar. I don't care what name you're going by now. You were Steven Simmons last month.'

Scott turned to me, a frown on his face. 'That's impossible. Ellie dumped me back in February. I've not seen her since.'

'You're lying! Don't listen to him, Lyddie! He's Steven Simmons, and he stole my money, and ...' Ellie slumped to the floor, her hands covering her face. I could only stare at her.

Scott drew me aside, his voice a whisper. 'I think I should leave. Your sister - she's not well, that much is obvious. You have to know, though. All that stuff she said - none of it's true. I've not seen Ellie for months, I swear. As for saying I stole money from her ...' He spread his palms in a gesture of incomprehension. 'She's lying, although I've no idea why.'

'She does, whenever it suits her. I'm so sorry, Scott. I had no idea she'd barge in here tonight.'

He leaned forward, dropped a quick kiss on my forehead. 'I'm no expert, but my guess is she needs psychiatric help.'

I nodded, tears in my eyes. 'I know you've had a lot of crap thrown your way this evening. But don't give up on me. That's all I ask.' My voice shook as I spoke.

When Scott didn't respond, desperation clawed at me. 'Promise me you'll give us another chance. Please.'

His expression grew wary. 'I need to consider how we'd make this work going forward. To be honest, I'm not sure we can.'

Had my heart been made of glass, it would have shattered. I stayed mute, unable to speak. Then he strode towards the door, pulling it open. The next second he had gone.

His departure slammed a wrecking ball into my gut. The world stopped turning, imploded into fragments. Despair wracked me, heightened by the certainty Scott and I were finished.

Later I couldn't remember how long I stayed frozen. After a while I became aware of Ellie's continuing sobs. When I turned around, she was sitting on the sofa, wiping her face with a tissue. Her cheeks were mottled, her nose red. In that moment, I hated her.

I walked over, wrenching her hand away with iron fingers. Ellie winced with pain, but I didn't give a damn. 'You bitch,' I snarled. Her only response was a sob.

'Wasn't it bad enough you invented a con man as the reason you're broke? When all the time it was your lousy business decisions? No,' I said as she began to speak. 'Shut the fuck up. No more lies.' I slumped beside her on the sofa, my grip on her arm still pincer-like. Energy drained from me like air from a balloon. Impossible to get my head around my sister's betrayal.

'I've always been there for you,' I continued. 'When you struggled at school, following the car crash, after the suicide attempts. So you can understand why I'm so angry.' My fingers tightened their grasp. 'You've lied, and that's bad enough, but I never thought you'd stoop this low. You tried to break up me and Scott, just to bolster your story about a con artist. Well, it looks like your plan succeeded.'

'I'm not lying,' she said, her voice hoarse. 'You've been dating the same man who stole my money.'

God, she was a fine actor, all right. 'That's impossible. The facts don't fit.'

'What do you mean? I swear Steven Simmons and Scott Champion are one and the same.'

'Shut the fuck up and listen. You told me the guy you dated had long hair. Dark, almost black, you said. You've seen Scott. Mid-brown hair, worn short.'

More sobs. 'He's dyed and cut it since I last saw him.'

I ignored her. 'His job's not right, either. He doesn't work in construction, but at a car dealership. What's more, he paints. Beautiful, incredible works of art.' I paused to draw breath. 'This guy you allegedly dated. Was he an artist?'

She shook her head.

'Didn't think so.' I spat the words out. 'Because he never existed, did he? You know where I saw Scott's paintings? At his home. He invited me there for a meal, and that's more than Steve Simmons ever did for you, isn't it?' She stared at me but made no reply.

'You told me he was evasive about his address, so you weren't able to track him down. Convenient, that. Because, like I said before, he never existed, did he?'

'You're wrong.' The words a mere whisper.

'There's more.' My urge to inflict hurt grew stronger. 'Scott has a sister, Darcy, and he wants me to meet her. You think a con man would introduce me to his family? Yeah, right. As if that would ever happen.'

No response. Ellie had become the frozen one, not me.

'Scott's the real deal, and you need to stop inventing all this nonsense about him.'

'I never ... I didn't ...'

'Oh, and I almost forgot. The final nail in the coffin of your pathetic lies. He's never asked me for money. Not the slightest hint of any financial issues. Hardly fits with him being a con artist, does it?' I was well into my stride by then, my voice rising ever higher. 'So don't you dare come here spouting your crap and trying to break up the best thing that's ever happened to me. I've had it with you, Ellie. Get the hell out of here.'

CHAPTER 12

I slept for maybe two hours at best that night, the events of the evening churning through my mind. Scott's expression when I told him the truth, Ellie's face as she spouted her lies. I lay in bed until almost morning, tortured by my thoughts. Could Scott forgive me? Would my relationship with Ellie ever recover? By the time the dawn light pierced my curtains, I'd persuaded myself the answer to both questions was no. Never had I felt more bereft.

Only one course of action seemed possible; I'd return to Spain on the next available flight. A couple of quick visits to Mum and Caroline, then I'd pack my stuff and get the hell out of the UK.

Such an option didn't sit well with me, though. I'd never considered myself a coward yet there I was, contemplating running away as an option. In that moment, resolve took over. Before I scurried back to Spain, my tail between my legs, I'd do my best to win Scott back. My fingers fired off a text: *All I'm asking for is a second chance.* I pressed 'send' before I could chicken out.

Decision made, I slept at last.

When I awoke, it was past eleven and my eyes were gritty with exhaustion. I hauled myself upright, my gaze straying to my mobile on my bedside cabinet. The blue notification light was flashing. Scott, was my first thought. Please God, let him still want me.

I had four messages, three of them from Ellie. I glanced through them; more protestation of her innocence, pleas for us to meet. I deleted each one. A long time would need to pass before I'd be ready to see my sister again.

The fourth message was from Scott. I hesitated, aware his reply held the power either to crush me, or glue me back together.

A second later, the knot of tension in my gut loosened as I read what he'd written.

Can we talk? Lunch at the Watershed, say twelve thirty?

That had to be good, right? He wasn't dumping me. Not yet, anyway.

Shit. It was already ten past eleven, and I needed to get going. I sent a quick reply. *Would love the chance to explain further. I'll see you in the upstairs bar.*

***

I arrived at the Watershed with a minute to spare, my palms clammy with nerves. The place was packed with the usual lunchtime crowd, but I couldn't spot Scott among the throng. I stood by the windows overlooking Bristol's Floating Harbour, taking deep breaths to calm myself. Twenty-five to one. I scanned the sea of faces in case I'd missed him first time, but no luck. The minutes ticked by. I wiped my sweaty hands on my jeans, willing Scott to appear. Maybe he'd had second thoughts. I checked my phone, but found no new messages. Right when my insecurities threatened to swamp me, he appeared at the top of the stairs. Relief poured through me.

He headed in my direction, the sight of him so wonderful it seared my soul.

'Sorry I'm late,' he said. 'I got held up at work.'

'It doesn't matter.' Grateful I could even talk, I didn't trust myself to say more.

He gestured towards the bar. 'We should place our orders.'

My stomach was clenched too tightly for food, but I couldn't refuse. I plumped for soup, with Scott opting for a Thai curry. Once we were seated at our table, awaiting our meals, I braced myself for what he might say.

'I admit I've been shocked by all this,' he began. 'First finding out Ellie's your sister, then you not being who you said you were. Then last night, when Ellie came round ... You mentioned she's been unwell but not the details. I take it she suffers some form of mental illness?'

'Something like that.' I told him about the car crash, and described the effects of her brain injury.

When I finished, Scott shook his head. 'It's not her fault, I guess. She can't help herself.'

'It gets worse.' If we were to re-establish our relationship, he had to know the full truth where Ellie was concerned. So far he'd only heard about her latest suicide attempt. Despite the fact she'd hate me for it, I told him about the first two.

Scott's face betrayed his shock. 'I'd not realised your sister was so disturbed. The last time she tried to kill herself - was that after she dumped me?'

'Not because you wouldn't lend her money,' I hastened to reassure him. 'It happened months after you two split, anyway. She did it because she'd backed herself into a financial corner and couldn't cope.'

He was silent for a few seconds, his gaze fixed on the table. I held my breath, not daring to speak.

'This does change things,' he said at last. 'And thank you for being honest. Everything makes more sense now.'

'You understand why I lied? Why it's a one-off and won't happen again?'

He nodded but still looked troubled. 'What's wrong?' I asked.

'If we carry on seeing each other, will Ellie's behaviour be a problem? If she continues these weird delusions about me?'

'No.' My reply was automatic. No way would I allow Ellie to break us up. Besides, my focus was on his words: *'if we carry on seeing each other'*. Maybe we stood a chance after all.

He blew out a breath. 'I guess if she gets psychiatric help, then perhaps things might work out. I can't deny I'm worried, though.'

'She's been seeing a counsellor for years. I'll email the woman, let her know Ellie's trapped herself in a web of lies, with you the villain of the piece.' I drew in a deep breath. 'Her counsellor won't talk with me directly, not with confidentiality issues to consider. And I can't deal with my sister myself, not while she's behaving this way.'

'Sounds like a plan.' Scott smiled, but only with his mouth. His eyes remained shuttered.

I screwed up my remaining courage. 'What about us?'

He frowned. 'Don't get me wrong, Lyddie. I understand your motives for lying. You were trying to protect your sister. I get that, along with you not realising how unstable she'd become. Promise me, though. No more deception.'

'No more deception,' I echoed.

'That Liam guy? He really meant nothing to you?'

'No. I swear on my life. He's history.' *I hope*, a small voice inside me said.

Scott smiled, and the sight switched on a thousand light bulbs within me. He wasn't giving up on us after all.

'Then we're okay,' he said. 'If that's what you want. I know I do.'

I closed my eyes, my heart hammering with relief. All was well in my world again.

We made plans, both of us in agreement that our relationship was too new for me to move back to England so soon. Instead, I'd ask my neighbour in Spain to keep an eye on my villa while I considered my options. For now, I'd continue to enjoy the privacy the Harbourside apartment offered. As for money, I possessed a healthy chunk in savings as well as my rental income from Amelia and my stock market investments. I'd be fine financially, at least for the time being. Anyway, what did my bank balance matter when I had this perfect man?

***

The next day dawned bright and warm, prompting me to take a walk around the Harbourside. My body craved fresh air and exercise, although my taste buds voted for a bowl of the Watershed's excellent chilli afterwards. A perfect morning beckoned.

Sunshine bathed my skin as I strolled towards the Arnolfini, my mood buoyant, my mind fixed on Scott. As well as lunch we'd spent the previous evening together, drinking wine and eating tapas at a bar in Clifton, and I couldn't have been happier. Our hands clasped, we'd chatted about anything and everything. The rest of the world could have vanished and neither of us would have noticed.

Lost in my thoughts, I turned the corner past the Arnolfini, heading for the bridge that led to the M Shed. With an *oof!* of surprise, I slammed hard against a man's chest. I stepped backwards, an apology on my lips. Then I saw who it was. Liam Tate.

Neither of us spoke for a moment. Until I found my tongue.

'You bastard. You're following me again.'

What appeared to be genuine astonishment crossed his face. 'What the hell are you talking about?'

'That day I had lunch at Bella Pasta. All the other times you've stalked me. As well as here, now.'

A sneer replaced surprise. 'Oh, yeah? How come I'm not behind you then?'

'Don't play the smart-arse with me!' My voice was approaching all-out yelling, and people were staring. 'Give me one good reason I shouldn't call the police.'

'Let's get something straight.' Anger filled his expression. 'I've better things to do than stalk a two-timing bitch like you.'

I stared at him. Shock rendered me speechless as I clocked the contempt in his eyes. My gut instinct told me he wasn't lying, however.

'I've just visited a potential development site with a client.' He waved a hand in the direction of the old warehouses lining the river. 'As for Bella Pasta, my bank is on the Triangle. I spotted you as I walked up Park Street to get there. I've not been following you, or whatever nonsense your overheated imagination has conjured up.' He threw me a look of scorn before striding off.

Dumbfounded, I watched him disappear into the distance. I remembered the night Scott thought we were being tailed. Had that been Liam, I'd have been bombarded with accusations of infidelity afterwards. He'd not said a word, though. Meaning it couldn't have been him. Had I jumped to conclusions about the guy?

If so, whispered a voice inside me, might Rick Montgomery be my stalker instead?

Don't go there, I told myself. *He can't have found you. No way.*

I reminded myself I'd not received any more texts from him. Maybe Rick-The-Dick had given up on me.

As for being stalked, Liam must be right – I'd imagined the whole thing. What an idiot I'd been. I'd turned a few random guys in hoodies into a full-blown drama.

***

Over the next couple of weeks, Scott and I saw each other often, although not as much as I'd have liked. He told me he needed to work late several nights and put in overtime at the weekends. 'Not my choice,' he said with a grimace. 'The motor trade is cut-throat, and I'm under pressure to sell as many cars as possible.' He'd looked so tired, so defeated, and my idea of helping him into a new career as an artist gathered force.

Each time we met, erotic tension pulsed through the air. Ah, sex, a seductive yet scary prospect. The chemistry between us burned fiercely, but we'd not been dating long. After such a prolonged dry spell I was nervous. No rush, I told myself. First I'd get better acquainted with this wonderful man. To my relief, Scott didn't press the issue.

Ellie continued to text and leave me pleading voicemail messages, each one perpetuating her lies, but I ignored them all. My phone calls with Mum reassured me that my sister seemed okay and that Ellie, thank God, hadn't told her about our quarrel.

In the meantime, I snatched every spare minute Scott had available. We had so much in common besides art. Both of us loved music from the eighties; he favoured Fine Young Cannibals whereas I adored Rick Astley. When it came to the cinema, Jason Statham flicks were our top choice. Like me, Scott preferred dogs to cats, red wine over white, curry rather than sushi. We agreed to differ over complementary medicine, once I'd admitted my belief that much of it worked.

'We're like that Chinese symbol,' he told me over cocktails one evening. 'Black and white, all intertwined. Can't think of its name.'

'Yin and yang. Apart from one thing. The thorny question of who played the best James Bond.'

'No contest. Roger Moore all the way.'

'It's Daniel Craig, you idiot.' He laughed, and as the banter between us batted back and forth, I couldn't have been happier. What made our relationship special, I decided, was the absence of jealousy. Not once had I suffered the chronic level of suspicion I'd endured with Richie. Just the occasional twinge - I was human, after all - but I managed to quash any pangs that arose, determined to learn from my past mistakes.

My new trusting self was the product of more than sheer resolve. Scott didn't realise the huge debt of thanks I owed to a woman called Maria Holmes. After I moved to Spain, I thought long and hard about how I'd behaved. All the jealousy, the accusations, how Richie hadn't deserved that crap. So I started online counselling. To my surprise, it went better than I'd dared hope. We'd talk via Skype once a week, and I'd rant about Gary McIlroy, how I couldn't allow myself to believe men weren't all liars. Over time Maria made me see I shouldn't judge all guys because of one dickhead. By our final session the green-eyed monster who had snooped through Richie's phone had gone for good. Thank God. That meant my new relationship wouldn't crash and burn the way my engagement had.

Little did I know I was about to get a painful reminder on that score.

***

One evening I was cooking paella at the flat, the kitchen fragrant with the smell of fried garlic. Scott was with Darcy, so I'd promised myself a Netflix binge once I'd eaten. As I added prawns to the pan, my mobile vibrated into life. 'Unknown caller' flashed onto the screen. I almost ignored it, but didn't.

'Hello?' My tone was curt. If the caller was selling double glazing, I wasn't in the mood.

'Hi, Lyddie.' Oh, God. That voice, laden with spice and overtones of sex, still sent shivers through me.

'Richie.' I drew in a deep breath. 'I'm guessing Caroline gave you my latest number.' I'd be having words with my friend about that.

'It was good to see you the other day. How are you?'

'Fine.' An awkward silence. Just as I was about to ask why he'd called, he spoke. 'Are you free tonight? I can explain later, if you'll let me come round.'

'You can't tell me now?'

'Please. I'd rather not do this on the phone.'

Anxiety hit me. 'Caroline's all right, isn't she? She's not sick or anything?'

He laughed. 'Relax. No self-respecting germ would go anywhere near my sister. She's fine.'

Curiosity got the better of me. 'You can come round now if you want.' When I gave him my new address, he whistled, but didn't comment.

'I'll be there in half an hour,' he said.

While the paella cooked, I paced the kitchen, disturbed about why my ex wanted to see me. I hoped Caroline wasn't trying to match-make again.

Thirty minutes later, my doorbell announced Richie's arrival. When I answered it, he stood before me, dressed in tight jeans and a T-shirt the exact blue of his eyes. God, had I ever loved him once.

'Come in,' I said. Once inside, he glanced around. 'Feck me. This is one posh pad, so it is.' Like Caroline, Richie had also acquired a few Irish speech patterns from their grandfather. He sniffed the air. 'Something sure smells good.'

'I'd better check it's not burning. Come on through.'

He followed me into the kitchen, his eyes alighting on the paella pan. 'Looks great. I've not had seafood for ages.'

Was that a hint? It would be rude not to offer. 'Would you like some?'

'Sounds good.' He grinned his sexy smile, and my knees turned to mush.

I grabbed an extra plate, cutlery and wine glass and set them on the table, conscious of the bottle of wine I'd opened before Richie's phone call. An air of intimacy pervaded the scene, which made me antsy. How would Scott react if he knew I was drinking wine with my ex?

We made small talk while we ate, catching up on each other's lives. For some reason he appeared nervous, which bothered me. Had Caroline misled him into thinking I was still available? The more we spoke, the greater my unease became.

'I'll make some coffee,' I said, once we'd both finished our second plateful of paella.

When I returned with two mugs of Kenco, Richie cleared his throat. 'You must be wondering why I called.'

'Are you planning on telling me?'

His gaze slid away, and I recalled how self-effacing he was, despite his stellar looks. 'Like I told you, it was great to see you again.'

'And?'

'And I can't help hoping we still have a chance. Just hear me out,' he said, as I began to speak. 'I understand Gary McIlroy screwed with your head. But that aside, we were good together, Lyddie. Weren't we?'

'Please don't say anymore.' Tears pricked at my eyes. After our breakup, I'd have given anything for Richie to tell me he still wanted me. Now Scott filled my entire world.

'There's something you should know,' I said. 'I'm seeing someone.'

Silence. Those baby blues I'd once adored filled with sadness. 'That's, um, that's great, so it is. I'm pleased for you.'

'Caroline should have mentioned something.'

'Yeah, you're not wrong there. Are the two of you happy together?'

I nodded. I hated to hurt him, but what choice did I have?

Richie got up from his seat. 'I should go.'

'I'm sorry.'

'Don't be. My timing's lousy, that's all.'

'If I'd not met Scott ...'

'But you have.' He came round my side of the table to kiss my cheek. 'Take care of yourself, Lyddie.' Before I could answer, he headed towards the door.

That night I cried myself to sleep.

***

Richie wouldn't quit my thoughts the next day. Until Scott called me from work, driving all memories of my ex from my mind. 'I have a suggestion,' he said, nervousness in his voice. 'Remember I said I'd like you to meet Darcy? How about tomorrow?'

Oh my God. Every vestige of hurt faded away, to be replaced by delight. 'I'd love that.'

'Good. Because I've already told her I'm bringing you.' He laughed. 'Presumptuous of me, right?'

'Let's call it optimistic.'

'I should warn you what to expect. Darcy gets exhausted easily. And she doesn't look good. Well, of course she doesn't, not after chemo and being so ill. She's excited about meeting you, though.' He laughed. 'Being sick hasn't softened her tongue. When I told her how lovely you are she asked why you bothered with an old fart like me. Sisters, hey? Gotta love them. Even if they drive you nuts.'

After we finished the call, I berated myself for not telling him about Richie. No deception, we'd agreed, but did a lie of omission count?

I persuaded myself Scott was better off not knowing. Why risk our growing closeness by voicing something that didn't need to be said?

CHAPTER 13

Scott picked me up at seven the following evening. On the way to Darcy's place he told me more about his sister. How she'd refused his suggestion she should live with him in Southville, protesting her need for independence. Her stubbornness denied her the opportunity to be picky over where she lived, thanks to her reliance on government benefits. Hence her home being a tiny rented flat in the Greenbank area of the city. Every so often, Scott would repeat his offer, always to be met with the same answer.

'She says she might as well die now if the only option is me playing nursemaid to her.' He laughed, but it sounded hollow. 'A tough cookie, is Darcy, despite her issues. You'll see.'

We pulled up outside a terraced house tucked down a side street. Paint peeled from the windowsills, the brickwork chipped and crumbling. Scott took a key from his pocket and inserted it in the lock, ushering me into a communal hallway. Ahead was a flight of stairs leading to another flat, but Scott led me towards a door on the ground floor.

'Darcy?' he called. 'Darce, hon, it's me.' He knocked twice, then used a second key in the lock. After the door swung back a whiff of boiled vegetables reached my nose. To my left I saw a cramped galley kitchen. The wallpaper was in need of replacement, the carpet under my shoes dark with dirt and age. To my right the doorway into the living room stood open.

Darcy was sitting by the window, the evening light playing over her features. Shock stilled my tongue as she struggled to her feet. Her skin was dull, sickly, its hue almost transparent. Her face appeared stripped of all bar a thin layer of flesh, the outline of her skull prominent. She might only be twenty-seven, but she looked in her forties. Her jeans sagged loose on her hips and a long-sleeved top floated over her arms. She wore a scarf around her head, wrapped tight above where her eyebrows had been. Her eyes were devoid of lashes. I thought of my own hair, tried to picture it falling out in clumps, and failed. Empathy rose within me, swift and thick. I swallowed hard.

'Scotty!' Darcy moved towards her brother, and they hugged. Then he drew back, wrapping one arm around my shoulders. 'Darcy, this is Lyddie. My girlfriend.'

Two words that gladdened my heart. 'It's nice to meet you,' I said.

She smiled. A genuine one, but it seemed to require a supreme effort. 'Likewise, chick. He talks about you all the time, you know.'

I laughed. 'I'll take that as a good sign.'

'Not sure you should. Honestly, Scott's hopeless. You agree, right?'

Sibling banter, I decided. Okay, I'd play along. 'Meaning?'

'The fact he once thought you were called Lynnie, not Lyddie. Not to mention believing you were an accountant instead of an artist.' Mischief played across her wasted face. Scott's rueful grin betrayed his embarrassment.

Time to help him out. 'Many people get confused by my name. And I once spent every working day immersed in figures, so he was half right.'

'Thank you,' Scott mouthed at me, out of Darcy's line of vision.

She sat down, exhaustion in every line of her body. 'You must excuse me, chick. Today's not a good day, I'm afraid.'

Scott fixed coffee for the two of us and fetched a glass of water for Darcy. Afterwards we sat in her tiny living room, making small talk. She asked about my paintings, her interest sincere from what I could tell, and I relaxed a little. I hadn't realised how much I wanted us to establish a connection, for Darcy to approve of her brother's choice of girlfriend. As time progressed, though, her energy levels flagged even further.

'Sorry I'm such lousy company,' she said after one too many yawns. 'Before I got sick nothing could hold me back. Scott will confirm what a live wire I was.' She took a sip of water. 'Now I struggle through every day. Chemo is a killer.' Her smile was devoid of humour. My heart hurt for her.

'That's why I've decided not to suffer any more of it,' Darcy continued. 'Oh, don't look at me that way, Scotty. You have no idea what cancer is like, or what passes for its treatment. Feeling sick twenty-four-seven, having your hair fall out, looking deader than a corpse. It's crap, every single minute of it, you hear me? I refuse to treat my body like that anymore.'

I stayed silent, figuring this was between the two of them. Out of the corner of my eye, I saw Scott chew his lip, clearly struggling for words.

'Chemo will give you your best chance,' he said. 'You're right. I have no idea what having cancer is like, other than that it must be hell. But you can't mess around with leukaemia, Darce. You need to fight it with all guns blazing.'

Darcy huffed out an impatient breath. 'The disease came back. Hardly a resounding success for chemotherapy, is it? I'm not putting poison in my body any longer. I'll find a natural healing centre instead, one that specialises in cancer care. And nothing will change my mind.'

Scott fixed her with a glare. 'And how do you propose paying for this nonsense?'

Her lips set in a thin line, and she didn't reply. Silence hung over us for a few seconds. God, this must be rough on Scott.

Darcy stood up, her complexion grey in the light from the overhead bulb. She leaned on a nearby table for strength, a tremor running through her body. 'I don't mean to be rude, but can you go, please? I'm exhausted.'

'Of course.' Scott's tone was apologetic. 'We'll see ourselves out. I'll call you tomorrow, Darce.'

He slammed his hands against the steering wheel once we were back in his car. 'She's going to die,' he said, his voice a strangled whisper. 'If I can't talk her out of this complementary therapy nonsense, that is. It's not as if she can afford that crap anyway.' With a flick of his wrist, he switched on the radio, and I understood the topic was closed, at least for the time being.

In my pocket, my phone vibrated. I pulled it out, angry when I found another text from Ellie. *Please can we talk? I swear you're dating the guy who stole my savings.* I deleted her blatant lie, pained that my sister could malign Scott, this caring boyfriend and brother, for her own selfish ends. All I could do was ignore her spite.

***

The next evening, Scott called me with the news that Darcy had found a treatment centre located in California and had made enquiries. The therapy they offered was based on fasting, natural juices and organic food, with two hours of daily meditation, the rest of the day being taken up with what he dubbed 'wacky stuff'.

'Chakra balancing, for God's sake,' he told me, derision in his tone. 'What the hell is that, anyway? And aura cleansing? This crap might be all very well if you're healthy, but Darcy's a sick woman.' His breath hitched, and compassion filled me.

'Maybe it's something she needs to get out of her system,' I replied, aware I needed to tread with care. 'If alternative treatments don't work, or if she can't afford them anyway, then she might be persuaded to consider another round of chemo.'

'If she stays alive that long.' Despair had replaced derision in his voice. After having seen for myself how ill Darcy was, I understood his concern.

'That wasn't why I was calling,' Scott continued. He paused. 'I wanted to ask you something.'

'What?'

I heard him take a deep breath. 'Whether you'd come away with me one weekend.'

I'd not expected that, although I'd hoped for it. The physical side of our relationship had been limited to passionate kisses so far, and part of me yearned to take things to the next level. Scott pushed every one of my buttons with an expert touch. This man had reignited fierce emotions in me - ones I'd thought had died with my engagement to Richie. I yearned for Scott in a way that both thrilled and terrified me.

A small voice inside me protested I was out of practice in the bedroom. I shushed it, telling myself sex was like riding a bicycle. You never forgot how to do it, right? It was time, despite my worries over my cellulite and stretch marks.

'I'd love that,' I replied.

'I was thinking Somerset or Devon, somewhere by the coast. Not so far from Bristol that I can't come back if Darcy needs me.'

'I know the perfect place.' The Hunter holiday home ticked all the boxes, and I never tired of staying there.

Scott's enthusiasm was infectious when I told him about the cliff-top walks, the local pub, how close the cottage was to the sea. We made arrangements to go the following weekend, the hint of sex filling the gaps in our conversation. After we ended the call, excitement bubbled within me. Two nights in Devon, each one spent making love with this gorgeous man? Bring it on.

The rest of the week dragged. Scott and I didn't have any evenings when we were both free; he was either seeing Darcy or working, or else I'd arranged to visit Mum or Caroline. I spent my daytimes painting, shopping or going for a drive. Each time I walked to my car in the underground parking area, I recalled how paranoid I'd been about weirdos in hoodies, and I couldn't help but laugh at my behaviour. My worries about being stalked had long since evaporated.

Not so with the sinister texts. Over the course of that week, I received two. I'd convinced myself Rick Montgomery must be too busy fleecing some other gullible female to bother with me, but it seems I was wrong. '*I'm closing in on you*,' promised one. '*Watch your back, bitch*,' the second one warned. I refused to reply, persuading myself the bastard was all bluff. He'd soon tire of baiting me if I ignored him long enough.

I didn't mention the texts to Scott, being too worried about the can of worms that would open. Another lie of omission, but I judged it wiser to say nothing.

Instead, I concentrated on our weekend together. On Wednesday afternoon I drove to Cribbs Causeway, browsing the lingerie departments of various stores and buying several sets of expensive underwear. In the fitting rooms, I winced when I realised I'd gained a few inches of flab since my return to the UK. *Relax, Lyddie*, I told myself. *He likes you the way you are. Would he have suggested a weekend away if he didn't fancy you*?

After I arrived home from my shopping trip, I deleted my profile on Premier Love Matches. It had served its purpose, and I was overjoyed with the result. To add to my delight, I found Scott had already removed his. No love-cheat, my wonderful boyfriend, of that I was sure.

As for Love Rats Exposed, I logged on intending to erase my profile, but didn't. Out of interest, I scrolled the latest posts, stopping when I saw a thread started by Sophie's mother Anna, called 'At last!' Curiosity filled me as to whether she'd persuaded her daughter to inform the police.

It turned out she had. Despite Sophie's reluctance, she'd agreed to report the fraud she'd suffered.

'We're a long way off getting a conviction,' the post ended. 'But I'm optimistic. She has stuff with his fingerprints on, along with evidence from her phone calendar of their dates. What with CCTV being everywhere, there's a fair chance they've been captured on camera together. We just need to convince the police about the scam he perpetrated.'

Great news, I thought. Ellie might not have been conned, but other women had. If Sophie shopped this bastard to the cops, she deserved a medal for performing a public service. *And when I find you, and I will, you're dead, bitch.* The memory of Rick Montgomery's text still frightened me.

I needed to know how things developed on that front, promising myself I'd check in again soon with Love Rats Exposed. By the time I logged out my profile was still intact.

***

On Thursday evening I agreed to catch up with Caroline. I'd not seen much of her since my return to Bristol, and I missed her forthright manner, the way she made me laugh. We'd not planned anything special other than sharing a bottle of wine. As I drove to her house, my anticipation bubbled high at the thought of wowing her with further details of my romance with Scott. I might not have seen him that week, but sexual tension was building between us with every text. Scott wasn't as reticent on his phone as he was in real life. Nothing explicit, but an erotic undercurrent pervaded his every message. Same with my replies, and I couldn't have been happier. Soon we'd be a couple in every sense of the word.

Can't wait to get you all to myself, one text read. *You're beautiful, Lyddie.*

With love on my mind, my mood was buoyant when I parked outside Caroline's house bang on eight o'clock. My high didn't last long.

I realised she was upset the second she opened the door. Her face wore that pinched look she got when she had something difficult to say but didn't know how. For someone so straight-talking, that didn't happen often.

She didn't waste time in getting to the point. She sat on the sofa, with me perched on the edge of an armchair. Once she'd poured us both a glass of wine, Caroline leaned forward.

'I had a visit from Ellie earlier,' she said.

Shock hit me. My sister and Caroline knew each other, with me their mutual link, but weren't friends as such.

'She told me stuff. Things that concern me. About this guy you're dating.'

I swear if Ellie had walked into the room right then, I'd have slapped her, and hard. As things stood, fury roiled within me, white-hot and boiling. It was bad enough she was continuing her absurd story, but to involve Caroline? Was there no limit to her spite? Ellie had overstepped the boundaries by a mile. Or ten.

'It's all a pack of lies,' I said. 'Whatever she's told you.'

'The thing is …' Caroline's voice was strained, and tension sat around her eyes. 'I believe her, Lyddie. To get a visit from her out of the blue came as a shock, as you can imagine. Meaning I took notice of what she said.'

'That's playing right into her hands. She's insecure, don't you see? Craves attention.'

She took no notice of my outburst. 'Ellie swears your boyfriend's the one who duped her. Said she'd met him at your place, told me he's the same man, no doubt about it. She seemed so devastated. Why won't you listen to her?'

'Because she's a liar,' I spat out. If Ellie wanted to play dirty, then fine. I'd not hesitate to fill Caroline in on my sister's lousy finances.

So I did. 'She lied to Mum and me,' I finished. 'I don't know if I can forgive that. Or her.'

Caroline twirled her wine glass between her fingers. 'Whatever the reason, she tried to kill herself, Lyddie. Never forget how desperate she must have been.'

My friend was right. The memory of Ellie's white face, her fragile body under the duvet at Southmead, burst into my mind. Ellie was a liar and messed-up in the head, but like Scott with Darcy, I couldn't bear to lose the sister I still loved, despite her deceit.

'How well do you know this man?' Caroline asked.

'Well enough,' I shot back.

'But you've only been dating a few weeks, right? Seen each other a handful of times? How can you be so sure Ellie's lying?'

I needed every ounce of self-control I possessed to keep my temper. Why was Caroline taking Ellie's side? Did she value my judgment so little?

My tone terse, I outlined the same arguments I'd flung at Ellie. How I'd visited Scott's home, met his sister. How he'd never once hinted at money issues or asked me for cash.

'You should see him with Darcy,' I said. 'He cares so much about her. He's devastated about her illness. If Scott's a con artist, I'm Jabba the Hutt.'

'These men are skilled liars, Lyddie. Remember that.'

'You don't think I can spot a bullshitter? Not after Gary McIlroy?'

'Just be careful. That's all I ask. Don't give your heart to this man until you're one hundred per cent sure he's the real deal.'

'He is. I'm certain of it.' My heart was a lost cause anyway. I couldn't wait for our weekend in Devon. No way could I mention it to Caroline anymore without sullying it.

I stood up, set my half-empty glass of wine on the windowsill. 'Time I was going.' Impossible to hide the irritation in my voice.

Caroline got up, moving to hug me, but I stepped back. Hurt flashed across her face.

'Don't be mad at me, lovey,' she said. 'If there's even a chance this guy isn't legit, then of course I'd be worried.' She gave me a shaky smile. 'All I want is to see you happy.'

'I know you do.' She meant well. So why did I suspect our friendship had suffered a serious setback?

CHAPTER 14

When Scott arrived on Friday evening, I wrapped my arms around his body, holding him tight. 'God, I've missed you,' I murmured against his neck. He smelled of shampoo and soap, an enticing blend of citrus and coconut, and I breathed him in, filling my lungs with his essence.

He laughed as he disengaged himself, his hands gentle. 'That's quite the greeting. I could get used to this.'

'Sorry. It's been a strange week.'

He frowned. 'Is everything all right?'

I nodded. 'Shall we get going?' I didn't intend to mention Ellie's appalling behaviour in visiting Caroline, or how my best friend had betrayed me. This weekend was about Scott and me, not them.

As we were about to leave, he reached out a hand, his fingers tracing the fake gold beads of my bracelet. 'I love the fact you wear this so much,' he said. 'One day I'll buy you the real thing, I promise.'

The journey to the cottage was smooth, the traffic sparse, and we arrived just after eight that night. The light was fading from the sky, the horizon a dusky pink, a hint of ocean salt in the air. After we got out of the car, the breeze turned chilly and I hugged my silk wrap around myself. The distant sound of waves crashing over rocks played in my ears, and I felt the tension drain from my body.

Scott stood to one side of me, staring at the cottage. 'Wow,' he said. 'Your family owns this? It's gorgeous.'

He was even more appreciative after we'd taken our bags inside, letting out a low whistle when he spotted the oak beams, the wood-burning stove. A moment of awkwardness settled around us when I showed him into the master bedroom, placing my suitcase by the left side of the bed. Scott set his down near the right, and my brain fast-forwarded to when we would make love. Heat rose into my cheeks.

'Come on,' I said, concerned my face would betray me. 'I'll introduce you to the local pub.'

Over fish and chips in the Royal Oak, washed down with cider, we made plans. A walk along the coastal path on Saturday followed by a picnic lunch on the cliff top, then a boat trip around the bay, our afternoon ending with a stroll on the beach. The weather forecast for Sunday was mixed, so we decided not to plan that far ahead. So long as we were together, nothing else mattered. Everything except the man beside me slipped away, and I couldn't have been happier.

Once we finished eating, Scott patted his jacket pocket, a frown on his face. 'I could have sworn my wallet was in here, but it seems to be missing. Maybe it fell out inside your car.' He stood up. 'Let me grab your keys so I can check.'

I fished them out of my bag. 'Here you go.'

While I waited for him to return I browsed the dessert menu. My mobile was on the table, next to my glass. As I went to take a swig of cider, it pinged with an incoming message.

My thoughts still on Scott, I picked up my phone. The next second my fumbling fingers sent it crashing to the floor.

Hello, friend. Don't assume you can ignore me. When I catch up with you, you're history.

I retrieved my mobile before anyone trod on it. Another ping. *Those who play with fire get burned, as the saying goes. You'll regret ever threatening me with the police.*

Oh, I already did. I'd been wrong - blind and foolish - to hope Broken and Betrayed's ex might tire of our little game. Although I knew the dickhead was toying with me, that he couldn't have uncovered my identity, I was scared. Angry, too.

A third ping. *Guess what? I think I know who you are.*

Impossible. He was messing with my head, right? No way could he have tracked me down. But he could, of course.

I pictured the unidentified hooded man near Caroline's house, at the Harbourside, by the car park entrance. Perhaps I'd not imagined being stalked after all.

Panic engulfed me. My fingers still trembling, I deleted every text the fucker had sent me, then put a block on his number, something I should have done the day I realised Steven Simmons had never existed. Maybe I should have kept them as evidence to show the police, should the threats ever escalate, but terror had trumped common sense.

'What are you doing?' Absorbed with my phone, I'd not noticed Scott returning from the car park.

'Nothing. It doesn't matter.' I refused to allow Rick Montgomery to sour my weekend with this wonderful man.

'Are you all right?' He took my hand and squeezed it in his. 'You look upset.'

'Can I have a hug? Please?'

'Of course.' Scott pulled me to my feet, and I lost myself in his embrace, his heartbeat a steady lub-dub of comfort in my ears.

'Thank you,' I murmured against his chest.

'Is something wrong, Lyddie? You can tell me.' He sounded so concerned, and I hastened to reassure him.

'Nothing you need worry about.' I saw no point in telling him about the texts. They belonged to the past – or so I hoped, despite the evidence to the contrary - and Scott was my future. 'Did you find your wallet?'

He patted his pocket. 'Yeah. It was on the floor under my seat, thank God. Shall we head back? You look all done in.'

He took me in his arms the moment we stepped through the door of the cottage, his kiss urgent and insistent. 'Lyddie,' he breathed against my hair. 'Let's go upstairs. Now.'

Both my body and mind were one hundred per cent on board with that idea. All traces of nerves faded away, along with the vile texts, leaving only desire. I led him towards our bedroom, my thoughts on the silk camisole with which I'd tease him. Not that I planned to wear it for long.

And I didn't. Any initial awkwardness vanished in seconds, lost in kisses and exploring hands. Our bodies soon grew slick with sweat. I held my man tight, desperate to dissolve into him, make us one flesh. I no longer cared where I ended and Scott began. Before long his breathing turned harsh and noisy, which drove my own pleasure higher. My entire being shuddered with the force of my orgasm, one that melted every muscle in my body. Afterwards we lay in each other's arms, sticky and sated, the moment perfect beyond words.

We never made it to the coastal walk the next day, or had our picnic lunch. Neither did we manage the boat trip or stroll on the beach; it was three o'clock before we eventually emerged from bed. Instead, we spent what remained of the afternoon in the garden, the sun hot and strong on our faces. Gulls swooped overhead, their squawks harsh and loud, the sound of the sea a distant roar as we hatched more plans. I pitched the idea of opening an art gallery in Bristol, Scott displaying an endearing modesty when I mentioned stocking his paintings. He told me he'd been his dealership's top salesman so far that year, how he'd whisk me away somewhere special when he received his performance bonus. All thoughts of Ellie and Mum, of Caroline and Richie, vanished. Nobody existed besides the two of us.

***

Sunday dawned overcast and cool, a hint of rain in the air. We got up about one o'clock this time, with me insisting on a coastal walk even if we had to don waterproofs.

As we approached the path that led to the cliffs, Scott's mobile pinged with a text. He frowned. 'Do you mind if I check that? It might be from Darcy.'

'Fine by me.' His devotion to his sister always touched me to the core.

Scott's face was a mask while he entered his pass code, then read her message. He tapped out a reply, his fingers quick and urgent.

'Is she okay?' The selfish part of me prayed she was all right, that we wouldn't have to cut short our Devon idyll. He nodded, but his expression remained tense.

'Yeah. It's just that ...' He exhaled noisily, shaking his head. 'She seems so set on this mad scheme of hers. Of risking this alternative therapy place in California instead of another round of chemo.' He sounded so defeated. 'I doubt anything I say will make a difference.'

'Remember what I said before. Perhaps she has to do this, however misguided it may seem to you. After all, healthy food and massages can't worsen her illness, can they?'

'Maybe you're right.' He didn't look convinced. 'But they sure as hell won't cure it either.'

A stiff breeze hit us once we reached the cliff top, whipping my hair around my face. I took Scott's hand as we stared out over the sea, watching the waves crash against the rocks. His body was rigid with tension, and I yearned for a magic wand to erase his worry. From nowhere, a realisation struck me - how much I loved him. Yes, I, Lyddie Hunter, the woman who once swore she was done with the male sex, *loved* this man. My fingers entwined in Scott's, I swore always to support him. Especially where Darcy was concerned.

The first few drops of rain interrupted my thoughts. 'Come on,' I said. 'Looks like we're heading for the pub again.'

We got inside before the downpour began in earnest, laughing as we ran through the door, our shoes spattered with mud. The two of us tucked into a late lunch, lasagne for me and steak for Scott, washed down with the local beer. As I forked my food into my mouth, I sent covert glances his way, my love a secret treasure in my heart. Over the last couple of years I'd noticed the clock ticking within my womb, its sound increasing in volume whenever I remembered I was in my thirties. I pictured Scott playing with our children, the weekends we'd spend as a family at the cottage. Perhaps I was getting ahead of myself, given the newness of our relationship, but I was certain Scott felt the same. Neither of us had vocalised the words, but they were implicit in every kiss we shared. As well as the way he held me, so tender and warm, after we made love.

'How about dessert?' he asked, once we'd finished our meals. 'I reckon I've room for some apple pie.'

I laughed. 'You go ahead. I'm stuffed.' At that moment, another ping sounded from Scott's jacket. His expression grew tense as he pulled out his phone and entered his pass code. He scanned the text, then shoved his mobile back in his pocket. I waited, concern squeezing my gut.

'She says she wants my approval. How the hell can I give her that?'

I squeezed his hand, not knowing what to say. Scott took a swig from his glass, setting it on the table with such force his beer slopped over the rim. He dabbed at the mess with his napkin, his movements flustered. 'Do you mind if we call at her place on the way home? I won't sleep tonight if I don't try to talk her out of this madness. Make her see she can't afford it, plain and simple.'

'Sure. We'll leave right away.' If the traffic was light, we'd be back in Bristol by seven o'clock. I didn't think Scott could change Darcy's decision, so he needed to accept it until she realised chemo was her best option. I prayed he would, for his own peace of mind, if nothing else.

A ping from my own mobile. A text from Caroline, pleading with me to call her. And a missed one from Ellie, in similar vein. I deleted both without replying.

***

When Darcy opened the door, she seemed a different person from the sickly woman I'd seen before. Her face was still pale, her skin dry and flaky, but excitement shone from her eyes. The flat smelled of pine air-freshener rather than boiled potatoes. The duster and can of polish on the table told me she'd been on a cleaning binge. If this was what the prospect of a Californian healing centre did for her morale, then perhaps treatment there wasn't such a terrible idea.

Once we'd sat down, Scott didn't waste time in launching his attack. 'About this alternative therapy place ...'

'Let me show you their website.' Darcy tugged him towards a laptop on a desk in the corner of the room.

Scott hung back, reluctance in every line of his body. I stepped forward instead, not wanting to upset Darcy. The place was situated near San Diego, with yurt accommodation housing up to twenty people. Its website boasted photos of women, all looking in perfect health, meditating cross-legged beside the ocean. I skimmed though diagrams of the body's chakras and meridians, read headlines about the benefits of enemas. Nowhere was there an actual mention of cancer - I guessed they weren't allowed to claim they could provide a cure - but the underlying message was implicit. The sales pitch was so convincing I almost signed up myself.

The final detail I clicked on was the price. Wow. To have a tube inserted in the rectum while working on one's chakras didn't come cheap. The twelve-week package cost a shade less than ten thousand pounds, once converted from US dollars.

I stepped back, aware of Scott beside me, his body taut with tension. Darcy appeared oblivious, however. 'Doesn't it look great, chick?' she said. 'This will cure me, I'm certain. How can it not?'

I had no answer to that. And neither, it seemed, did Scott.

***

We drove back to the Harbourside in silence, Scott clearly preoccupied with his sister. She was fixated on going to California, and while I understood his reservations, there didn't appear to be much he could do to dissuade her. Besides, the place in San Diego might prove him wrong and cure her cancer.

Once I'd parked up, I squeezed his arm, desperate to wipe the concern from his face.

'Are you staying?' Selfish of me, but I reasoned that a bout of hot sex might shift his focus off his sick sister.

He shook his head. 'Sorry, sweetheart, I'm shattered. Time for an early night.'

'I get that.' I gentled my tone. 'You're upset about Darcy, aren't you?'

'Yeah.' He shifted in his seat. 'When she makes up her mind, nothing can talk her out of it. The miracle cure she wants isn't possible though. I'm worried the disappointment will crush her once reality hits home.'

'Why won't it happen? The treatment might work, remember.'

'I'm talking about the money side of things, not the goddamn yoga and colonic irrigation. Darcy hasn't worked for the last two years and her savings are zero. She survives on benefits and living hand to mouth. She insists she'll get a loan, but no bank will lend her the money, and I can't either.' He spread his hands in a gesture of futility. 'I only bought my house last year and the deposit I put down cleaned out my savings. Even if I thought it was a good idea, I'm not in a position to come up with ten grand.'

Darcy's wasted face came into my mind, and I ached with sadness. Carried away on a wave of optimism, she'd obviously overlooked her shaky finances. Scott was right; she'd be devastated when her bubble burst and she realised California wasn't an option. When I lay in bed that night all I could see was the excitement in Darcy's eyes, a sharp contrast to the hurt in Scott's.

***

The next day I got a phone call from my mother. We'd not spoken much recently, given my preoccupation with Scott. Mum had no idea I'd begun dating again. She meant well, and she loved me, but her tendency to control was woven into her DNA. She'd demand to know why I'd not told her about Scott, perhaps interpret our relationship as a sign I was moving back to the UK, something for which she'd long been angling. While I suspected my return to Bristol wasn't far off, part of me rebelled against her being proven right.

She didn't bother with preamble. 'Eleanor called me last night. I must say, Lydia, I'm disappointed in you.'

Pack your bags, Lyddie, I thought. *Time to go on a guilt trip*.

While I struggled for a response, she continued her attack. 'I wish you'd told me about this Steven Simmons guy.'

'It wasn't my story to tell.' I couldn't prevent a defensive note from creeping into my tone.

'And now you're dating the same man who stole her money. Refusing to listen to reason.' My mother's voice grew sharp in my ear. 'Have you no sense, Lydia? Didn't I raise you better than that?'

Fury rose within me, so thick and fast I couldn't reply. How dare Ellie spout her lies to our mother, knowing Mum would never let it drop?

True to form, she pressed her knife in deeper. 'If your father were alive, he'd be shocked and upset by all this.'

'Ellie's lying,' I said.

'That's absurd. Why would she make up a story like that?'

I almost told her, but didn't. Taking petty revenge on Ellie would only escalate our feud. My sister's financial problems would remain a secret from Mum, even though the temptation to reveal her business had failed was huge.

A full-blown argument was on the cards if we continued talking. 'I have to go, Mum. I'll phone you soon.'

Before she could reply, I ended the call. One day soon I'd take Scott to meet her, so my mother could judge for herself what calibre of man he was. The kind I'd been searching for my entire life.

***

Scott held me in his arms on my sofa in the Harbourside flat that night. A sense of easy familiarity hovered in the air, as though we'd been a couple forever. Safe in the blanket of cosiness it provided, I gave voice to my worries, certain Scott would know what to do.

'Ellie and I aren't talking. Now Mum's muscled in on the act. She called me earlier.'

'What happened? What did she say?'

I outlined our conversation. 'The unfairness of it bugs me like crazy,' I admitted. 'Why does Mum believe Ellie over me?'

'Don't forget your sister tried to kill herself not long ago.' He squeezed my shoulder. 'For your mother, that has to be hell on earth. Which means her sympathies flow towards Ellie rather than you.'

How come I'd not figured that out? While I remained annoyed with her, my mother's behaviour made more sense in the light of Scott's words.

'You know why?' he continued. 'Because you're forged from stronger stuff, Lyddie. You've got your act together in a way Ellie hasn't. And your sister can be an expert manipulator when she wants something.' He shook his head, his expression rueful. 'I found that out first-hand, remember.'

'I don't want to be around either of them right now,' I admitted.

'Then don't, sweetheart. Spend time with me instead.'

He was right. It was pointless talking further with Ellie while she continued to lie about Scott. As for Mum, she'd discover the truth, and soon. Same with Caroline. In the meantime, I'd concentrate on Scott, and to hell with anyone else.

I drew him close, the scent of his shampoo strong in my nostrils as his cheek brushed mine. His arms tightened around me. Everything else faded away to leave just us, united against the world. When Scott pulled back, love was in his eyes, so much so I struggled to bear the tenderness they held. His fingers tucked a stray strand of hair behind my ear, his touch gentle. A simple gesture, but nothing had ever made me feel so cherished.

His hands moved lower, slipping under my T-shirt to stroke the skin beneath, and I lost myself in him, our mouths hungry and urgent as we tumbled onto the floor. All I could concentrate on was this wonderful, incredible man, who occupied my entire world. Tears leaked from my eyes when my orgasm surged through me, and I floated away on a cloud of pure Scott.

Afterwards we lay on the carpet, the sweat cooling on our bodies as our breathing slowed to normal. Then he spoke the words I'd been longing to hear. The ones I was too much of a coward to say myself.

'I love you, Lyddie.' Scott's voice stroked a soft caress over my heart. He stared into my eyes, his own filled with adoration. My smile was so wide my face almost split in two.

Only one response was possible. 'I love you too.'

CHAPTER 15

Scott had invited me for a meal at his house in Southville the next evening. 'I'm not the world's best cook,' he told me as he pulled a dish of charred stuffed peppers from the oven, his expression apologetic. 'With luck this may still be edible. If not, there's a kebab shop two streets away.'

I wound my arms around him while he prodded the burned peppers. 'You have other talents,' I murmured against his T-shirt.

Scott's mobile rang out, causing us both to jump. From the corner of my eye, I saw Darcy's name and picture appear on the screen.

'Sorry,' he said. 'Let me see what the little madam wants, then we'll eat.' He sank onto one of the kitchen chairs, the phone pressed against his ear.

From what I could make of the conversation, it involved California. And money. Scott pinched the bridge of his nose, exhaling his frustration. 'I've told you already, Darce. I don't have that kind of cash to spare.'

Darcy continued to plead her case. I could hear her voice, even if I couldn't make out exactly what she was saying. 'I can't magic money out of thin air,' Scott insisted. The conversation carried on, growing ever more heated. When he ended the call, Scott's expression looked hunted. 'You'll have guessed what she wanted.'

I lowered myself onto his lap, holding him close. I hated seeing the man I loved so unhappy. An idea buzzed at the back of my mind.

'This isn't the first time she's asked me for money,' he continued. 'I've not said anything because I hate to burden you with my problems.'

'We're a couple now. I want you to share stuff with me, the bad as well as the good.'

'It's torturing me, Lyddie. To see her so ill, knowing she needs to continue the chemo, all the while hearing how California's her only hope.'

Before I knew what I was doing, the words rushed from my mouth. 'What if I funded Darcy's treatment? Gave her the money?'

Scott pulled away from me, shock in his face. 'Sweetheart, no. I couldn't ask you to do that.'

'Let me help. I can't bear to see you so worried.'

He didn't speak for a while, simply stared at me. 'Please,' I said.

Scott shook his head. 'I can't accept your offer. Even if it's beyond generous.'

'Why not? I have the cash available, so you might as well use it. All I want is for Darcy to get well.'

'We've discussed this, remember? All that weird crap - fasting, enemas, chakra balancing - I don't buy it.'

'But it's not about what *you* think, is it?' I was a woman on a mission. 'Or me, or anyone else. Darcy believes alternative therapies will work, and maybe she's right. Mind over matter, and all that. From what I've seen, if she has to go through more chemo, she won't deal well with the emotional aspect. Let alone the physical.'

'You're not wrong.' Scott still looked unsure though.

I tried again. 'Let me help her. Please.'

'I can't take your savings.' His jaw was set tight.

'Yes, you can.'

'It doesn't feel right.'

'Why ever not?'

'You'll be wasting your money. That's why.'

'Not your decision to make.'

A pause. 'You're certain about this?'

'For the hundredth time, yes.'

'I don't deserve such a wonderful girlfriend.' His voice was thick with emotion.

'Tough. You're stuck with me.'

'Wow.' He shook his head. 'I won the jackpot when I met you, didn't I?'

I laughed. 'Yeah, you struck gold all right.'

'That performance bonus I mentioned? The firm will pay it to me by Christmas. If you can wait until then ...'

'Not a problem.' The money Darcy needed, while a decent-sized sum, was well within my means and I didn't doubt Scott intended to repay me as soon as possible.

'I'll make it up to you.' He kissed me, his worry replaced by excitement. 'We'll go abroad over New Year. Lanzarote, perhaps. What do you say?'

My heart leapt at the idea of sex in the sun with him. 'I say yes. With bells on.'

'We'll tell her the good news tomorrow.' Scott hugged me. 'Together.'

A lovely idea. As we ate our burned peppers, he raised his glass of wine, clinked it against mine.

'To the future.' Such tenderness in his eyes. 'I love you, sweetheart.'

***

Scott took the following morning off work. 'This is huge,' he said on the drive over to Greenbank. 'Managing the dealership can take a back seat for a while.'

'I can't wait to see her face.' I'd lain awake the night before, picturing her reaction.

'She'll be delighted. You'll see.'

When Scott and I walked into her flat, Darcy seemed paler, more exhausted, than the last time we met. The flat had that stale closed-in smell again. 'Sorry for not getting up from this chair,' she said. 'I'm all done in today.'

Scott sat beside his sister. 'We have good news, Darce.' His eyes sought mine, a smile on his lips. 'Tell her, sweetheart.'

Embarrassed, I stayed silent. When I didn't speak, he continued, 'Lyddie has offered to pay for you to go to California.'

Her mouth fell wide with shock. 'What? Are you serious?'

'Yes. If you give her your sort code and account number, she'll transfer the money to your account today.'

She stared at me. 'I can't allow you to do that.'

I knelt beside her chair, gazing into her wasted face. 'Why ever not? Please let me help you, Darcy.'

She continued her protests, until Scott and I eventually convinced her. Once we did, Darcy's grin could have outshone the sun. I'd done the right thing in offering her the money.

'How can I ever thank you, chick?' She grasped my hand, her fingers dry and bony against mine. 'With any luck, I can leave for California at the end of the week.'

'So soon?' I hadn't expected her to go that quickly.

'The treatment centre emailed me this morning. They've had a cancellation.'

'That's great.' I couldn't be more pleased. I promised her she'd get the funds, along with the cost of her return flight, that afternoon.

'I'll make a firm booking the second I get the money,' Darcy said. 'The universe meant for this to happen, don't you see, chick?'

I mentally rolled my eyes, although delighted for her. Behind his sister's back, Scott pulled a face, then grinned. Despite his concerns, I knew he was pleased for her.

I hugged Darcy, her body bird-like against my sturdy frame. 'You take care of yourself, you hear?' I studied her face as I stepped away. Excitement had lit a fire inside her, but her skin remained pasty, in contrast to the inky smudges under her eyes. I prayed Darcy would find the miracle she sought in California.

***

I didn't see Scott on the Friday of that week. He was taking the day off to drive Darcy to Heathrow, so that evening I went to Caroline's instead. Things between us had stayed tense since our last meeting. She'd texted several times, suggesting we get together, and after the fifth message I capitulated, sending a quick reply.

I'd missed her; the rift in our friendship was unprecedented. As for my sister, she hadn't called, texted or emailed for several days. That was fine by me. Mum had left several voicemail messages, each more strident than the last, urging me to see sense and ditch Scott, but I'd ignored them all. My mother and I would carry on the way we always did, with her trying to run my life and me evading her attempts any way I could. Dysfunctional, sure, but weren't most families?

Maybe I could mend my relationship with Caroline, however. I rang her bell at eight, a bottle of wine in my hand. To my dismay, her expression seemed strained when she opened the door. Her body was tense as we hugged, her smile forced.

'Come in,' she said, waving me into the living room. She grabbed the wine, extracting the cork and pouring large measures into two glasses. I sat opposite her and we made small talk, avoiding any mention of Scott. Caroline appeared distracted, her gaze often flitting to the clock on the wall.

'You okay?' I asked. She wasn't her normal self at all.

'I'm fine, so I am.' It was unlike her to lie.

When the minute hand hit the half-hour mark, the doorbell rang. Caroline sprang to her feet, her eyes avoiding mine as she rushed into the hallway. Was that guilt in her face?

A familiar male voice reached my ears.

'Richie was just passing.' The lie was obvious, and fierce resentment filled me. So Caroline was match-making again, was she? More like meddling, in my view. I plastered a fake smile on my face.

He nodded in my direction. 'Lovely to see you, Lyddie.'

'Likewise.' My irritation must have been evident in my clipped tone, but I didn't care.

Richie sat in the armchair nearest the door, his legs sprawled in front of him. Damn, he looked good. A tight-fitting T-shirt in a soft shade of blue intensified the azure of his eyes, its fabric stretched over his hard muscles. His dark hair flopping across his forehead, the waft of spicy cologne, that uncertain manner of his – they all stirred up memories of better times. I clamped down hard on my traitorous thoughts. Richie might well look delicious enough to tear apart and eat with my fingers, but the guy was off limits. So was I. I'd already found my dream man.

'So, Lyddie.' Caroline's voice held tension, nervousness evident in every syllable. 'Are you still seeing that bloke? Scott, Steven, whatever he's called?'

Irritation flared within me. Her words were a subtle dig, the way she'd paired Scott's name with that of Ellie's fake con artist. Caroline was being a manipulative bitch and I refused to play her game, especially in front of my ex.

'He's called Scott.' My tone was freezer-frigid in its coldness. 'And yes, we're still an item. What's more, it's serious. We love each other.'

Dismay flew into Caroline's expression. Richie remained silent. Had he spoken, I couldn't guarantee I'd keep my temper.

'Isn't that a little soon?' Caroline hesitated, no doubt clocking my sour face, but she ploughed on anyway. 'I mean, you've only been going out together a few weeks, right?'

'That is none of your business. Whom I date, and for how long, is not your concern.'

She took a gulp of wine. She looked ready to cry, but I steeled myself against possible tears. Caroline had crossed a boundary, and if our friendship suffered, she was to blame, not me.

'You're like a sister to me, so you are,' she said. 'What Ellie told me, though - I believed her. I'm fecking worried about you. So is Richie.'

Fury spewed from me with the force of a volcano. Goddamn my blabbermouth friend and her latest treachery. 'You gossiped about me to Richie, of all people?' I yelled. 'How dare you betray me like that?'

'Lyddie.' Richie's tone was calm, despite the tightness around his mouth. 'Caroline's right. I'm concerned. We both are. We only want to help.'

'By patronising me? Giving me unwanted advice? Believing my mentally unwell sister instead of me?' I didn't give a damn if I was shouting. 'What is this? Some kind of American-style intervention?'

'Lyddie, please.' Caroline was crying for real by then. 'I meant well.'

'You had no right to tell Richie.'

'Just answer me this.' Wariness had crept into her voice. 'Has Scott ever asked you for money?'

'No.' I injected a truck-load of triumph into one short word. It was the truth - Scott had never asked me for funds. I didn't have to lie, unlike Ellie.

Caroline looked taken aback. 'Are you sure?' She grimaced. 'Feck, I'm sorry. That was a stupid question.'

I huffed in exasperation. 'I've already told you all the reasons Scott isn't who Ellie says he is. The way he cares about his sick sister, the fantastic artwork he creates. None of it ties up with the shit Ellie's spouting.'

Richie spoke. 'Then why is she saying these things?'

I clung to the vestiges of my loyalty to my sister, reluctant to divulge what Scott had said about Ellie's demands for money. I'd acted out of malice before in telling Caroline, but I refused to repeat such spite with Richie, however angry I was. Besides, my so-called friend had doubtless already blabbed the details to him.

'I can't tell you that. But she's wrong. Scott's the real deal.'

'So this guy you're dating has never asked you for money?' Richie's scepticism was obvious. 'A couple more questions, Lyddie, and then we'll let it drop. Yes, we will,' he said, shooting a warning glance at Caroline when she tried to interrupt. 'This sister of his. Darcy's her name, yeah? Am I right in thinking she's seriously ill?'

The change in direction threw me off-balance. 'That's correct. She has leukaemia.'

'Is she in remission? Or getting chemo?'

'She's on her way to California right now. To an alternative therapy centre. Conventional medicine hasn't worked for her.'

Richie didn't respond at first, and I got the impression he was choosing his words with care. 'And who paid for her stay in California?'

'What?' I stood up, my foot kicking over my wine by accident, but I was past caring. 'You have no right to ask such questions. Scott's sister, and how she funds her treatment, is none of your business.'

'Sit down, Lyddie. Please,' Richie said. 'Just hear me out. Take this guy's job. He manages a motor dealership, right? How do you know that for sure? I'm guessing you only have his word for it.'

'I trust him. He's honest, caring, loyal.'

It was as if I'd not spoken. 'These men are experts at their game,' Richie continued. 'Devious and without scruples. This guy probably changes tack with each woman. That's why he appears different to when he conned Ellie.'

'Really.' I made no effort to disguise my sarcasm. 'So what's his game this time? How does he intend to defraud me?'

'Through his sister.'

That was a step too far. Ice dripped from my next words. 'She has leukaemia, for fuck's sake. Are you suggesting she's pretending?'

'That's exactly what I suspect.'

I gawped at him. 'I've met Darcy. She looks like death. Pale as putty and thinner than a toothpick. No way is she faking.'

'Wouldn't be the first time someone feigned a serious illness for fraudulent purposes. Which brings me back to what I asked earlier. Who's paying for her treatment in California?'

My silence gave me away.

'Lyddie?' Caroline prompted. 'Please say you haven't given her money. Oh, my God. You did, didn't you? You've paid for a trip she'll never take, because she's part of the scam, don't you see? They're working you together.'

'No.' My mind clamped shut against her words. 'You're wrong. Yes, I gave Darcy the funds for her treatment. I'll do so again if needs be.' Caroline's sobs grew louder. 'But that proves my point, don't you see? Because Scott has never asked me for money.

Neither has his sister. I offered because I wanted to help. It was my decision - nobody forced me. Scott intends to repay me by Christmas.'

'Oh, Lyddie.' Such love in Caroline's voice, yet it burned me like a blowtorch. 'He'll be long gone by then. So will she.'

'I told you my coming here tonight would be a mistake.' Richie's words were aimed at his sister. 'Didn't I say Lyddie would never listen to reason?'

I'd been right. They'd cooked this up between them. Devious, manipulative behaviour, but I'd show them.

'Answer me one thing.' If this didn't convince them, nothing would. 'Scott couldn't have known Ellie and I were sisters. We were both flabbergasted when we discovered the truth. Why would he tell me he'd once dated Ellie, if his aim was to fleece me of money? How could that help him?'

My question was met with silence. Caroline and Richie glanced at each other, uncertainty in their expressions. 'I'm not sure,' Caroline admitted.

Patience was never my strong suit, and she'd pushed me too far. 'You've crossed a line. We're no longer friends.'

'Don't say that. Please.' She was still crying as I shoved past her, heading towards the door. But Richie blocked my way.

'Be careful, that's all I ask,' he said. 'I'm worried this man is using you. We both are. Please don't give him or his sister any more money.'

Who the hell did he think he was? 'You're jealous, aren't you? You broke off our engagement, but you can't bear to see me happy with anyone else. Well, fuck you.' I swept past the man who was once my world, desperate to escape him and his sister.

CHAPTER 16

I lay in bed at the Harbourside flat, unable to sleep, my brain churning. My dominant emotion was anger. Two people I'd once loved had stabbed me in the back, and God, was I angry. Fucking furious, in fact. One thing was certain. Although it pained me, my friendship with Caroline was over unless she admitted she'd been wrong about Scott. Twenty years of closeness gone in one evening, and it hurt like mad. As for Richie, fury filled me at his sheer arrogance. How dare the man who'd dumped me dispense advice on my love life?

Well, screw him. Screw Caroline, Ellie and my mother too. They could all go to hell. So long as Scott and I were together, I'd be fine. What was it he'd said when I'd told him I didn't want to be around Mum or Ellie? *Then don't, sweetheart. Spend time with me instead.*

That sounded good to me. Wonderful, in fact. Thank God for Scott. He made everything in my world bigger, brighter, better.

Should I call him? It was almost midnight, so I decided not to, despite being tempted like crazy. This wasn't the time to inflict my problems on him, not when he must be wrung dry of emotions after taking Darcy to Heathrow. For another hour, I tried to sleep, but my brain refused to shut off from the events of the evening.

After a while I retrieved my laptop, hoping to lose myself in the internet. For the next few minutes I checked my emails and social media sites. Then I remembered Love Rats Exposed, curious as to whether Anna had posted an update about Sophie. I logged on, scanned through the latest threads, looking for her name, and found it. I clicked on the post and started to read.

Oh, my God. Horror shuddered through me, my breath suspended in shock. The words were bleak, written by a woman steeped in grief.

'Too upset to write much. My beloved Sophie is dead. Her body was discovered in an alleyway last weekend. She'd been stabbed to death.'

A slew of posts followed, all expressing sympathy. One asked whether Sophie ever got the chance to inform the police about the man who defrauded her, a post I considered insensitive in its timing, although I'd wondered the same thing. The dead woman's mother had posted a brief reply. *'No, she didn't.'*

I switched off my laptop, leaning back against my pillows. Could Sophie's murderer be Michael Hammond, the man who'd conned her? Had he discovered she planned to unmask him to the police? The more I considered the idea, the more unlikely I judged it. For one thing, her ex had broken off contact with her once he'd syphoned off her money. How would he have known what she intended, unless she'd texted him in a fit of fury? The simplest explanation was the most likely one: she'd fallen victim to a random attacker.

A thought struck me. Sophie had been murdered during the weekend Scott and I spent at the cottage. She might have been stabbed at the same time as we made love. While we strolled along the cliff top, perhaps. Or as we held hands in the pub. The hideous contrast choked me up, swelling my heart until it almost burst from my ribcage. Tears flowed, unchecked, down my face. I sobbed for the dead woman, her grieving mother, my hurt over Caroline and Richie, until I cried myself to sleep.

***

The next day was Saturday, and I spent the morning sketching, determined not to dwell on Sophie's death. Scott texted me at lunchtime, saying he'd be working on a new painting all day, but asking whether I was free to get together the following evening. A perfect end to the week. We'd drink beer, I'd catch up on Darcy's progress in California, then we'd make long, slow love. Just what I needed.

'See you tomorrow,' I texted back.

That afternoon I drove over to Bedminster. The area was fun and funky, filled with eclectic street art, and it had been a while since I'd visited the deli on North Street. If I was honest, I had another motive - Bedminster was close to Southville where Scott lived. As I shopped for stuffed olives and artichoke hearts, I battled with myself over whether to call round unannounced. What if he was one of those artists who hated to be disturbed while working? I wasn't some double-glazing salesperson, though - I was his girlfriend. God knew I needed the comfort he could offer, and I couldn't wait until tomorrow.

I made a decision. Within the next hour, I'd be with the man I loved. A huge grin settled on my face as I drove the short distance to Southville.

I parked up near Scott's house, unable to spot his Toyota. He must have left it around the corner. Parking was difficult in Southville and I'd been lucky to bag a space. As I lifted the iron door-knocker, my mind was running on his hands, how they would undress me. Another sappy grin curved my mouth. Footsteps sounded in the hallway. The door opened.

The man standing before me wasn't Scott. The grin faded from my lips.

We stared at each other. He was shorter and much older than Scott, his hair grey and bushy, his eyes brown, not blue. He was dressed in paint-smeared jeans and T-shirt. When I didn't speak, a frown crossed his face.

'Yes?' he said.

From somewhere I dredged up the words. 'I, uh, I'm looking for Scott Champion. Is he home?'

'That's me. I'm Scott Champion.'

I stared at him, unable to process the situation.

'Can I help you?' Impatience hovered in his voice.

'But ...' This was Scott's house, where I'd seen his incredible paintings, the letters addressed to him, what seemed a lifetime ago. I hadn't mistaken the address.

'You're Scott Champion?' I said.

'Yes. What can I do for you?'

I stared at his jeans, spattered with what appeared to be artists' acrylic paint. A sliver of understanding stabbed me, followed by denial.

'I came to this house twice recently.' My voice almost cracked with emotion. 'To visit a man who said his name was Scott Champion. He told me he lived here.' Once I'd spoken, I realised how weird my words sounded.

The man's brow creased. 'What did he look like?'

When I described Scott, understanding dawned in his expression. 'That sounds like Steve Simmons. He stayed here not long ago.'

'When?'

He pulled a face. 'Can't remember the date he arrived. He left on Wednesday, if that helps. I get so many people passing through it's impossible to remember the details.'

'Passing through?' I echoed.

'Airbnb. Short-term rentals, you know? I let out my spare bedroom via their website. People come, they stay a while, they move on.' He shrugged, before sympathy crossed his face. I realised how it might look. To this man, I must be a two-night stand of the other Scott, a woman who refused to accept she'd been a casual pickup. Shame filled every part of me.

'Thanks,' I mumbled, before hurrying back to my car. Cocooned in its sanctuary, I sat behind the wheel, frozen with shock. Should I call Scott to demand an explanation? There had to be one. Hadn't I lied at the start of our relationship? What if he'd done the same?

My mind ran through possibilities. Suppose his mortgage lender had foreclosed on Scott's home and he'd been too ashamed to admit it? Hence needing to use Airbnb? Or what if the other man claiming to be Scott Champion suffered from mental illness? Both scenarios seemed unlikely, yet my heart still clung to a sliver of hope.

Then I remembered the paint-smeared jeans. The guy with whom I'd spoken a few minutes ago had created those incredible paintings, not the man I'd been dating. Besides, there had been his reference to Steven Simmons. However much I longed to deny it, his name was too great a coincidence to ignore. The truth slammed into my brain. Scott was a lowdown piece of shit, his duplicity unmasked by my surprise visit. The Southville address had served its purpose in convincing me he owned his own home, that he, not the real Scott Champion, was a talented artist. No doubt he planned to rent the spare room there on future occasions when it suited him and the owner was absent. How well he'd played me.

I cracked wide open then. With my head against the steering wheel, I bawled like a baby. The confident version of Lyddie had exited stage right, leaving behind a blubbering wreck. If I'd thought Gary McIlroy had deceived me, his betrayal was small potatoes compared with this. I'd been suckered to the hilt, played by a master at his game. Screwed in every sense of the word, and I couldn't say nobody had warned me. Too headstrong to listen, instead I'd gift-wrapped myself, added a silk bow, and presented myself as a willing victim to Scott Champion.

After I cried myself dry, I sat there, numb with shock. An endless loop of Scott ran through my brain; the magic of his kisses, the adoration I'd glimpsed in his eyes. How could he have faked such passion? But then I remembered the posts from Love Rats Exposed. All those women had been convinced their boyfriends' declarations of love were real. Blinded by arrogance, I was no better. Hadn't I boasted about being able to spot a dirt-bag at a hundred paces? Of course I'd never become a victim like them, not after Gary McIlroy. Instead I'd set out to catch a rat and ended up being bitten by one.

You're dead, bitch. God, those awful texts. He'd sent them, every damn one. Scott had been Mr Weirdo Stalker too, even lying about us being followed. All done to scare me – I guessed he got pleasure from frightening women - as well as keep tabs on my movements. Once our relationship turned serious, he hadn't needed his spy tactics.

Ellie had been right all along but I hadn't listened, mired too deep in bullshit to admit the truth. Same with Mum, Caroline, Richie. I'd behaved like a fucking idiot; I'd given precedence to a silver-tongued rogue over my family and friends. So easy to write Ellie off as a delusional liar, Mum a control freak. Caroline, though? Hadn't she always been loyal and supportive? Why had I been so swift to kick her in the teeth?

My face flushed with shame when I recalled shouting at Richie about him being jealous. He'd only wanted to protect me. I found it hard to accept how badly I'd fucked up.

Then I remembered Darcy. What had Caroline said? *She's part of the scam, don't you see? They're working you together.*

Who could she be, I wondered. I doubted she was Scott's sister; no family resemblance existed that I could recall. How stupid I'd been not to notice. Not his girlfriend, either. A man that handsome could bag himself any woman he chose. Why would he settle for someone as drab and emaciated as Darcy?

I started the car, dread pooling in my belly. Somehow I drove to Greenbank, ignoring every red traffic light I encountered on the way. All I could focus on was Darcy, the certainty I'd find her at home, not enduring colonic irrigation in California.

I parked opposite the house where I'd visited with Scott and rang the doorbell. Nobody answered. I peered through the letter box, my ears alert for any sound from inside. Nothing. The place was empty. Darcy wasn't home. I returned to my car to wait.

Even then, hope continued to defy common sense. Might she be in San Diego after all?

But no. The idea was ridiculous, the chances zero. I'd been conned, plain and simple.

I stared at the shabby house across the street, my hands clamped on the steering wheel as I continued my vigil. My patience was rewarded after an hour. I didn't recognise her, not at first. This woman had dark straggly hair, with no sign of the scarf Darcy had worn around her skull. She was the right height and had the same bird-like build, her shoulders hunched as she carried her shopping bags along the street. As she drew closer, I saw the unhealthy pallor of her skin, the darkness under her eyes. Above them, she'd drawn clumsy brows to replace the ones she must have plucked before I visited. Any vestiges of doubt I had vanished.

Darcy took a key from her pocket and inserted it in the lock. Within a few seconds, she'd disappeared from view.

Another crushing wave of betrayal swept over me. I didn't care about the money I'd lost, but I did about my self-respect. That lay shattered into tiny pieces, demolished when the real Scott Champion opened his door to me. And again when Darcy - if that was even her real name - closed hers behind her. The two of them must have laughed their guts out at gullible Lyddie Hunter. Oh, the shame of it.

Humiliation gave way to anger. I lowered my window all the way down, then tugged the fake gold bracelet from my wrist. The cheap elastic snapped under the force of my fingers, sending beads flying in all directions, peppering the pavement and bouncing along the gutter. I watched several land close to a nearby drain and disappear into its foetid depths.

'Fuck you, dickhead,' I snarled. Then I started the engine and drove towards Caroline's house.

***

My friend took one look at me after opening her door, and pulled me swiftly inside. At the sight of her face, so loving and concerned despite my shabby behaviour, I broke down again. Caroline enfolded me in her arms, holding me tight. We stayed that way until I hiccupped to a stop, her T-shirt soaked from my tears.

'Come inside,' she said, walking me towards the living room. 'I should warn you, though. Richie's here.'

I didn't care. Wasn't he one of those to whom I owed an apology?

Richie stood up as Caroline steered me into the room. Shame made it impossible for me to acknowledge him. His voice reached me, warm and soothing, although afterwards I was unable to remember a thing he'd said. I simply stood there, shaking and sobbing, Caroline's arms around me.

At last I found the words I needed. 'I should have listened to both of you. About Scott. Or whatever his real name is.' Humiliation swelled in my chest, my sense of betrayal so great it threatened to choke me.

Both my friend and my ex treated me better than I had any right to expect. They heard me pour forth my anguish, never once saying 'I told you so'. For that, I was grateful.

'There's so much I don't understand,' I wailed. 'Why didn't he ask for the money in cash like he did with Ellie? Why tell me he'd once dated her? That's what I don't get.'

'Me neither.' Richie's voice was thick with anger.

'He told you to stir up trouble,' Caroline said. 'To drive a wedge between the two of you.'

That made sense. I remembered what I'd read about how men like Scott operated. Divide and conquer, in a bid to separate victims from their family and friends. He'd done that so well.

I wiped away a tear. 'You're right. He knew I'd believe him, not her.'

She nodded. 'You need to go to the police, and soon. What with your evidence, and Ellie's, they'll be able to nab the bastard. And he doesn't know you've sussed his little game, does he? This is your chance to get the fecker put in prison, so it is.'

I shook my head. 'I can't, not yet.'

'You have to.' Richie still sounded furious. 'Caroline's right. This guy needs to serve jail time.'

By then, my initial shock had worn off. An idea was forming in my mind, but not one I cared to discuss with Caroline or Richie.

'Thank you,' I said, my voice hoarse with emotion. 'For being so kind after I've behaved like a complete fool.'

'Always,' Caroline replied. Richie didn't speak, just reached out a hand to squeeze my arm.

'Let us know if you want us to come to the police with you,' Caroline continued. She clearly assumed I'd opt for that route, and I chose not to correct her.

'I need to get going,' I said. 'I'll be in touch. Soon.' I fiddled with the hem of my jacket, too embarrassed to catch Richie's eyes. *Mend those fences*, I reminded myself. 'Maybe the three of us could go for a drink one night. Or a meal. Or whatever.' I felt my cheeks redden.

Caroline nodded. 'Yeah, we'll do that. When you're feeling better, lovey. I'll call you, all right?'

***

I'd not long arrived back at the Harbourside when my mobile pinged in my bag. A text from Scott.

Darcy just called. All good in California. She's starting treatment tomorrow. You still up for Sunday night? Love you, babe. xoxo

'Fuck you,' I growled, the urge strong within me to hurl my phone across the room. What a bastard, piling lies on top of bullshit. So Darcy was in San Diego, was she? Yeah, right.

I was done with crying. Fuck that. Anger had replaced my tears. If Scott been in front of me I'd have torn him to pieces, then pissed on his remains.

A second ping from my mobile. This time from Ellie, ending her recent silence - another text begging for us to get together. How badly I'd treated my sister, despite what I'd promised Dad. I'd been harsh with her when she was recovering from an attempted suicide, and she deserved better. I prayed she'd forgive me.

I pulled up her number and placed the call. She answered straightaway. 'Lyddie? Thank God you've finally got in touch.' She sounded nervous. 'We need to talk.'

'Hey, Els.' Relief swept over me. My sister still loved me. We'd be okay.

'I'd like us to get together soon,' I said, not giving her the chance to interrupt. 'I have some news to tell you.'

'Has something happened?' Concern in Ellie's tone. Time to hedge around the truth, otherwise she'd fret about me.

I kept my voice cheerful when I replied. 'Yes. Nothing for you to worry about, but I can't go into it over the phone. Can we meet up?'

'I'd love that. Although I'm busy most of next week. Several bags and purses to make for a rush order. I won't be coming up for air until they're finished.'

A stone sank in my gut. I'd hoped to see her as soon as possible.

'Listen, Lyddie ...' She tried again to discuss our quarrel, but I deflected her attempt. We'd have time for all that later. We ended the call with an arrangement that I'd phone her on Thursday to arrange lunch the following weekend.

'I love you,' I said as we wrapped up the conversation. To my relief, Ellie said it back.

Next came my mother.

'Didn't I tell you so?' was her initial reaction. Annoyance sparked in me, but she'd been right and I'd been wrong, so I needed to suck it up and move on. By the time we finished talking, our relationship seemed on a firmer footing. I made her promise not to discuss my disastrous love life with Ellie, not until I'd spoken to my sister myself.

I headed off to bed, my mobile in my hand. The Lyddie staring at me from the bathroom mirror was a very different creature to the one who'd watched a fake cancer victim walk down the street earlier. Inside me burned a determination for revenge. Go to the police? Sure, I could do that, but I wasn't convinced it would result in justice. With Sophie dead, the available evidence had dwindled. None of Scott's other victims, including Ellie, were willing to involve the law. Apart from me, the bastard had conducted his scams via cash, and the bank transfer to Darcy linked me to her, not Scott. No paper trail existed for the cops to follow to his door, wherever the hell that might be. Not in Southville, that was for sure.

I kept circling round to the same argument; the police would need more proof to secure a conviction. Besides, I was dealing with two expert swindlers. I didn't doubt the pair of them would claim the money had been a loan or a gift, pitting my word against theirs. Scott, or Steven, or whatever his goddamn name was, would wriggle off the hook somehow. That brought me back to the idea I'd formed while at Caroline's.

I'd beat Scott at his own game. I already had a notion of how to accomplish that. One thing worked in my favour. He had no idea I'd discovered the truth.

Yes. I was going to do this. Revenge would taste sweet, and he'd never see me coming.

Time to return Scott's text.

Sorry I didn't reply earlier. I'd love to get together tomorrow. Maybe a curry? Love you too.

CHAPTER 17

Scott and I arranged to go to Monsoon Spice, an Indian restaurant I told him I wanted to try, on Sunday evening. Revulsion churned in my stomach at the thought of playing the loving girlfriend a second longer; it had been difficult enough when he called after getting my text. I reminded myself to stick to the plan, picturing Ellie's pale face in her hospital bed. How determined I'd been to get justice for her. The devastation I'd suffered at Scott's hands. The dose of his own medicine I'd shove down his throat would taste bitter indeed.

We'd agreed he'd pick me up at eight. When my doorbell rang, I drew in a deep breath and wiped my sticky palms on my jeans. 'You can do this,' I told myself.

'Hello, beautiful.' Scott stood before me, a smile on his mouth and love in his eyes. The latter was so convincing I doubted myself for a second. God, he was good at this.

'Hi, handsome,' I said, stepping into his arms. Our lips met, and my resolve almost shattered, although through anger, not desire. I yearned to slap the prick so hard they'd hear it in California, then drive straight to Bridewell police station. Cool logic overrode instinct, however. *Remember the plan*, I reminded myself. So I poured myself into the kiss, smiling at him when we pulled apart.

'Shall we go?' I patted my stomach. 'I'm hungry for that curry.'

Once we were seated in the restaurant, I took Scott's hand from across the table. 'Any news from Darcy?'

He nodded. 'We spoke on the phone earlier. It was still morning in California, and she was so excited, like you wouldn't believe. Beats me why anyone would be thrilled about only drinking prune juice for three days, but anyway. I can't thank you enough, sweetheart.'

'My pleasure.' I squeezed his hand, a Judas grin on my face. Time to increase the stakes. 'I'd do it again, if she needs more money. Anything to make you happy. You're such a good brother to her.'

Was it my imagination, or did Scott's eyes narrow when I mentioned giving Darcy more cash?

'I couldn't ask you to do that a second time,' he said. 'You've been more than generous already.'

I smiled at him, all lightness and love. 'I would, though, in a heartbeat. If this round of treatment isn't successful. Should Darcy find she needs longer in California ...'

He shook his head. 'I don't deserve an angel like you.' He raised my hand to his lips, planting a kiss on my palm, his eyes fixed on mine. His expression spoke of tenderness, devotion, gratitude. The Lyddie of two days ago would have swooned at the sight. Instead, hatred filled every cell of my being. I'd enjoy playing this bastard at his own game.

His mobile, set beside his cutlery on the table, vibrated with an incoming message. Scott laughed. 'I bet that's Darcy.'

I bet it is too, I thought. A pre-arranged text, sent to deepen the deceit and convince me his sister was thousands of miles away sipping prune juice. And I was right. Scott entered his pass code, read the text with a grin, then handed me his phone.

Bile seared my throat when I read the message. *Everything great here in sunny California!!!! Just done yoga on the beach!!!! Off for an enema next - don't you envy me?!!!!!!! Talk soon, xoxo*

The bitch, I thought sourly, annoyed as much by the proliferation of exclamation marks as the deception they represented. 'Sounds like she's off to a flying start,' I said, schooling my features into a suitably gratified expression. In my head, I made a mental note of his pass code, or what I thought it might be. His mobile had been upside down and Scott's fingers had pressed the numbers with lightning speed. 1507, I decided, perhaps his date of birth.

Useful to know. The chances were good I'd need to snoop though his phone at some point.

We continued the charade while we scoffed our food.

'Aren't vindaloos incredibly hot?' he asked. 'Are you sure you can eat something so spicy?'

I waved a dismissive hand. 'I'm tired of playing it safe with curries. Time to crank up the heat.' As our meal progressed, I made a show of struggling to eat my lamb dish, yet reassuring Scott I was fine whenever he feigned concern. My stomach handled fiery food with ease, but he didn't know that. All part of the plan.

Once we were seated in Scott's Toyota, I clutched my belly, grabbing his hand in mock alarm.

'That vindaloo might have been a mistake,' I said, my voice low and pain-wracked. 'Too hot and oily by far. Can we go home, please? Now?'

'Of course.' We drove in silence to the Harbourside, with me scrambling from the car the minute we arrived. 'I need a toilet,' I gasped, faking a retch. 'Huge apologies, but I think I'm going to be sick.'

'Can I come in? Make sure you're all right?'

A vehement shake of my head. 'I'd rather not subject you to whatever's going on in my stomach. Way too embarrassing.'

More bogus concern. 'Please, sweetheart. I just want to help.'

My hand gripped my belly again. 'Oh, God. Sorry, but I really need to go.' I flung the last words over my shoulder as I ran to the entrance door, yanked it open, and stood on the other side, hidden by its wooden panels.

Within a minute I heard Scott restart the engine and drive away. Slowly and with care, I opened the door and peeped outside. After I watched his taillights disappear around the curve of the car park, I scurried to my rented Audi. My fingers shaking, I switched on the ignition and set off after Scott.

I stayed three cars behind him as we drove in the opposite direction to Southville. Instead, he headed up Park Street towards the Triangle. I maintained my distance, tailing him along Clifton's

Promenade, a road lined with Georgian mansions and reeking of wealth. Most were rented out as offices. Scott indicated right, turning into the car park of a building called Clifton Heights. I recognised it as a block of serviced apartments I'd rejected when conducting my search for somewhere to live. The location was too far from the Harbourside and the prices were eye-wateringly expensive. Such a place would suit Scott, though. The apartments in the Clifton Heights building, like the Airbnb address, could be rented on a short-term basis, making it ideal for his itinerant lifestyle.

So this was where he planned to enjoy the high life until he'd drained me of my savings. I didn't doubt a further stay in California would be required for Darcy, then another, all at my expense. Bastard. My resolve strengthened.

I had yet to discover which apartment he had rented but that could come later. It was too risky to snoop around while Scott was in the building. Satisfied I'd done everything possible for the time being, I drove back to the Harbourside. The minute I arrived I typed a quick message to Scott, aware of the importance of maintaining appearances. *Sorry about earlier! Stomach still iffy, so off to bed. Will text once I'm better. x*

Sleeping wasn't an option. I switched on my laptop, searching for the website for the block where Scott was staying. I checked the availability of apartments, starting from the next day. My luck was in. One of the flats was vacant, so I reserved it for a week, certain I'd accomplish my plan long before then. A few minutes after making my booking, I received an automated email giving me the entrance code to the front door and a temporary one for the apartment. The message informed me I could check in whenever suited me after 2pm.

'I'm coming for you, dickhead,' I said.

***

The next morning I got up early and drove to Clifton, arriving at Scott's block of apartments by eight o'clock. I parked close enough to watch the front door but not so near he might see me. I chose a spot under a tree, the Audi obscured by its shade, and settled in to wait. I wondered how Scott spent his days, given that the job at the car dealership must be as false as everything else he'd told me. Did he visit Darcy - the two of them plotting the next part of their scam? Or did he scour the dating websites for his next target? My skin prickled with repulsion. I couldn't wait to wreak my revenge on him.

Time ticked by. Nine o'clock, ten o'clock. No sign of Scott. My fingers drummed a staccato beat against my thigh, my nerves stretched tight. At last I spotted movement behind the glass windows fronting the second floor - a man walking down the stairs. Scott emerged through the main door, heading towards his Toyota.

Once he'd driven off, I got out of my car, striding towards the building, my eyes flicking to where Scott had been parked. Bay number six. From what the introductory email had said, the numbers corresponded to those of the apartments. Meaning I knew which one the bastard had rented.

I glanced at my watch. Eleven o'clock; three hours until check-in, meaning I had time to kill. With that in mind, I walked to the main part of Clifton. I'd do some window shopping and then have lunch while I honed my plan. I had no idea when Scott might return, so I didn't dare try anything that day. Instead I'd check in at 2pm and scout out my apartment in the hope the layout and furnishings would be the same throughout the block. One thing in particular I needed to locate, an item mentioned in the website's list of amenities provided for the tenants.

At two o'clock I was at Clifton Heights again, skirting the approach to the building with care in case Scott's Toyota was back in its space. It wasn't, but I'd need to be quick in case he returned. No way could I explain my presence there if we met in the stairwell. My fingers tapped in the access code to the front door, then I sprinted up the stairs to the first floor. Another round of tapping, and I stepped inside the apartment I'd rented. Number four.

And what a smart place it was, the quality of the furnishings justifying the steep charges. Solid oak bookcases, two glass and marble coffee tables, Egyptian cotton sheets, a huge sleigh bed. Everything spoke of opulence and understated wealth. The layout consisted of one bedroom, a bathroom, lounge, kitchen and dining area. While I walked through the rooms, my eyes searched for, but didn't spot, what I was after. Once I checked my emails on my phone, I realised my mistake. I crossed the lounge to a cupboard set within one of the oak bookcases, reaching up to open its doors. Inside the cupboard, out of sight to casual eyes, was a safe. Sturdy, capacious, with a keypad on the front. I didn't doubt the one in Scott's apartment held a copious amount of cash, none of which was rightfully his.

A safe that, if my plan succeeded, would soon be empty.

CHAPTER 18

Scott contacted me that night. Bile rose in my throat when his name flashed onto my phone. I almost rejected the call, then I remembered - hadn't I been intending to text him anyway, ready for the next stage of my plan? I swallowed my anger, stepping into my role like a seasoned Hollywood star.

'Hi there,' I said, my tone light and breezy. 'I was just about to call you.'

'How are you, sweetheart? Feeling better?' Like me, the man deserved an Oscar. Had I not known otherwise, I'd have sworn that was concern in his voice. As matters stood, I guessed all he felt for me was contempt.

'Fine.' I barked out a short laugh. 'My stomach's much more settled, thanks. I won't be eating anything that spicy again, that's for sure. How about you? Did work go okay?'

'Busy. I started at seven and didn't stop until five.'

What a fucking liar. Fury flared within me.

'The day went like a dream. I sold four high-end cars,' Scott continued. 'That bonus I'm getting at Christmas? It just got bigger, babe. I'll be able to repay what I owe you, with plenty to spare for our trip to Lanzarote.'

'Wonderful,' I managed. 'How's Darcy? Have you heard from her?'

He laughed. 'Several texts, yes. She's craving a burger with all the trimmings, but is sticking with the prune juice. More enemas, too. Thank God she didn't go into details. They'd probably make your vindaloo problems sound tame.'

My anger skyrocketed, but I reminded myself to stick to the plan. If everything went well, the fucker would soon regret ever messing with Lyddie Hunter. Instead, I laughed too. 'Rather her than me.'

'Can I see you tomorrow? Another meal out, perhaps?'

'Sorry. I have a school reunion to attend.' Followed by a theatrical groan. 'I'm dreading it, believe me.'

'Wednesday, then?'

'Sure. I'll call you after I get back.'

***

By Wednesday morning I had several texts and three missed calls from him on my mobile. I waited until lunchtime, then decided I'd made him sweat enough.

He answered on the first ring. 'Are you all right, sweetheart? Why didn't you phone me last night?'

I ignored his question. 'Can we get together this evening, like we mentioned?'

To my relief he agreed straightaway. 'What did you have in mind?'

'How about going for a beer somewhere in Southville? Maybe The Hen and Chicken on North Street?'

'I'd love to. You don't sound yourself, sweetheart. Are you sure you're all right?'

'I'm fine. But I have something to tell you.'

'Okay.' Hesitation in his voice. 'What did you want to say?'

'It, um, it can wait until I see you.' Had I projected the right amount of nerves?

Scott cleared his throat. 'Everything's fine between us, isn't it?'

I sighed, loud enough for him to hear. Another misdirect. 'I'd rather hold off on telling you until tonight, if that's all right. Shall we say eight o'clock?'

We ended the call with everything in place from my point of view. Before he said goodbye, Scott told me he loved me. I didn't respond other than a quick, 'see you later.' My lack of enthusiasm clearly rattled him, which was the intended effect. Besides, after tonight I'd never have to endure the prick ever again.

***

That afternoon I packed up my stuff at the Harbourside apartment and transported it back to my house in Kingswood. Amelia didn't comment, being used to me coming and going as I pleased. God, did it feel good to be back in my old home, its surroundings as comfortable as well-worn pyjamas. I needed every inch of the sanctuary it offered.

That evening I dressed in ancient jeans and a faded top. For what I had planned, comfort, not style, was in order. Once I'd grabbed an old rucksack, I was ready. At 7.30pm I was back at the Clifton Heights building, parked so I had a view of the entrance and Scott's car. I figured he'd leave within the next few minutes. Ah, there he was, crisp and slick in tight-fitting trousers and a sugar-white polo shirt, a leather jacket slung over one arm. He strode to his car, its lights flashing as he unlocked the door. Then he was driving towards the exit, never once glancing my way. Within seconds he'd vanished from sight.

I got out of my car and headed towards the building. Cameras covered the parking area and entrance, but they didn't bother me. I was a paid-up resident of number four, so I had a valid reason for appearing on any security footage. On my last visit I'd established that no cameras existed on the upper floors - the management must have decided the separate pass codes for each flat and the front door offered sufficient protection. Sloppy of them, but I'd use such negligence to my advantage.

I headed to the second floor, to number six. My breath hitched in my chest with the enormity of what I was about to do. This was burglary - no matter how I tried to rationalise it, I was planning to become a criminal. I, Lyddie Hunter, who'd always played a straight hand. Not anymore, though. I pulled on the woollen gloves I'd brought with me while I scanned the hallway to check a second time for cameras. None. No sounds came from the apartment opposite, and no car had occupied its parking space. Everything was on track with my plan.

A light flashed on the entrance keypad to Scott's apartment, the small red bead a challenge. My wool-covered fingers hovered over the buttons, my mind recalling Scott unlocking his phone to read Darcy's text during our curry. I was gambling on him using the same four-digit code for most things, the way I did. Bank cards, phone, car immobiliser. What numbers had he used? I was certain the first three were one, five and zero, but wasn't sure of the last digit. Seven, perhaps? I inhaled a calming breath before tapping in the numbers. One. Five. Zero. Seven.

The red light flashed at me three times, a warning sound accompanying each flash. Shit. I'd got it wrong.

My heart thudding in my chest, I tried again. One. Five. Zero. Six. More flashes, the beeps shredding my nerves. Dear God, what if the keypad only allowed three attempts before it alerted the central security system? I closed my eyes, sending out a prayer I'd get it right next time. If God existed, I doubted he'd condone burglary, but desperation was biting at my heels. I touched my fingertips to the keypad, sweat dampening my palms under the thick wool. One. Five. Zero. Five.

The light turned green. A click sounded from within the lock. I sent a silent thanks to the universe.

My fingers closed over the handle, pushing open the door to step into Scott's apartment. As I'd predicted, his flat was a mirror image of mine. Little evidence existed of him in the kitchen and living area. An upturned mug in the dish rack, a car magazine on the table, a T-shirt slung over an armchair. I padded into the bedroom, where an open suitcase sat on the floor, betraying his peripatetic lifestyle. The wardrobe door stood ajar, a few clothes occupying space on the hangers within. In the bathroom, Scott's razor was plugged in and charging, his shaving foam and shampoo next to it. A faint whiff of his musky cologne hung in the air and I breathed it in, transported to the cottage in Devon, to our love-making, the passion in which I'd almost drowned. Self-disgust surged through me before I reminded myself why I was there.

'You can do this,' I told myself. Then I walked back into the lounge.

Across the room stood a heavy oak bookcase, complete with a small cupboard. I opened the doors to reveal the safe within, another red light above its keypad. My fingers tapped out the same four numbers again: one, five, zero, five. Bingo. The light turned green, a whirring sound came from the mechanism, and the safe door swung open to display its contents. Cash. A lot of it.

I reached in a gloved hand. The bundles of notes were sorted by denomination, most of them fifties and twenties but a few tens and fives. I did a quick count; the safe contained over twenty thousand pounds. Ten thousand of which was mine - the rest possibly what remained of Ellie's savings. I ran my fingers over the notes, a grin on my face. Then I transferred the bundles to the rucksack I'd brought with me.

Four mobile phones lay beside the cash. I didn't doubt that on one of them I'd find the vile texts he'd sent me. They went into my rucksack as well.

The safe also contained a large envelope. I opened it, finding several credit cards inside. Obtained via identity theft, I surmised, and a necessity for joining premium dating websites. Each bore a different name. One Scott Champion, another Steven Simmons. Rick Montgomery and Michael Hammond as well, aliases familiar from Love Rats Exposed. I'd been right; the same man had conned me, Ellie, Sophie, and Broke and Betrayed. Under the guise of John Hayes and Chris Talbot, the names on the remaining cards, he'd doubtless defrauded two more. At least. I took the envelope and added it to the contents of the rucksack.

Mission accomplished. It was almost time to go.

One last detail remained. On the outside of the safe were instructions on how to create a new pass code. All I needed to do was to shut the door, type in a different code and press 'enter'. My fingers tapped out a random four-digit number, then confirmed it as instructed. I wanted Scott to be unaware for as long as possible that he'd been robbed, hoping he'd assume the safe had malfunctioned when he was unable to open it. The building was managed off-site, so even after he complained the problem wouldn't be rectified for a while. By the time Scott discovered his loss, I'd be long gone from his life.

Job done, I left the apartment, satisfaction in every cell of my body. Still no sound from the flat opposite, and nobody passed me on the stairs or in the entrance lobby as I walked out. It was five minutes after eight o'clock; Scott would be at The Hen and Chicken, wondering where I was. I hurried back to my Audi, then pulled out my mobile. A quick text was in order. *Car problems. Have called breakdown service. Sorry, won't be able to make it tonight.*

His reply came straightaway. *Hope you're OK. Anything I can do? Should I drive over?*

My fingers got busy typing. *Thanks, but I'm not in the best of moods. It's been a frustrating evening.*

Too bad. Really wanted to see my special girl. Let's meet up tomorrow instead.

His special girl. Ugh and double ugh. I typed another message. *Text me when you're home so I can call you.* Then I drove to Kingswood. After I stepped into the hallway, my mobile pinged.

'I'm tired,' I told Amelia. 'Think I'll grab an early night.'

Once in my bedroom, I emptied my rucksack onto the bed, thick wads of money tumbling out along with the envelope and mobiles. Among them was my own phone. As I'd predicted the text was from Scott, saying he was back home and asking me to call. I braced myself, knowing this wouldn't be easy.

He answered straightaway. 'Hi, sweetheart. How's your car?'

'Don't ask. I've been told the clutch needs a new part. I'm sorry I couldn't make it tonight.'

'Me too, darling. Can we get together tomorrow?'

'I'm afraid not. Remember I said I had something to tell you?' I drew in a theatrical breath. 'Oh God. This would be much better done in person.'

A pause from Scott. Then: 'You're worrying me, Lyddie. Have I upset you?'

When I failed to reply, he continued, 'You mean the world to me, sweetheart. Talk to me, please.'

'It's just that ...' Another dramatic intake of breath. 'I never meant to mess you around, I swear.'

'What are you talking about?'

'Remember I mentioned I had a school reunion to attend?'

'Yeah. What about it?'

'I ran into my ex-boyfriend there. The place taught both sexes, you see. While we were doing our A-levels, we dated. For several years afterwards too.'

He exhaled noisily. 'I don't like where this is heading. Should I be concerned?' He sounded genuinely worried.

I gave a loud sigh, designed to show my remorse. 'I never meant this to happen, believe me.'

'What?' Spit it out, for God's sake, can't you?'

'I still have strong feelings for him. We spent the night together.'

'What the hell are you saying?' His Mr Nice Guy mask had slipped, it seemed. 'You cheated on me?'

'Yes. I can't tell you how sorry I am.'

'So what does this mean? Are you breaking up with me?' He was pissed off all right. For a second, unease bit deep into my flesh.

'I've realised I belong with him. We share so much history. I can only apologise and hope you don't hate me.'

He didn't respond. 'Say something,' I prompted.

'I told you I loved you.' His turn for a theatrical sigh. 'You said you felt the same. Why are you doing this?'

When I didn't reply, he continued, 'I hoped we'd get married one day.'

That was laying it on thick, even for him. 'Please forgive me. I didn't intend to hurt you.'

'Are you sure about this, sweetheart?' Mr Nice Guy had returned. 'We were good together. Or so I thought.'

'Don't make this more difficult. Please.'

Another pause.

'Maybe you're just confused, Lyddie.'

'My mind's made up. I'm sorry.' Then I fired my killer shot. 'One other thing. You don't need to bother repaying my money.'

He'd not expected that, I could tell. 'Really?'

'Yes. If Darcy's cured, I'll consider it well spent.'

'Well, if you insist ...' He cleared his throat. 'That's very generous of you.'

'I hope you don't think too badly of me.'

'I can't say I'm happy you want us to break up. But if you're certain ...' His mask was back in place, his former anger gone. With any luck, once he'd calmed down, he'd decide he was up ten thousand pounds and free to pursue some other gullible woman. An easy win.

'I'm certain.' Time to sever this twisted relationship. 'Goodbye, Scott. Take care of yourself.' With that, I ended the call.

I flopped back on my bed, my relief intense. I'd done it. I'd conned a con man, and now I was free of him forever.

***

My initial euphoria soon wore off. I couldn't share my triumph with anyone, and a sense of deflation seeped through me. Then I remembered Love Rats Exposed. Those women would love to hear I'd hoodwinked Scott fucking Champion.

I logged on, checking the recent threads. Dozens of people had commiserated with Anna over her daughter's death, and I added my own belated sympathies. Then I located the thread I'd started before and began to type.

'I was wrong,' I posted. 'Turns out I'd been dating the guy who swindled my sister after all. Remember Scott, the man I hoped was Mr Right? Well, it was him all along. He tried it on with me too, and almost succeeded. Not quite, though. I can't go into details, but he's choking on a fat wedge of humble pie because of me. Now I've dumped the bastard, and good riddance.' Then I closed my laptop.

I packed the bundles of cash into my rucksack again and hid it at the back of my wardrobe, to be dealt with tomorrow.

The mobile phones got shoved into an old shoebox and stashed beside the money. From my cosmetics bag, I took out my nail scissors. Then, with deliberate cuts, I destroyed the credit cards. My scissors halved Scott, Steven, Rick, Michael, John and Chris, my fingers vicious.

'Die, you bastard,' I said, as I chopped Scott Champion in two.

After I finished, I checked my laptop, curious to see what responses I'd received. Quite a few, it seemed. *Good for you! Don't be a tease - tell us how you managed it!* from Broken and Betrayed. *Wow! You rock, girl! The bastard had it coming to him*, from Heartbroken Helen. Satisfaction sparked in me at their obvious admiration, although I wouldn't be revealing how I'd delivered Scott's comeuppance. Some things, like burglary, shouldn't be disclosed online.

A good evening's work. I slept well that night.

CHAPTER 19

I awoke early the following morning, satisfaction deep in my belly. If I'd been a cat, I'd have purred for hours. Instead I enjoyed a lie-in while I planned my day. First I'd head over to Mum's, given that we'd not seen each other for a while. Next would come a trip to the bank to deposit my half of the money, then I'd drive to Ellie's, assuming she was available, to deliver the rest to her. After that, I'd call Spain, let my neighbour know I was heading back, albeit only for a short while. Just as long as I needed to close the gallery and vacate my villa, ready for its sale. I had my sister, Mum and Caroline to consider. My disastrous liaison with Scott had made me realise how much I needed them. Not to mention Richie. A man who, unlike Scott, was the real deal. Bristol was where I belonged. Not Spain.

I grabbed my mobile, fired off a quick text to Ellie. *You around later? We need to talk.* With that, my stomach rumbled, causing me to head downstairs into the kitchen. My sister's reply came as I polished off a plate of bacon and eggs. *Great! I could use a break from making all these purses. One o'clock?*

After I showered and dressed, I took the rucksack from my wardrobe and transferred the money to my handbag. Then I drove to Mum's house.

She seemed pleased I'd called round. I didn't stay long, just enough time to reassure her that I'd dumped Scott. No mention of my decision to move back to the UK. I judged it too soon for that particular revelation.

'Thank God you've seen sense,' she said.

'Amen to that.' For once, my mother and I were in agreement.

My next stop was the bank. Once inside, I hesitated. Ellie had lost all her savings whereas I had plenty left. Her business was young, and I wasn't convinced she'd freed herself from her financial quagmire, no matter what she claimed. Part of me realised I was attempting to ease my guilt at having misjudged her, but I didn't care. I'd give my sister the whole twenty thousand, and to hell with my motives. She deserved it.

With that sorted, I returned to my car to head to Ellie's. Love for her filled my heart, along with relief I'd been granted a chance to fix our relationship. In that moment, life tasted sweet. Scott was history, and the temptation of Richie hovered on the horizon. Not right away – I'd been too damaged by recent events – but a girl could hope, couldn't she?

The hug Ellie gave me after she opened the door threatened to crack my ribs, even though she was so slight. Thank God my sister was so forgiving. We'd be fine, a fact that almost forced me to my knees in gratitude.

'Come inside,' she said. I followed her into the living room.

'I've missed you.' My voice was thick with emotion.

'Likewise.' She smiled, and so did my heart.

'I love you,' I said.

She laughed. 'Likewise again.' Then she stared at me, a frown on her face. 'You don't seem yourself. What's wrong?'

I drew in a breath. 'You were right. We dated the same man, and he's an evil lying rat.'

She swallowed a gasp. 'How come you changed your mind? Did Caroline convince you?'

'Let's just say I've seen the light.' Some things - Darcy and the faked cancer - Ellie wouldn't hear from me. 'It's over between us.'

She frowned. 'Weren't you crazy about him? Why the sudden change?'

'I prefer not to talk about it, okay? But I'm sorry for the way I've behaved.'

'You believe me now? About Scott, or Steven, or whatever his name is?'

'Yes. I should never have doubted you.'

'At least you didn't lose your savings to him.' My dismay must have shown in my face. 'Tell me you didn't. Please.'

I couldn't lie about the money, not after telling Caroline and Richie I'd funded Darcy's treatment. 'Yeah, I got taken for a ride, just like you. Not for as much though. It's worth it to get him out of my life.'

'Will you go to the police?' Her voice held fear; no doubt she was terrified I'd mention her own shame.

'No.'

'That's good.' She smiled, her relief obvious. 'You want something to drink?' Without waiting for an answer, she disappeared into the kitchen.

Ellie remained full of questions about Scott as we drank our coffees, especially about how I discovered his duplicity, but I refused to answer them. I didn't care to dwell on the extent to which he had duped me. 'You were right, I was wrong,' I told her. 'That's all you need to know. I'm finished with the prick.'

'Thank God.'

'I have a surprise for you.' It seemed an appropriate moment. My handbag sat on the floor next to my chair, its presence a silent plea: *give me to Ellie*. I hauled the bag, fat with the bundles of cash, onto the table. With a grin on my face, I pulled it open, exposing the thick wads.

'It's for you,' I said. 'All of it. Twenty thousand pounds.'

Ellie stared at me, her confusion obvious. 'I don't understand.'

My moment had arrived, and I planned to savour every second. I'd intended to tell her I won the money on the National Lottery, but found I couldn't. Too many lies had soiled our relationship already. Besides, how could I explain a bag of cash rather than a bank transfer between us, if I'd won it on a lotto ticket? No, I'd tell the truth, and to hell with it.

'I stole it from Scott.' Shock replaced confusion in her face. Before Ellie could speak, I ploughed on. I confessed my anger at Steven Simmons after her suicide attempt, how I'd decided to exact revenge on the bastard who'd driven her to such despair. How convinced I'd been that Scott was genuine.

'Then I discovered the truth. He's a ruthless con artist, just like you said.' I told her about my determination to play the bastard at his own game.

'I found out where he was living,' I continued. 'So I broke in and stole the money. All of it.'

Ellie remained silent. 'Say something,' I urged.

Her lips quivered. 'You did that for me?'

'Yes. If you're worried about him finding out, you needn't be. I've covered my tracks.'

'Are you sure? Oh, my God, what if he comes after you?'

I cursed myself for causing her worry. 'It'll be okay, Els. He doesn't know where I live, remember. Not now I'm back in Kingswood. Even when he discovers the money's missing, he won't link its disappearance to me. He'll never twig that I'm onto him.'

'You're certain?'

'Yes. He'll think it's an inside job by one of the maintenance crew at the apartment block. And there's no way he'd involve the police. It'll be all right. You'll see.'

She shook her head. 'I can't believe you'd go to such lengths for me.'

I emptied the bag onto the coffee table. 'Take the money. Please.'

She didn't respond, but didn't say no, either.

'You don't need some extra cash?' I asked. 'I bet you do.'

Ellie nodded. 'I won't deny that.' The notes remained where I'd left them, however.

Then she shrugged. 'I'm not thrilled about accepting this money, I'll admit.'

'Why ever not?'

'Because it's been tainted. By *him*.'

'It's yours now. Do what you want with it. Donate it to charity if you're that bothered.' I was past caring.

***

Once home, I fixed myself some lunch, then slumped on the sofa. Amelia was at work and I was grateful to have the house to myself. Before long I drifted off to sleep.

When I awoke, a sense of having overlooked something vital nagged at my gut. What, though?

For several minutes, I ran through everything in my mind, telling myself I was imagining things. *It's over*, I reassured myself. *You're free of him and so is Ellie.*

Then the reason for my worry sledgehammered me between the eyes.

Anna's daughter Sophie had been murdered, and a horrible suspicion was growing inside my head. Her mother had posted that Sophie never got the chance to inform the police about the fraud. My earlier concern resurfaced that she might have texted Scott, whom she knew as Michael Hammond, about her intentions. If so, did that impulsive gesture, no doubt done in a 'fuck you' moment of anger, result in her death at Scott's hands? Had he decided on drastic action to ensure her silence?

I considered the facts. Okay, so we were at the cottage the weekend she died. We'd returned early from Devon, though, on the pretext Scott wanted to check up on Darcy. Then he'd pleaded the need for sleep. Scott could have killed Sophie after he left me that Sunday night. Anna hadn't specified when her daughter had died, only that it happened that weekend.

I forced myself to breathe, long and slow, to ease the tightness in my chest. Might Sophie's stabbing be a coincidence? I had no proof Scott was a killer, just my gut instincts. They were screaming a warning at me, sirens blaring and lights flashing.

Oh, God. I ran to the bathroom, only just reaching the toilet before I vomited up my lunch.

Once I finished heaving, I went to my bedroom, switching on my laptop and navigating to Love Rats Exposed. The thread from Anna about Sophie's murder was at the top, with at least a dozen new posts on it. I clicked on it, refreshing my memory about when her daughter had died. I was right; Anna hadn't given details, just that Sophie was murdered the same weekend Scott and I spent in Devon.

Impossible to function until I discovered the truth. I retrieved my laptop, typing 'murder of Sophie in Melksham alleyway' into Google. Too bad I didn't know her surname.

The first item was a link to the local newspaper, which reported Sophie's death as taking place on the Saturday of my weekend with Scott. Her last name was Hannigan, it seemed. Other sources corroborated the date. Thank God. I heaved a sigh of relief. I had overreacted. Scott had been with me when she died. He was a fraudster, sure, but not a killer.

CHAPTER 20

By evening, my mood had turned buoyant, my earlier concerns gone. Tomorrow I'd book my flight to Spain, making sure I saw Ellie and Mum again before I left. What made me smile as I fixed myself a bowl of pasta had less to do with them than it did with my best friend. Caroline had phoned just before I started cooking.

'How are you doing, lovey?' she asked.

'Fine. You mustn't worry about me. I'm over Scott. Ready to move on.' A little optimistic, perhaps, but so what?

'Already? Feck, that was quick.'

'The sooner the better, I'd say.'

'So long as you're not bottling up your emotions.'

I smiled at Caroline's scepticism, but then she remained unaware of the revenge I'd exacted. 'Nope. Definitely not.'

'Have you been to the police yet?'

'No.' A heated debate ensued, one that only ended when I reminded her about Ellie. 'I won't do anything to jeopardise her mental health,' I insisted. 'She'd never cope with the police investigating Steven Simmons.' To my relief, Caroline agreed.

'The reason I'm calling ...'

Was that nervousness in her words? Or excitement? 'That last time Richie and I saw you,' she continued. 'You mentioned about the three of us going for a drink. Or a meal.'

Oh, God. Please, please, please, I prayed in silence.

'There's a pub he wants to try in Thornbury that does a Sunday carvery. How about we all go this weekend?'

Delight filled me. *Yes, yes and triple yes!* No wonder Caroline had sounded excited. Perhaps Richie only wanted us to be friends, given how badly I'd behaved, but I couldn't stop the sense of hope that filled me. First I'd heal the wound Scott had inflicted – Maria Holmes, who'd helped me so much before, came to mind - and then maybe we'd get a second chance at love.

We wrapped up the call and I carried my spaghetti bolognese, along with a glass of wine, into the living room, chose an armchair to slouch in and turned on the television. The local evening news had just started. I forked meat and pasta into my mouth as the title sequence finished, unaware of the shock awaiting me.

The camera focused on the male anchor. 'In tonight's programme, we reveal how the death of a local drug addict is linked to a recent murder in Melksham.' I shovelled in more spaghetti, still oblivious.

'Twenty-seven-year-old Darcy Logan, a long-term heroin addict, was found dead at her home in Greenbank yesterday. The police officers who were called to the house discovered jewellery and other items belonging to Sophie Hannigan, a resident of Melksham who was murdered recently. Unconfirmed reports say Darcy Logan's description matched eyewitness accounts of a woman spotted fleeing the scene of the crime.'

The fork dropped from my hand, the bowl of pasta spilling onto the carpet as I jerked upright in my seat, not caring about the mess at my feet. A photograph flashed onto the screen. In front of me was the woman I'd known as Scott's sister.

'Police describe the circumstances surrounding Darcy Logan's death from a heroin overdose as suspicious and have not yet ruled out foul play. They are also liaising with Melksham police investigating the murder of Sophie Hannigan.' The camera then panned to the female newscaster, who began the next item.

My throat closed over with shock. All rational thought fled my brain. Scott was far more dangerous than I'd given him credit for. Instead of getting his own hands dirty, he'd persuaded Darcy to murder Sophie. He'd been so damn clever, every step of the way. His accomplice's heroin addiction fitted perfectly with posing as his sick sister. The long sleeves she'd worn each time I'd met her - not to keep a dying woman warm, but to cover the needle tracks on her arms. No wonder she looked so gaunt, so unhealthy. With her hair concealed under a scarf, her brows plucked and her eyelashes cut off, she'd easily fooled me into believing she suffered from cancer.

I wondered how much money Scott had offered her to play the role. Not a lot probably, given her addiction. Same with murdering Sophie. And now Darcy was dead. She'd served her purpose, and Scott couldn't risk her blabbing the truth.

I couldn't find it in me to hate her. She'd been another of his victims, just in a different way.

A thought struck me. Was I in danger? Two women were already dead, and I'd acted in a fashion guaranteed to piss off their killer in a big way. I gulped down the rest of my wine, in need of an alcoholic crutch. Then I leaned back in my chair, closing my eyes, my brain a mess. I thought long and hard, outlining everything in my head before coming to some conclusions.

Fact one: as far as Scott was concerned I was a success story. He'd fleeced me of a sizable chunk of money, hadn't he? He'd probably already moved onto his next victim.

Fact two: He had no reason to consider me a threat. The dickhead still believed I was clueless about his real identity.

Fact three: he had no proof I'd taken his money. My original theory still held good - he'd attribute the theft to the maintenance staff at the apartment block.

Fact four: Scott didn't know where I lived. In a city the size of Bristol, he'd never track me down.

From whatever angle I looked at it, it appeared I was safe. A mantra kept repeating itself in my head: *he doesn't know where I live. He doesn't know where I live.*

Or maybe he did. Oh God. He'd stalked me several times, including before I moved to the Harbourside. The chances were good he'd discovered my Kingswood address in the process. Fear gripped my bones, squeezing terror into my core. Should I involve the police in order to protect myself?

Followed by another consideration: two women had been murdered, and I possessed evidence that could help their enquiry. Richie was right - Scott Champion deserved to be behind bars. I didn't care about the fact I'd have to admit to burglary and theft in order to tell the whole truth. Worst case scenario? With no criminal history and a reasonable explanation of my motives, I'd probably receive a suspended sentence rather than actual jail time.

Decision made. I'd tell the police everything and point them towards Scott's other victims on Love Rats Exposed. I'd turn over the ruined credit cards in my waste bin, the mobile phones in my wardrobe, give them his Clifton Heights address. Maybe they'd catch him, maybe they wouldn't, but either way I'd have done the right thing.

My only regret was that I'd have to drag Ellie into the whole sorry mess, despite her reluctance to involve the police. I dreaded to think what that might do to her mental health.

I'd talk to my sister as soon as possible. With any luck she'd understand. She might even come with me to the police.

My mobile was on the coffee table. I fired off a quick text. No details, just asking if she was free tomorrow morning, saying we needed to talk further.

Armed with cloths and cleaning spray, I tackled the mess on my carpet, my ears on alert for a reply. Nothing. I considered my options. I'd go to Ellie's place in the morning whether I'd heard back from her or not. If she wasn't home, I'd have to text her, then head to Bridewell anyway. Whatever happened I'd be unmasking Scott to the police in the next twenty-four hours.

***

I awoke the next morning after a fractured night's rest, my sleep punctured with nightmares. Sophie, bleeding to death in a filthy alleyway. Scott, forcing a syringe of heroin into Darcy's arm. A whisky and wine hangover pounded at my temples, causing me to groan when I lifted my head from my pillow. The first thing I did was check my mobile. No response from Ellie. Concerned, I fired off another text. And waited. Still nothing.

By lunchtime I'd sent several messages and called twice, only to be met with her voicemail. Panic mounted within me at the thought she might have attempted suicide for the fourth time. The police would have to wait. First I needed to ensure Ellie's safety.

I drove to her flat in St George. I had a key, so I let myself in, checking each room. No sign of her, although everything appeared in order.

I phoned Mum, outlining the reason for my concern. 'Has she called you?' I finished.

'No. I've not heard from her for a couple of days.' Anxiety sounded in her voice. 'Oh, God. Where can she have gone?'

I blew out a breath. 'I've no idea.'

'Let me know the moment you find her.'

'I'll call you straightaway.'

I paced the floor all afternoon, willing my mobile to vibrate into life. At six o'clock, my prayer was granted.

Sorry didn't get back to you before. Have taken the train to the cottage. Needed time to think.

I fired off a reply. *You OK?*

My mobile pinged. *I just want to die. Hurting so much.*

Terror shot through me. I dropped the phone, scrabbling to retrieve it from the floor. My mouth dry with fear, I called Ellie's number, but it went straight to voicemail.

I just want to die. What had been the catalyst this time? Had our recent estrangement pushed my sister over the edge? But we'd rescued our relationship, hadn't we?

Another ping from my mobile. *Can you come to the cottage? Not sure I want to live anymore. Too much guilt over Alyson.*

So that was the reason. Her best friend would have turned twenty-five next week had she survived the crash. I was betting that was why Ellie had plummeted downhill so suddenly. Thank God she'd reached out for help this time, not tried to kill herself. It was progress, and hadn't I intended us to talk face to face anyway?

This way was better. Surrounded by the lush Devon scenery, Ellie and I could work through her issues. No way would I tell her about Darcy and Sophie's murders, or my plans to involve the police, not while she was so fragile.

I grabbed my bag and car keys. Within a couple of hours, I'd be on the south coast, depending on the traffic.

I tried calling her again. To my relief, this time she answered. 'Lyddie?' Her voice was a murmur, no more.

I forced calm into my tone. 'Just hold on, okay? I'll be there as soon as I can.'

'Devon seems a good place to end my life.' Such exhaustion in her voice. 'Remember how steep the cliffs are?'

'No,' I whispered. 'Don't do anything stupid. Please.'

'I need you. Please come.'

'I will. Right away.'

'Don't bring Mum. I can't face her right now.'

Once I ended the call, I tapped out another text. *Leaving home now. Will be with you soon so we can talk. I love you. X.*

Next I phoned our mother.

'Oh, no. I'd so hoped Eleanor was on the mend. Help her, Lydia. For God's sake, stop my baby girl from hurting herself.' Mum's sobs tore at my heart. I promised I'd do whatever it took to drag my sister back from the brink.

Time to pack. I crammed clothes into a suitcase before hurtling into the bathroom. Five minutes later I ran down the stairs and out of the door.

The drive to Devon took longer than I'd hoped, the traffic being heavy all the way, and I didn't get there until 8.30pm. I arrived frazzled, but as I turned down the lane to the cottage my thoughts remained optimistic. I switched off the engine, stepped out of my car and grabbed my suitcase from the boot. As I did, I glanced at the cottage, seeing the curtains twitch in the living room. Thank God. My sister hadn't killed herself, and my knees almost buckled, so great was my relief. I took my key from my handbag, inserted it into the lock, and pushed open the door.

'Ellie?' My voice echoed up the stairs and through the hallway, only to be met with silence. My ears detected no other sounds in the cottage. Overwrought as I was, I must have imagined seeing the curtain move. I squashed the thought she might be at the cliffs, intent on killing herself. Hadn't she promised she'd wait for me?

She must be in the back garden, I decided. I dumped my suitcase on the floor, then started towards the kitchen, before stopping halfway. A faint whiff of fragrance teased my nostrils, made me inhale a slow, deep breath. As my lungs filled, recognition sparked in my brain. Followed by denial.

Impossible. Wasn't I tired, stressed, concerned about Ellie? I was imagining things, surely.

Time stopped after I released the lungful of breath I'd been holding. I took another, smaller inhalation. Still the same hint of fragrance, the musky aroma causing my nails to sink deep into my palms. Aftershave, without a doubt, its scent familiar. Slowly, and with caution, I turned around.

And looked straight into Scott Champion's eyes.

CHAPTER 21

'Hello, Lyddie,' Scott said. 'So glad you could join me.'

I couldn't speak, my mouth drier than cotton-wool as I stared at him. Gone was the mask he'd worn before. In front of me stood the real Scott, a smirk on his lips, malevolence in his eyes. His wide-legged, thumbs-hooked-in-belt stance reeked of arrogance served with a side dish of menace. He'd positioned himself between me and the front door. I didn't even try to run to the rear entrance. He'd overpower me before I made it halfway. Besides, there was Ellie to consider. Oh, God. Had my sister already become his third victim?

As if he could read my mind, Scott stepped forward, that damn smirk still on his mouth. 'You'll be wondering about Ellie. Where she is. Whether she's still in one piece.'

'If she's not, I'll kill you myself, you fucking bastard.'

He laughed. 'Well, aren't you the feisty one? Be careful, Lyddie.' He took another step towards me. 'You'll need to keep me sweet if you hope to see that sister of yours alive.'

Relief overwhelmed me on hearing my sister wasn't dead. My eyes glanced around, searching for possible weapons. Nothing. The hallway was devoid of furniture apart from a small table, on which stood the landline and a vase of dried flowers.

'You'd like that, wouldn't you? To see Ellie?'

'Where is she?'

'Not here. I have her close by, though, and she won't be going anywhere. She's tied up, all safe and secure.' He gestured towards the living room. 'Shall we? You first.'

I complied, the familiarity of my surroundings suddenly alien. The furniture appeared the same, the way the sunlight streamed through the windows, but he'd polluted everything by his presence. The cottage was no longer the sanctuary it had always been. In my peripheral vision, I checked the room. A solid table lamp to my left, a heavy marble vase to my right, both possible weapons.

'Sit.' Scott pointed at the armchair furthest from the door. I obeyed, my eyes never leaving his face. He squatted in front of me.

'I have a question for you,' he said.

'Where the hell is Ellie?' I demanded.

He shook his head, his smirk widening. 'You think you're so clever, don't you? The great Lyddie Hunter, believing she'd pulled the wool over my eyes. But I'm smarter, sweetheart. I've been ahead of you every step of the game we've played with each other, and hasn't it been fun?' His grin morphed into a glare, one that pierced me with hatred. Fear sparked in my belly. I recalled Sophie, Darcy, aware I couldn't relax my guard for a second. Not if Ellie and I were to survive.

Scott stood up, then leaned over my chair, his hands on the arm rests. He brought his face so close to mine that his breath fanned my lips.

'I ask the questions, not you,' he said.

'What have you done with my sister?'

'Oh, Lyddie. Didn't I make myself clear?' With that, he stepped back, his hand cracking a vicious blow across my left cheek. A cry of pain issued from my mouth, my body twisting after another slap landed on my right side. A stinging pain exploded through my face, and with it, rage. To hell with this shit. Instinct kicked in and I launched myself at him, my fists pummelling his chest, fury in every cell I possessed. He was too big, too strong, however, and within seconds he held my wrists tight in a savage grip.

'I'll tell you again. I ask the questions, not you. My first is: where's the money you stole from me?'

That puzzled me. If he'd abducted Ellie, why hadn't she told him I'd given it to her? My fragile sister wouldn't have lasted five seconds with *this* version of Scott before she crumbled. He must know she had the cash. Perhaps he'd killed her in a fit of rage before getting his answer, and my legs buckled with terror. If Scott hadn't been gripping me so tightly, I'd have dropped to the floor like a discarded tissue.

'And I have a second question. How did you find out I wasn't the loving boyfriend I pretended to be?'

I snorted in derision. 'I paid a surprise visit to the real Scott Champion in Southville. After that, everything fell into place.'

A frown twisted his lips. 'I did wonder whether I'd overplayed my hand in renting the Airbnb room. Not that it matters anymore.'

'You cocky bastard. Yeah, you overreached yourself all right.'

'You need to watch your mouth,' he ground out, his spittle landing on my chin. 'I have the advantage here, remember. How did you discover where I was living? Open the safe?'

Despite his warning, I couldn't help myself. 'I have a question for *you*, dickhead. How did you guess it was me who took your money?'

Another harsh laugh. 'I knew straightaway who the thief was.'

His words stunned me. Impossible, surely? I wetted my dry lips. 'How?'

'You really don't know?'

'No.'

'Let me see. What did her last post say?' His voice rose high in a parody of a woman's. '"Wow! You rock, girl! The bastard had it coming to him".' He grinned. 'Recognise that, do you?'

Bitter understanding hit me, another piece of the puzzle falling into place.

'Heartbroken Helen isn't so heartbroken, it seems. She's proved very helpful.' Another grin.

I was stunned. 'She's one of your stooges? Like Darcy?'

'No. Not like Darcy.' He stood watching me, that smirk back on his lips. When I didn't reply, he continued, 'You stupid bitch. Don't you get it? *I'm* Heartbroken Helen.'

If I hadn't been so terrified, I'd have cried. For Sophie, and her mother, both betrayed by Anna's posts on Love Rats Exposed. And for myself, unmasked by my own revelations.

Scott laughed. 'There you were, bragging about how you got the better of me. Who's the one choking on humble pie now?'

My gaze shot daggers into him. 'I hate you.'

'Never try to con a con artist, Lyddie. I guess you've learned that lesson the hard way.'

Yes, I had. I'd been blind, and stupid, and arrogant. A mere pawn, when I'd fancied myself queen of the game.

'You should see your face,' he jeered. 'Not that long ago you were flashing those cow-eyes at me, banging on about how you loved me. God, that made me laugh. I suckered you well and truly, and you were too moonstruck to realise.'

'Fuck you,' I ground out. 'You killed Darcy, didn't you?'

'Never trust a drug addict. She'd have set fire to her own mother to get her next fix, but she'd served her purpose.'

'And Sophie Hannigan. You murdered her too. Through Darcy.'

'She had it coming to her. The bitch was intending to blab to the police.'

Scott lowered me back into the chair, leaning over me once more.

'You have something that belongs to me,' he said. 'I want my money back.'

'I don't have it anymore. Ellie does.'

'That's not what she told me.' Confusion filled me; why had she lied? She'd known the danger this man posed. Why risk her life that way?

'You have my money. I have Ellie. A fair swap, wouldn't you say?'

I thought fast. The bundles of cash must still be at her flat, surely?

Scott leaned over me, his face a mere inch from mine. 'Answer me, bitch.'

'I don't have it, I swear.'

'That doesn't matter. You can get it for me.'

'How?'

'You're not exactly poor. From your savings, of course.'

He was right. Most of my funds were tied up in stock market investments, but I kept a healthy chunk of money in a bank deposit account. Enough to give the arsehole what he wanted.

'Here's what will happen,' Scott said. 'You'll log onto your bank from your phone and transfer the cash. I'll be watching you, so don't pull any stunts. Just return what you stole and we'll call it quits. Then you'll get your sister back. Alive.'

I nodded. What else could I do? Although a sliver of hope flickered within me.

'That'll create a trail,' I said. 'From my account to yours. And that's good. You know why? Because it'll act as an insurance policy. If I go missing, and the police investigate, they'll find the bank transfer and dig deeper.'

His lips curled in contempt. 'You stupid cow. Don't you think I've thought of that?'

I stared at him, unable to spot any flaw in what I'd outlined.

'You reckon Darcy was the only junkie who'd do anything I asked to get her next fix? I've already made arrangements with a coke-head I know. It'll be her bank account I'll use. She and I go way back but the police will never connect us. I'll collect the money in cash from her tomorrow.'

'Good luck with that. Your tame druggie will do a runner with it.'

A snort of derision. 'The bitch knows I'd slice her into a thousand pieces if she ever double-crossed me.'

God, had I underestimated him. My main concern was Ellie and how best to ensure we both survived. I promised myself I'd rescue her somehow. After all, I was a strong, well-built woman, with a car waiting outside. I'd need to act fast, and on instinct, then outrun him and make it to my vehicle. First, though, I needed to know her location.

'I'll transfer the money,' I said. 'On one condition. That you let me speak with my sister. Proof of life and all that.'

He grinned. 'I thought you might make such a request.'

I waited. He didn't move, simply stared at me.

'Let me speak with her,' I repeated.

'Persistent bitch, aren't you? I'm a decent guy, though. Sure, I'll allow you to talk to Ellie.'

Surprise, mingled with relief, filled me.

He pulled his mobile from one of his jacket pockets. 'Everything's set up for you two to chat. I've taped her phone to her hand. She can move her fingers enough to answer calls and put them on speakerphone. With any luck, she'll be conscious by now.' He tapped a few times on his mobile before laying it on the side table. Within two rings, Ellie's voice, high and panicked, sounded into the room.

'Lyddie?' My heart twisted with love and relief. 'Lyddie, is that you?'

'I'm here, Els. What the hell happened?'

'He broke into the cottage not long after I arrived. He didn't expect me to be here, of course. Called it an unexpected bonus.' A strangled sob. 'I told him you were on your way, and that you'd phone the police, but he just laughed. Told me he intended to lure you to the cottage anyway. Said he liked how isolated the place is.'

I shuddered at the implication. 'He'd better not have hurt you.'

Another sob. 'He knocked me unconscious and tied me up. Blindfolded me too, so I can't see anything. There are rats here though. One of them ran over my foot.' From my peripheral vision, I saw Scott grin.

'He wants the money. Why didn't you tell him where it is?'

'Because I don't have it anymore.'

'You see my problem, don't you, Lyddie?' Scott said.

'What do you mean, Els?'

'The bag of notes you stole from him. I couldn't help thinking the money was tainted. So I gave it away. Like you told me to.'

I wasn't sure I'd heard correctly. 'You did what?'

'Yeah, that was my reaction too,' Scott interjected. 'The stupid bitch took a bus into town, found a few down-and-outs, and handed them bundles of cash. *My* cash. Wasted on a load of bums who'll blow it on drugs.' Fury burned in his eyes.

Typical Ellie. Impulsive, her judgement often poor following her head trauma, she'd taken my suggestion of donating it to charity literally. The result? Both of us had become pawns in Scott's game and he'd almost forced us to checkmate. Unless I found a way to overcome him.

'I'm so frightened. Please help me, Lyddie—'

Scott leaned over, cutting Ellie off mid-sentence. Then he rummaged in my bag, bringing out my mobile. He thrust it into my hand. I stared at him, my sister's words playing in my head. She'd mentioned rats, hadn't she? Scott had already said he was holding her somewhere close. That brought to mind the woodshed that belonged to the cottage. One that had a door that bolted from the outside. The obvious place to hold her captive.

Scott reached into his inside jacket pocket. And brought out a knife. He held it to my throat.

'Time to repay what you stole from me. I have the upper hand here, remember.'

I forced a bravado I didn't feel. 'You'll never get your money. Not unless you let Ellie and me go.'

He laughed. The blade scraped over my skin, then pressed against my jugular.

'You reckon?' Scott said. 'Think again.' His fingers pushed down harder on the blade, almost enough to pierce my skin.

'Oh, the damage this knife could inflict. You'd do anything I asked, believe me.'

Scott stepped away, then thrust the knife back into his jacket. 'What are you waiting for? Log into your bank account. I'll give you the details of where to transfer the money.'

'What happens afterwards?' I said, fighting to keep the fear from my voice. 'That's when you kill both of us, right?'

Scott grinned. 'Transfer the money, bitch,' he said. 'All twenty grand of it.'

'And if I don't?'

'Either you give me back what you stole now, or later. After I've had some fun.' He patted his jacket pocket, the one containing his knife.

'I'm not scared of you, you bastard.' I was playing for time. Could my mobile be a weapon? What if I smashed it into his teeth while I kicked his legs from under him?

'Maybe *you're* not. But Ellie's terrified of me.'

I couldn't breathe. He'd found my Achilles heel.

'She's close to here, remember. I'll bring her to the cottage. You can watch while I go to work on her.'

Terror froze my heart. 'Don't hurt her. Please. I'll do whatever you want.'

To my frustration, Scott moved behind me to monitor what I did with my phone. So much for my idea of ramming it into that goddamn smirk. My fingers shook as I tapped the screen on my mobile. Three bungled attempts later I managed to access my bank's website. He leaned closer, his eyes taking in my balances. Between my current and savings accounts, I had over forty thousand pounds.

Scott let out a low whistle. 'Looks like I've hit the jackpot. The price of seeing your sister alive just doubled.' He grinned. 'Transfer the lot. Every penny.'

No way could I argue. Panic caused me to fumble as I sent the entire balance of my savings over to my current account. Then I waited for his instructions.

'You ready?' he asked. 'And remember, bitch, I'm watching your every move.'

He read out a sort code, account number and name from his mobile. I entered them, then set up a new recipient. When that was done, I typed in the amount to transfer, and tapped the 'submit' button.

Up came a warning message. I couldn't move more than thirty thousand pounds in any twenty-four-hour period unless I used my bank's fee-based service. That would take one working day to complete.

'Do it, bitch,' Scott said. 'You won't be alive in twenty-four hours, anyway.'

What choice did I have? Within minutes, I'd set up the transfer. I'd now lost fifty thousand pounds to this bastard. Not that the money mattered, not with Ellie tied up and helpless. With him behind me, the path to the doorway was clear. I thought fast. Smash the marble vase against his head. Run like hell, get to the woodshed ...

'Thanks for that,' Scott said. 'It's been fun, hasn't it? The game stops here though.'

He grabbed my phone, tossing it back into my bag, before walking back in front of me again. His fingers travelled towards the pocket containing the knife, a grin on his face. Only seconds separated me from being stabbed to death, and I acted from pure instinct. My hands seized my handbag and swung it towards his head. The bag didn't contain much weight, but I was counting on surprising him while my right foot kicked towards his ankle. A futile effort. Scott deflected the bag's trajectory and side-stepped my foot, his other arm shooting out to grasp my wrist.

'You'll pay for that, bitch.' Every word a snarl. Terror pounded through me. Scott had his money, and no reason to keep Ellie and me alive.

A sound reached my ears from outside. Scott's too, from the way his body went rigid. The noise of gravel crunching underfoot, approaching the cottage.

'Help!' I screamed. 'Whoever you are, please help me!'

The front door opened. Footsteps echoed in the hallway.

Ellie walked into the room.

CHAPTER 22

I stared at my sister. Her expression was calm, as though she hadn't a care in the world. The woman who stood before me wasn't someone who'd been knocked unconscious and held captive in a woodshed. Her wrists bore no signs of having been tied, no angry welts marring her pale skin. She smiled at me.

'Hello, Lyddie,' she said. She walked over to Scott, planting a kiss on his mouth. 'Hi, darling.'

A billion neurons short-circuited in my brain. I could barely compute what was happening.

'What are you playing at?' Scott grabbed Ellie's arm. 'This isn't what we agreed. You were supposed to wait in the car.'

Ellie laughed. 'Does it matter? We'll soon be long gone. Besides, why should you have all the fun? Don't I get to enjoy any?'

'I don't understand.' A quiver sounded in my voice, and I hated myself for it. Deep inside, I knew the truth. I'd realised it the instant Ellie addressed Scott as 'darling'. All I lacked were the details.

It seemed deception wore many faces. One of them my sister's.

'Talk to me, Ellie,' I pleaded. 'What has he done, or said, to you?'

A harsh laugh escaped her. 'All the right things, believe me.'

'I don't understand,' I repeated. 'I thought you loved me. Why are you doing this?'

Her mouth twisted with contempt. 'You have to ask that? Really?'

No love was visible in my sister's expression. Quite the opposite. Pain, followed by bewilderment, swept through me. Why did she hate me so much?

'Fuck it. If you don't know, I can't be bothered to tell you,' Ellie said.

Stupefied, I stared at her. Scott stood to one side, watching us, that damn grin back on his face.

'You reckon you're so smart, don't you?' my sister continued. 'You were stupid enough to hand me that bag of cash, though.'

She'd not given the money to the homeless, of that I was sure. Odds were the whole twenty thousand was back with Scott. 'You said he conned you out of your savings. Was that another lie?'

She nodded. 'Steven loves me. We're going to be married. The only one he's tricked is you.'

Oh, he'd conned Ellie, all right. Once the prick found out about her inheritance, that she had a sibling with money, he'd have planned a double scam. All the while promising marriage to my vulnerable sister.

When I didn't reply, she carried on, 'I loaned him money to help him through a lean patch, like any supportive girlfriend would. Steven means the world to me.'

'If you're so happy with him, why the suicide attempt?'

She snorted. 'That wasn't real. I swallowed a few pills, then phoned Mum, knowing she'd call an ambulance straightaway.'

She keeps asking for you. Our mother's words after I arrived at Southmead. 'So I'd come back to Bristol. You played me.'

'Yep.' God, how manipulative she'd been.

'I don't understand. Why tell me he stole your money?'

'That was Steven's idea. So I could get revenge on you.'

'Revenge? For what?'

She ignored me. 'The plan was to convince you I'd been conned out of my savings. So you'd give me the cash you thought he'd taken from me. Instead you banged on about sorting my finances and setting up spreadsheets.' Acid filled her tone. 'The one time I needed you to play the big-sister role, you failed me.'

Aghast, I stared at her.

'Then Steven told me he'd spotted your picture on Premier Love Matches. He recognised you after seeing a photo of you at my flat. That's when he suggested he should pretend to date you, said he'd get money from you that way.'

How could she be so gullible? 'And you didn't wonder why he was browsing a dating website? If he wants to marry you?'

Scott stepped forward. 'I was deleting my profile,' he said. 'I joined several sites when I decided to search for my soulmate. But then I met Ellie, and we fell in love.' He wrapped an arm around her shoulders. My sister gazed at him, adoration in her eyes.

'You see?' Ellie said. 'He loves me. We're planning on living in America after we're married.'

'That's impossible. There are strict regulations governing immigration into the USA. And what about Mum? Don't you care about her?'

Ellie didn't reply, but I saw shame creep across her features. Perhaps I was getting through to her after all.

'What about when you confronted him at my place? Was that just an act?'

'All part of the plan. Along with that crap about my business being in financial trouble. So you'd believe Steven and not me.' Her lips turned contemptuous. 'You must admit I can play a role pretty well. I should have been an actor.'

'And it didn't bother you? That he dated me at the same time as you?'

'Ellie knows I love her,' Scott said. 'Isn't that right, darling?' Over the top of her head, he winked at me.

'Steven would never cheat on me,' Ellie said. 'I trust him with my life.'

'You may well end up giving him your life.' Bitterness seeped into my tone. 'Others have. Darcy Logan, for one.'

My sister gave a mock laugh. 'That drug-addled bitch. She died of a heroin overdose, pure and simple. Scott's not a murderer.'

'He killed Sophie Hannigan too. By proxy that time.'

Ellie stared at me. 'Who's she?'

'Another of his victims.' I warmed to my theme. 'He's a con artist, don't you see? The bastard's worked his wiles on a string of women and if any of them threaten to contact the police they end up dead. He's already admitted he paid Darcy to stab Sophie. All because she intended to blow the whistle on him.'

Ellie stepped out of Scott's embrace, fury sparking from her eyes. 'You're a liar. Steven could never kill anyone.'

Oh, how little she knew him. He'd played her like the master of his game he was. To protest further would be pointless - Scott had snared Ellie so tightly in his trap she'd not listen to a single word I uttered.

'I still don't know why you hate me so much,' I said.

'Go to the car, darling,' Scott said. 'Wait for me there. Lyddie and I will finish our little chat, then she can drive back to Bristol all safe and sound, like I promised you. And we can start our new life in America.'

Like the puppet she was, she moved towards the door. I had to act, and fast, because Scott was planning to kill me, then her. Of that I was certain.

'Ellie. Don't leave me. Please.' She ignored me, heading into the hallway. A second later I heard her feet crunch over the gravel again. I was alone with Scott.

Perhaps that was a good thing. Better one opponent than two. Time for a little role-play of my own.

I shrank against the back of the chair, injecting fear into my tone. 'Please don't hurt me. I won't tell anyone, I swear.'

He laughed. 'Yeah, right. Now why don't I believe you?' He stood there for a couple of minutes, our eyes locked in a battle to establish who'd look away first. All the while his hand stroked the pocket containing his knife.

'Such a shame we can't spend longer together,' he said at last. 'But Ellie has a date with my sharp-edged friend here.' Said with a drumbeat of fingers against the blade. 'It's time to end our little game.'

His hand dipped into his pocket, and I knew the moment had come. With lightning speed I leapt forward, my foot kicking hard against his ankle. Then I shoved him aside with every ounce of force I could muster. He crashed against the marble-topped mantelpiece, groaning in pain as I ran towards the doorway. I hurtled into the hallway and wrenched open the front door, banging it shut behind me once my feet touched the gravel outside. With only a few seconds' advantage, I'd need to be quick. I'd left behind my handbag, containing my keys and my phone, meaning my only option was to flee on foot.

By then it was dark, the night illuminated only by a sliver of moonlight, clouds obscuring most of the sky. A faint drizzle filled the air. In my peripheral vision, I spotted the woodshed. I darted inside, drawing the door shut, the odour of old timber strong in my nostrils. In the half-light I glanced around. Against one wall stood an axe, dull from disuse. My hands grasped its handle, my heart hammering in my chest. I waited.

Seconds later the door to the cottage slammed back on its hinges, then banged shut again. Frantic footsteps sounded on the gravel path. Three possibilities existed. One: he'd run down the lane in the direction of the cliff top to find me, once he realised I'd not taken my car. In which case I'd sprint back to the cottage, bolt the door behind me, grab my mobile and call the police. Two: he'd assume I'd headed towards the village and follow the path that led there. Ditto as to my reaction. Or three: he'd spot the woodshed and guess I was hiding inside. My money was on him checking that option first. He must have heard the direction in which my footsteps had taken me, thanks to the gravel outside the cottage. If I was right, he'd receive one hell of a greeting.

My fingers tightened around the axe handle.

Footsteps. Coming my way. I dragged in a lungful of air, praying for strength as they moved closer.

'Lyddie, Lyddie, Lyddie,' Scott chanted, his tone high and mocking. 'The longer it takes to find you, the more you and Ellie will suffer. You may as well come out now.' The proximity of his voice told me he was almost at the entrance to the woodshed.

The door opened. Scott Champion stood before me.

I'd not banked on the axe being so heavy. No way could I swing it high enough to deliver sufficient damage to fell him. I managed to hoist it off the ground by six inches, aiming it at him as he lunged towards me. The blade of the axe struck his left ankle. Scott collapsed to the floor, a chant of 'fuck, fuck, fuck' issuing from his mouth. His eyes were squeezed shut with pain. A wound gaped, red and angry, at the bottom of his leg, blood running from it. The axe had been too blunt, my swing too feeble, to inflict more than a flesh injury. While I stared, Scott started to haul himself upright. The axe dropped from my hand with a clatter. Before he could regain a standing position, I kicked out, my foot scoring a hard blow right on the gash, causing him to collapse in agony again. Then I ran.

My feet pounded over the gravel as I raced towards the cottage, my only thought being to alert the police. To my horror I remembered the door needed a key to open it from outside. And mine was inside, in my handbag. I couldn't dial 999 unless I broke in somehow. That might take time. With Scott hell-bent on revenge, I didn't have the luxury of that option. The track to the village, my other hope for summoning help, started from behind the woodshed, with my would-be killer between it and me. All I could do was run in the other direction. So I did.

The sounds of cursing faded into the distance behind me. Whether Scott could pursue me depended on how badly I'd hurt him. His injured ankle would hinder him but I didn't think it would stop him altogether. Fury might fuel his adrenaline, making him even more determined. The notion made my feet pound faster towards the dirt path leading from the cottage to the cliff. The earth had become muddy thanks to the drizzle, which was steadily worsening. Several times my legs almost slipped from under me, my gasps of panic loud against the silence of the night.

Behind me, I heard the rhythm of feet, the sound off-kilter, that of a man unable to move as fast as he'd like. A grunt of pain accompanied each laboured step. Thank God; the sound told me I'd outstrip him in any race. Apart from one problem. The track ended in the cliff-top walk I'd taken so many times with Ellie, from which the only exit was the stone steps that led to the beach. Impossible for me to consider swimming to the next bay and wading ashore. The tides were treacherous and the shoreline rocky. I doubted I'd make it halfway before drowning. I was trapped between Scott and the sea, with no way out.

CHAPTER 23

Besides the hazardous coastline, I faced another problem. Hidden on the lane ahead must be Scott's Toyota. He couldn't have left his car on the path that led to the village, or I'd have spotted it when I arrived. Ellie must be inside, and I didn't rate too highly my chances of appealing to her better nature. I'd have to skirt around the vehicle instead and pray she didn't spot me. The track was narrow, little more than the width of a car, and overgrown in places, difficult to follow in the darkness. Thick brambles on either side offered no opportunity for concealment. Behind me, I heard the grunts that signalled Scott was still in pursuit. My chest grew tight with panic, my breath coming in laboured gasps. The drizzle had turned into rain, my clothes sodden against my skin as I ran.

A dark shape came into view, tucked to one side under the hedgerow: Scott's car, a gleam of moonlight silhouetting Ellie in the passenger seat. I ducked to my right, keeping near to the ground on the driver's side, my breath held hostage in my chest. Every movement set off rustling noises through the brambles I hoped Ellie would ascribe to rats. Rodents terrified her; I doubted she'd leave the car to investigate the sounds. As I inched past, I heard a gasp of fear and knew I'd guessed correctly.

Once safely out of view, masked by the dark, I continued down the track. A hundred metres head of me, just visible around the curve in the lane, was the stone stile, its bulk dark and solid, forming a bridge between the bushes on either side. An idea sparked in my brain. I might not be able to escape either of them, but I could hide.

The stile comprised two slabs of stone set upright on their narrow edges, a third slab placed between them at right angles, so walkers had to step on and then over it to pass through. Numerous feet had worn the earth surrounding the stile into a dip and hedgerows fringed either side of it. My only chance was to slip through the stile and conceal myself behind one of the vertical slabs, tucking my body as far as possible into the vegetation. Scott wouldn't spot me en-route to the cliff, but once there he'd realise I must have hidden along the way. Even in the poor light, he'd see I hadn't taken the steps that led to the shore. Then he'd come looking for me, meaning I couldn't stay behind the slab. Instead, I'd have to run back and take the track leading to the village.

I heard a car door opening, then slamming. The sound of voices. Then footsteps, those of two people, headed my way.

I moved forward around the bend in the lane until I was level with the stile but out of sight from Ellie and Scott. They weren't far away, meaning I needed to act fast. I placed a hand on one of the upright slabs, hauling my legs onto the cross section, then stepping through and tucking myself into the thickest part of the hedge. I crouched behind the protection the slab offered, almost but not quite concealed from view. If either of them happened to glance my way, I'd be screwed. My only chance lay in the fact Scott would most likely be looking ahead, not to one side.

His grunts of pain were moving ever closer, along with the two pairs of footsteps. My calves ached from squatting and my knees begged for relief. The hedge scratched my cheeks, drops of rain penetrating its bulk to slide down my face. My body shivered in the chill wind as I listened to the grunts and the uneven footsteps. Scott and my sister were almost upon me, and my lungs screamed their need to release the breath I was holding. I didn't dare risk it, though, and in that moment they reached the stile. I heard his hand strike the top of the slab near where I was hiding, his feet landing on the cross section, a fresh groan of pain sounding out once his weight pressed on his injured foot. Next came Ellie's softer step. Then the pair of them made it through, heading towards the cliff top.

Gratitude filled every cell in my body as I exhaled my relief. The thick clouds that had obscured the moon before had, for the most part, passed, leaving it only half covered. From my vantage point I saw Scott and Ellie silhouetted against the sky. He had his hands on his hips as he scanned his surroundings. Ellie stood next to him, one arm around his waist. The steps to the beach were signposted to their right, and as I had predicted, he shuffled towards them to check whether I'd escaped that way. My sister remained where she was, her back turned to me. I needed to make my move while they were distracted, my intention still being to summon help from the village.

I crept forward, keeping myself low until I'd almost cleared the hedgerow, its branches snagging my clothes and impeding my exit. My fingers tugged at the twigs holding me captive, my impatience mounting while I untangled myself to the point where I could almost, but not quite, stand upright. Then Scott turned, and I froze.

He was staring straight at me. Even at a distance of some twenty metres and in the dim light, I could see his feral grin had returned.

'Gotcha,' he shouted, triumph in his voice. Then he hobbled towards me, Ellie following, his speed faster than I'd have expected given his injury. As I unhitched myself from the last bramble, he reached me. His hands grasped my shoulders and spun me around as an iron fist slammed into my cheekbone. My face exploded with pain, fireworks flaring through my face. The blow knocked me off balance and sent me crashing against the thick stone of the stile.

'Steven, don't!' Ellie threw herself on him, trying to pull him away. Hope flickered within me. Maybe she didn't loathe me as much as I feared. And the punch might prove a good thing if it convinced her of his tendency towards violence. She clearly had no idea he intended to kill us.

Scott dragged me to my feet, his fist ready for another blow. Instead he erupted in a roar of agony when my foot slammed into his wounded ankle. His body crumpled against the stile, blocking my way. I ran, my only option being the steps leading to the beach. His furious curses sounded in my ears as I sprinted towards them. The night had grown dark again, thick clouds hiding the moon once more. As I approached the cliff edge, he was back on his feet and in pursuit of me. I hesitated as I neared the top of the steps, by then only a few metres away. They were steep, and must be slick with rain. Below me I could hear the sea bursting over the rocks, reinforcing my conviction I'd never survive a swim to the next bay. I turned around, hoping to backtrack and outrun both of them, but my feet slipped on the muddy ground. My body crashed with agonising force against a rock embedded in the earth. I hauled myself upright, gasping at the pain in my thigh while my eyes searched the blackness. Scott's injured leg was hampering him, and Ellie got to me before he did.

We stood facing each other, a myriad of emotions in my sister's face.

'He hit you,' she said. 'I never thought he'd hurt you. I - we - just wanted the money, nothing else.' By the time she'd finished speaking, Scott had reached us. He skirted around me to stand at the top of the steps, a few metres behind me. His intention was obvious: to block my escape that way. Ellie stood between me and the stile, but I still reckoned I could outrun her. I just had to pick my moment, when I was less winded.

'Get the fuck away from her, Ellie,' Scott growled.

'You punched Lyddie.' Anger and confusion reigned in my sister's voice. 'Why did you hurt her?'

'He's a monster, that's why,' I said. 'You do realise he slept with me?'

Shock registered in Ellie's face. 'You're lying.'

'Don't listen to her, darling,' Scott said. 'You're the one I love.'

She ignored him, her eyes fixed on mine. 'He wouldn't cheat on me. We're going to get married.'

'And we will, sweetheart. We're starting a new life together, remember?'

She didn't answer him, doubt written across her face.

'I'm not lying,' I said. 'But Scott is. He played both of us for fools.'

'He'd never sleep with you.' The words burst from her in an angry torrent. 'You're hardly his type. Steven prefers petite women, not overweight ones.'

Her barb hit home although I suspected she'd not meant to be cruel. Ellie was a cornered rat, desperate to bolster her image of Scott as Mr Wonderful.

The drizzle came down harder, wetting my face and concealing the tear trickling past my cheek. Everything was so fucked-up, and it was my turn to hurt her.

I drew in a breath. 'He has a birthmark. About a centimetre wide, near his left groin.' *Let's see how Mr Wonderful bounces back from* that, I thought.

The world stilled around us. Ellie continued to stare at me, her eyes wide. Then her gaze switched to Scott, her face crumpling in anguish. She dropped to the mud, her knees drawn to her chest. A series of moans issued from her lips. I'd been right in guessing she'd lied about not losing her virginity to him. My instinct was to comfort her, but I resisted, reluctant to turn my back on Scott for even a second. I glanced at the stile, weighing my chances. They seemed pretty good. I'd easily outrun both of them; Ellie was incapable of action and Scott wouldn't get far with his injured ankle.

He must have seen my eyes flit towards the path. 'Think again, Lyddie. You reckon it's a good idea to leave me with Ellie?' His hand patted the pocket containing his knife. I froze.

I couldn't risk it. I didn't doubt he'd kill her. My sister remained huddled on the ground between us, wrapped in her misery.

Scott's grin widened. 'Give me one reason I shouldn't slice the bitch anyway. Right here and now.'

Pure instinct drove me. I reached down to grab the rock onto which I'd fallen.

The perfect size to fit into my palm.

Light enough to throw.

Heavy enough to hurt.

'You fucking bastard!' I hurled the rock at Scott, aiming for his chest, but missed. The stone struck his head, wrenching a cry of pain and shock from his lips. The impact knocked him off balance, and he lurched to one side, his weight landing on his injured leg. A howl of agony split the darkness. Ellie's head jerked skywards.

Afterwards, when the police were interviewing me, the scene replayed itself in slow motion in my mind. Scott's body teetering backwards. His damaged ankle, unable to support his bulk. The ground that offered no traction as his feet skidded over the sodden soil, the edge of the stone steps inching ever closer. Scott, sliding on air in a desperate quest to regain his balance. His eyes held mine for a second before he plummeted over the edge. A tortured scream spiralled downwards, matched by the shriek that came from Ellie.

A series of thuds hit my ears: Scott's body as it slammed into the stone steps, one after another. Then a final thump, followed by silence.

For several minutes, I was incapable of movement. Frozen by shock, terrified of what I'd see if I looked down the cliff face, I stood motionless on the spot. Shivers coursed through me, but not from the chill of my wet clothes. Whimpers issued from my mouth, a stream of 'oh God, oh God, oh God' echoing into the night sky. Exhausted, I slumped onto the sodden grass, hugging myself into a foetal position, the rain soaking me even further. Out of the corner of my eye, I saw Ellie, also huddled into a ball. Moans that were barely human came from her.

At last I dragged myself upright. Despite my reluctance, I couldn't avoid the inevitable any longer. I needed to check if Scott was still alive, however unlikely the possibility.

I stumbled the few paces to the top of the stone steps, my eyes searching through the darkness. They didn't need to look far. Below me, on the shingle of the beach, lay his crumpled body, immobile, his limbs splayed at unnatural angles.

My journey downwards took forever, shock rendering my legs reluctant to work. At last I reached the bottom, Scott a metre in front of me. His face was turned my way, his eyes open and sightless. Blood streaked his right cheek from a gash on his temple. His arms lolled uselessly, his fingers grazing the pebbles. More blood oozed from the back of his head where it had hit the steps during his fall, mixing with the rain to form reddish swirls that disappeared into the shingle. I pressed my fingers against his throat, searching for a pulse, but found none. He was dead.

Once I'd made my way back up the steps, Ellie came into view, standing in the same spot where she'd been huddled over. She didn't speak as I approached; instead, she just stared at me. My face must have revealed the truth, because she let out a low moan, followed by a whole stream of them. I wrapped my arms around her and we clung to each other, the rain soaking us to the skin. She might hate me, but in that moment we merged into one person.

CHAPTER 24

My teeth began to chatter, my body shivering with cold. I took Ellie's hand. 'Let's get back inside, where it's warm.'

She didn't reply, just nodded. We stumbled along the track that led back to the cottage, stopping to collect her handbag and keys from Scott's car. Her suitcase, packed in readiness for America, was in the boot. Once through the door, I hustled her upstairs and into the bathroom, turning on the shower. Shudders ran through her, but she didn't move, her wet hair plastered to her skull, her arms wrapped around her body. She stayed there, immobile, while I pulled clean clothes from her suitcase.

'Get undressed,' I instructed. My tone warned her not to mess with me. 'Run the shower as hot as you can stand. Don't come out until you're warm.' Ellie complied without a word. Before I left the room, I removed every sharp object I could find. She wouldn't make a fourth suicide attempt on my watch.

I shut the door, then went into my bedroom. First I turned the radiator on high and pulled off my muddy clothes. Then I towelled heat into my frozen body before tugging on jeans and a thick jumper. A shower would have to wait. I had things to do.

Once dressed, I made my way downstairs. Apart from the sounds reaching me from the bathroom, the world around me was quiet, a blessed contrast to the terror of before. On the floor was my handbag, with my mobile inside. I grabbed it before walking over to stare out of the window. By then the rain had stopped, although the wind still rustled through the trees.

Footsteps padded across the landing above, towards Ellie's bedroom. I prayed she'd have the strength to deal with what was to come. I wasn't optimistic on that score.

Three things remained for me to sort. Number one was to phone Mum, assuring her Ellie was safe and well, that we were heading back to Bristol, and how I'd explain everything soon.

My second task was to call my bank. It provided round-the-clock telephone customer service, and I intended to avail myself of that particular feature.

'I want to reverse a pending transfer,' I told the woman who answered.

Number three was to inform the police. Oh, I could have sneaked back to the beach, removed any evidence from Scott's body, then driven Ellie back to Bristol in the hope his death would be ruled an accident. Which it had been, of course. But I'd had enough deceit shoved down my throat in recent weeks. I didn't intend to become a liar myself. Besides, I still needed to notify the police of everything I knew about Darcy and Sophie's deaths. A cover-up was not an option.

I drew in a deep breath. This was going to prove difficult.

And I was right. I finished by telling the officer on duty we were on our way back to Bristol, ending the call before he could order me to stay put. My top priority was to get Ellie home. Given how difficult the cottage was to find, we'd be gone before the police arrived anyway.

***

After that, my life imploded. Police interviews filled the next two days. I snatched sleep whenever I could, unable to switch off my brain at night. Confident Lyddie had vanished, replaced by a stranger I needed to keep under strict control.

Before the initial interview took place, the police noticed the bruise on my face, and I told them how Scott had punched me. The doctor who examined me also noted the damage done by the rock on which I'd fallen, his report supporting my testimony. That swung things my way, I suspected. Even so, the officers who questioned me at Bridewell were suspicious at first. No doubt they saw me - and Ellie - as scorned women, proving the 'hell hath no fury' theory.

'So you admit to breaking into this man's apartment and taking a considerable sum of money from his safe?' the senior detective remarked.

I answered with a decisive 'yes'. No more lies.

'Did your sister push her boyfriend to his death?' the same officer asked later.

Neither my gaze nor my voice faltered for even a second. 'No.'

'Then perhaps *you* did instead.'

I shook my head. 'It was an accident. I threw a rock at him, and he slipped in the mud.'

To my relief, the detective's tone grew less confrontational the longer the interview progressed. The following day he told me the evidence corroborated my story. Thank God the rain stopped when it did, because by the next morning the sunshine had dried the ground. Investigators discovered Ellie's footprints, the marks stopping several metres from the cliff edge. They also found the scrapes made by Scott's shoes as he fought to prevent himself from falling. His tracks were at a distance from hers that was longer than my sister's arms. It proved she couldn't have pushed him. My footprints were identified leading to the stone steps, but located far enough from Scott's to mean I wasn't a suspect on that score either.

They also found the scuffed earth where I fell and the hollow in the ground where the rock had been - further proof I'd not lied. Later, I was told my skin cells were on the knife they took from his pocket.

The same police officer informed me they'd uncovered evidence of Scott and Ellie's relationship: texts, emails, her hair and fingerprints in his car. I gave him the cut-up credit cards and the mobile phones I'd filched from Scott's safe, one of which I learned retained the vile messages he'd used to taunt me.

Everything Scott had admitted about his involvement in the murders of Darcy Logan and Sophie Hannigan went into my statement. No lies, no concealment. I hoped it would be enough to nail the bastard, even if only after his death.

A few days later, the police told me they didn't intend to prosecute me for assault, their view being that I'd acted in self-defence with the axe. When it came to me breaking into his flat and Scott's death, both matters had been referred up the chain of command as to how to proceed. In particular, whether my throwing the rock constituted manslaughter.

'He threatened to stab Ellie,' I insisted. 'I never meant to kill him.'

'It's possible you won't face charges. Not if you were defending your sister.'

That offered some relief. I could tell by the guy's manner he thought prosecution unlikely, but of course he couldn't offer any guarantees.

By the time we finished I only had one question left for the police.

'He had so many identities,' I said. 'Have you discovered his real name?'

'We're working on it,' was the reply.

Ah, well. He'd always be Scott Champion to me, Steven Simmons to Ellie. Besides, I had other priorities to sort.

***

Mum was one of those priorities. As soon as I could between talking to the police, I drove over to her house. I thought she might faint, so bad were the tremors that shook her when I told her the full story. When I revealed Ellie's deception, her face turned as pale as sleet. Although angry and upset over her daughter's behaviour, she refused to blame her.

'That bastard,' she said, her mouth set in a grim line. 'He took advantage of my girl's vulnerability, twisted it for his own purposes. How is Eleanor coping? More to the point, where is she?'

'She's in good hands.' I prepared myself to deliver less than wonderful news.

As I'd predicted, Mum didn't react well to the revelation that Ellie was back in Southmead's psychiatric unit. She'd been sent there by a doctor, a decision approved by the mental health worker in attendance when the police attempted to interview her. She'd lashed out at them, then turned inwards, refusing to talk. That didn't surprise me. Any authority figure scared her no end. She was being kept on the psychiatric wing for observation and her own safety.

When I left, Mum looked as though she'd aged ten years in two hours. My heart ached for her. I resolved that, whatever it took, we'd become closer.

***

Caroline, as ever, was my rock as far as Ellie was concerned.

'Have the police said anything more? Or her doctors?' The question came during one of my visits to her house.

I shook my head. 'She still won't talk to anyone.'

'Not even to you?'

'No.' Tears filled my eyes, along with memories of our previous encounter.

I'd not been optimistic that same morning when I entered Ellie's room at Southmead's psychiatric unit. Mum had met me at the door, distress implicit in the pallor of her skin, the dark smudges under her eyes. I doubted mine looked any better. I'd hardly slept the past few nights.

'She won't talk to me. Perhaps she will to you,' she said, an unconscious echo of her words when she'd broken the news of Ellie's third suicide attempt. I didn't share her optimism. My sister would probably give me the silent treatment instead.

I was proved right. When I walked in, she was curled up on her bed, her eyes glued to the floor. Then she rolled away, the curve of her back a definite snub.

'None of this was her fault,' I told Caroline. 'She's always been fragile, lacking in confidence. Ripe for a predator like Scott Champion.'

'Sounds like the fecker could charm gold from Fort Knox.'

'You're not wrong. I'm still worried the police will charge Ellie, though.'

'What for? Wasn't she one of his victims?'

'As well as his sidekick. She plotted with Scott to defraud me, remember.'

'Won't they let her off due to the brain damage? She can't be held responsible for her actions, right?'

'I hope not. But I can't be certain.'

'You're a saint, so you are. Head injury or not, if my sister shafted me like that, I'd be mad as hell. You're not angry with her?'

'Yes. No. Maybe.' My emotions had ridden a rollercoaster recently. 'I won't deny I'm hurt. She hates me and I have no idea why.'

'Oh, lovey, I'm sure she doesn't. That bastard turned her against you, so he did.'

'I'll visit her again tomorrow. With any luck she'll talk to me eventually.'

When the time came to leave, Caroline hugged me. 'I'll call you soon. Maybe we can go for that meal with Richie soon. Along with a stiff drink. Feck knows you need it.'

***

I went to see Ellie again the following afternoon. She was huddled under the duvet, her head the only part of her visible. When she saw me her lips curled in contempt and she turned her back on me once more.

To hell with that. I marched to the other side of the room, causing her to burrow further under the bedcovers. I sat in a nearby chair, addressing the shape in the bed.

'I don't understand. Why do you hate me so much?'

No response. I tried again. 'I only ever wanted to help you. To love you.'

This time she rewarded me with a restless shifting of her body. Encouragement of sorts. 'I'm hurting here, Ellie.'

Ellie threw off the duvet, hauling herself upright against her pillows. The anger in her eyes shocked me.

'I, I, I,' she said. 'Can you even hear yourself anymore? It's all about *you*. It always has been.'

Too stunned to reply, I stared at her.

'The wonderful Lyddie Hunter. You think you're so clever, don't you? With your business degree, your accountancy qualification, your stock market investments. Turns out you weren't that smart after all. You fell for the first man who showed you any interest since Richie. Couldn't wait to give Steven your money, could you?'

Pot, kettle, black, I thought.

'Always so keen to show your superiority.' Her voice rose high, in a parody of mine. '"Oh, Ellie, let me explain algebra once more. Here, I'll check your French homework for you." Stupid Ellie, who can't get anything right by herself. Who failed her exams while you collected top A-level grades. Always Daddy's little brain-box, weren't you?'

I gaped at her. 'Dad never said you were stupid. Mum didn't either.'

'But you all thought it, didn't you? You in particular. My perfect sister, who got off on patronising me, treating me like I was dim. Maybe I am. After all, Dad never invited *me* to drink whisky and discuss politics with him, did he?'

'You hate scotch. And talk about the government bores you.'

She carried on as if I'd not spoken. 'Okay, so I can't pass exams the way you can. I might not have as many IQ points. You were dumb enough to hand me twenty thousand pounds in cash, though.' She was on a roll, it seemed. 'Just so we're clear, I don't want your interference. I never did.'

From somewhere I summoned my voice. 'That's why you hate me? Because I helped you with your homework?'

'No,' Ellie said. 'Because of Alyson.'

Had I heard correctly? 'You're not making sense,' I whispered.

'If it weren't for you, she wouldn't have died. You're the reason I crashed my car.'

I floundered for words, so great was my shock. 'I had nothing to do with that.'

'You had everything to do with it. You think I didn't overhear what Dad said to you that night? How proud he was, just because you aced some stupid accountancy exams? Because you got to stick a bunch of letters after your name? Fuck you, Lyddie. I was eighteen, and about all I'd passed was my driving test. Hardly stacked up, did it?'

'But why blame me for the accident?'

'You want to know why? Because I got angry, madder than I'd ever been. So I texted Alyson, told her I needed to let off steam, picked her up from her place. All the time I was driving I ranted about what a cow you were, until I couldn't think straight. Alyson yelled something about how I should be on the left, not the right. Then the other car was coming at us, and, oh God ...' Her voice trailed away and in my head the truth clicked into place.

'It was you on the wrong side of the road,' I said. 'Not the other driver. That's why you swerved into the tree.'

She didn't deny it. 'But the whole thing was your fault, don't you see? You and those stupid exams. If you passing them with flying colours hadn't made Dad proud of his oh-so-clever daughter, I wouldn't have got mad, and Alyson would be alive. You killed her.'

No, I thought. *That's your injured temporal lobe talking. Not the voice of logic or reason.*

'Everything got worse after the accident. Thick, helpless Ellie was now brain damaged. The car crash gave you an excuse to meddle even further. That's when I started to resent you big-time.'

'I only ever wanted to help you,' I repeated, too stunned to take in what Ellie was saying. Every word pierced me with pain.

'I never asked for your fucking help. I just needed Dad to be proud of me, like he was with you. Fat chance of that, huh?'

I couldn't bear to hear any more. Tears blinded my eyes. I ran from the room.

CHAPTER 25

Back home in Kingswood, I paced my bedroom floor, Ellie still haunting my head. No matter how much I dissected my sister's words, I couldn't deal with them. Or even understand their rationale. Anger filled my every step as I marched to and fro. I was mad as hell, and who could blame me? I'd no idea Ellie resented me so fiercely, and for such screwed-up reasons.

Unfair, unreasonable and downright fucking out of order.

Yeah, I was angry all right. She'd tried to swindle me, hadn't she? Worse, though, was her utter selfishness. Our mother deserved better than to rush to save her daughter from suicide, only for the whole thing to be staged. Not to mention how Ellie had used Alyson's death to manipulate me into driving to Devon. Shameless, all of it. I didn't recognise the woman inhabiting my sister's body.

Back and forth I paced, unable to find out an outlet for my fury. Some things even a single malt couldn't help.

The notion of whisky brought Dad into my head. Thank God he wasn't alive to witness his youngest daughter's deceit. He'd have been ashamed beyond words.

I stopped mid-stride.

I'd once told Ellie Dad adored her, how she could never shame him. His words sounded in my head. *Promise me you'll look out for her. She'll need you more than ever.*

My attitude softened a little. Had he lived, our father would have done his best to understand Ellie's ugly behaviour. A good man, was Dad, and shrewd. He'd have grasped the power Steven Simmons had wielded over her, and why he'd gained it so readily.

Only one explanation fitted: her head trauma. Unable to deal with Alyson's death, Ellie had twisted the facts; her injured brain decided I was the culprit, not her. Cognitive dissonance at work. The sister I'd known before the accident would never have been so vicious.

Maybe I was deluding myself. Ellie had said she'd resented me for helping with her homework. Chances were the seeds of her dislike had been sown then, but would have lain dormant if not for the car crash. Or if she'd never met Steven Simmons.

Or if I'd not been so pushy.

However hard I might find it, I needed to keep my promise to Dad. To be the kind of daughter that would make him proud.

Time for a glass of Lagavulin. I headed downstairs, pouring myself a finger of amber smokiness. Its fiery taste brought my father to mind again. How he would have wanted me to forgive, not condemn, Ellie. Glass in hand, I sat on the sofa and examined the facts from a different angle. How could I blame my sister after all the discussions I'd had with her neurologist? Or for loving a con artist when I'd also succumbed to his wiles? My judgment had been as flawed as Ellie's. If I, with all my supposed intelligence, had fallen prey to the slick bastard, she wouldn't have stood a chance.

My perspective shifted closer towards understanding. Only one question remained. Did I still love her?

The answer was yes. With that realisation, my anger faded.

I couldn't stay mad at her. She'd lost the man she loved, along with her hopes - marriage, America, a new life. My sister must be devastated, struggling to cope, all without a fully functioning temporal lobe.

'I only wanted to help you,' I whispered, for the third time that day.

But were my intentions really so altruistic? I searched my heart for an answer, and came up with no. Deception, as I'd already learned, wore many faces. To my chagrin, I realised one of them was mine. Take the hours I spent with Ellie helping her with her homework.

I'd been so keen to play the caring older sister I'd never considered how patronised she must have felt. Instead I'd congratulated myself on how supportive I'd been. Time to admit that part of me enjoyed controlling Ellie. Like mother, like daughter, it seemed.

Deception had played a part in my relationships with men too. Hadn't I convinced myself Gary McIlroy was Mr Right? Persuaded myself Richie couldn't be faithful? Blinded myself to Scott's snake-like nature? Perhaps self-deception was the worst kind. Shame filled my soul.

Over the next few hours, I tossed everything around in my head, my former anger trumped by my determination to mend my ways. If Ellie and I were to forge a healthier relationship, I had to change, and fast. My sister needed me. Not the domineering, *I-know-best!* version, but a different, softer Lyddie. One who listened, who didn't attempt to control. I needed to take a step back in order to move forward. I swore to myself that in future I'd allow her to live life without my interference. If she required help, I'd give it, but not before she asked.

'I'll make you proud of me, Dad,' I said aloud.

***

Outside Ellie's door the next morning, I hesitated. She'd been so angry, and I was still hurting; might I be better off leaving her alone? Then I remembered my earlier resolution about how I had to change. Besides, wasn't I practising self-deceit again? If I was honest, I was dreading seeing my sister. Hence my procrastination.

Here's to the new improved Lyddie, I reminded myself. I opened the door.

Ellie was lying in bed, her back to me, a silent mound under her duvet. She didn't acknowledge my presence in any way while I pulled up a chair.

I gathered my courage.

'I know you think I'm a control freak,' I said. 'And you're right. I've been thoughtless, and insensitive, and I'm sorry.'

No response. I ploughed on. 'I love you. You have to believe me.'

Still no reply, but a slight shift of her position gave me hope.

'Dad adored you too. So does Mum. We all do.'

Another almost perceptible movement under the duvet.

'All I wanted was to take care of you, but instead I smothered you. I'll change, I promise.'

The shape in the bed moved again. Ellie rolled over, her head poking above the duvet, her eyes on my face.

'Will you give me another chance?' *Please, please*, I begged her in my head. 'A fresh start. That's all I ask.'

Hurt filled my heart when she turned away.

'I'll come back tomorrow,' I said.

When she failed to respond, I left the room. I hoped my words had sunk in, even if only a little.

***

'Can you pack some more clothes for Eleanor? And extra toiletries?' Mum asked when I phoned her that evening.

'Sure. I'll sort it in the morning.' I didn't mention Ellie's anger, her accusations. Our mother would get upset; besides which, telling her was pointless.

The next day I drove to my sister's flat in St George, intending to pack the extra stuff she needed. Inside her bedroom, I inhaled her essence, the hint of perfume and talcum powder that lingered in the air. On top of her wardrobe was a suitcase, and I pulled it down, placing it on the bed. I stuffed the case with jeans, tops, shoes, throwing Ellie's cosmetic bag on top. Underwear came next. I yanked open the top drawer in her dressing-table. Bras, knickers and socks filled the space, and I grabbed a handful. As I did, a glint of gold met my eye.

I reached in a hand, pulled out the object. 'Oh, Ellie,' I whispered.

In my fingers I held the bracelet Dad had given me to celebrate my accountancy qualification. The same night Ellie crashed her car, gripped by her conviction our father preferred me. My fingers traced over the engraved flowers, then the inscription inside. *To my daughter, with all my love, from Dad.*

I hadn't lost the bracelet in a moment of carelessness. Ellie must have stolen it once she left hospital after the accident. She'd hidden my father's gift where she thought no-one would find it. Then forgotten it in her haste to leave for America. Vulnerable, unstable, she couldn't allow herself to believe she'd always had his love. The bracelet became a substitute, with Ellie no doubt persuading herself the words were meant for her. With it nestled in my hand, I recalled the promise I'd made.

'I'll look out for her, Dad,' I told my father. 'I've screwed up, I'm well aware of that. But I'll make it right again.'

The bracelet went into my handbag, then I closed the suitcase. My watch indicated I had another two hours left before visiting hours at Southmead finished for the morning. If the traffic stayed light, I'd be there in half an hour.

***

Ellie was dressed this time, lying on her duvet. She didn't acknowledge me after I entered, but her expression seemed less hostile. I sat in the chair beside her bed, and placed the suitcase on the floor.

'I spoke to Mum on the phone last night,' I said. 'She'll visit you this afternoon. She said to tell you she loves you.'

Her fingers twisted around themselves, but she didn't reply.

Reluctant to reiterate my words from the day before, unwilling to mention Scott, I decided on a different tack.

'You act like you despise me. I don't think you really do, though. At least I hope not. Am I right?'

A flush rose into her cheeks. I hoped it might be from embarrassment, not anger.

'Be honest, Els. You may have found me a tad on the pushy side before you dated Steven Simmons, but you didn't hate me, did you?'

Her face reddened further. She shook her head. At last we were getting somewhere.

'I have something for you,' I said. My fingers extracted the bracelet from my bag. I laid it on the bed. When she saw it, Ellie turned pale.

I sat beside her, drawing her into my arms. To my relief, she didn't resist. 'Shhh,' I whispered into her hair. 'It's all right, Els. Really.'

She cried against my shoulder for a long time. When she pulled away, shame filled her expression.

'I shouldn't have taken it,' she said. 'It was wrong of me, I know. But I was so confused back then. I still am.'

I fastened the bracelet around her left wrist. *To my daughter, with all my love, from Dad.* What did it matter which one of us wore it? The sentiment remained the same.

She stared at me, confusion in every line of her face. 'It's yours,' I told her.

'Why?' she whispered.

'Because I love you. That's why.'

'I've been horrible to you. Behaved dreadfully, been a terrible person. You can't possibly love me.'

'Don't say that. You're precious to me. You always will be.'

She didn't reply at first. Then her eyes met mine.

'Can you forgive me?' Her voice was hoarse, her words a mere whisper, but God, how welcome.

I hesitated before replying, in an attempt to blend honesty with tact. 'In time, yes. It might take a while. You've hurt me, and badly.'

Relief flooded her face. 'Of course. I get that.'

'I won't pretend I can overlook everything that's happened. I do understand, though. You were in shock after what happened at the cliff. You didn't mean those things you said the other day.'

'What about at the cottage? Or before? I tried to con money from you. I'm every bit as bad as ...' She shuddered. '*Him*.'

I shook my head. 'Not even close.'

'How can I blame you?' I continued. 'I fell victim to him too.'

She gulped back a sob. 'I've never hated you. You have to believe me.'

'He was behind the whole revenge thing, wasn't he?' She'd already said as much during our argument at the cottage.

'Yes. He instructed me what to do, what to say. If he'd told me to dance naked through the streets, I'd have done it.'

'He groomed you. As well as pumping you for information about me.' I realised how Scott had known to play the 'shy guy' role, among other things.

She nodded. 'He twisted all of it into something bad. He said you were a lousy sister, persuaded me I should hate you. Insisted you were responsible for Alyson's death. In the end I hadn't a clue what was true and what wasn't.'

'That's how men like him operate.'

'Steven made the pain over Alyson go away, you see. If I blamed you, I couldn't be guilty. After that, believing everything else he said came easily.'

Wow. The bastard had reached parts of her I'd considered untouchable. That gave me something on which to ponder.

'I always felt so strong, so capable, when I was with him,' Ellie said. 'For me, that acted like a drug.'

'You became hooked on him.'

'Yeah.' A pause. Then: 'What happened?' She sniffed. 'On the cliff top, I mean. I heard him scream. The next minute he was dead.'

I drew in a breath. 'He slipped in the mud. Wasn't able to regain his balance. Not with his injured ankle.'

Pain crossed Ellie's face. It was important I tell her the whole truth, though. 'He had a knife. He would have stabbed you.'

Ellie shuddered. 'What was it he said? "Give me one reason I shouldn't slice the bitch".' Her eyes held so much hurt I ached for her.

I prayed my next words wouldn't alienate her forever. 'I threw a rock at him. That's why he fell.'

She stared at me, her eyes wide. 'All I wanted was to protect you,' I said.

'You killed him?'

I moistened my dry lips. 'I never meant to, I swear.'

Silence for a while. My nerves stretched tight with apprehension.

A sob. Then: 'I'm glad he's dead. You were right, and I was wrong.'

I pulled her into my arms again, figuring a hug would work better than words.

'I loved every inch of that man.' Sadness in her voice. 'Now all I feel for him is hatred.'

'Me too.'

'I felt so ashamed after you left yesterday. That thing you said about only wanting to take care of me? I knew it was true, however much I pretended otherwise.'

'Remember what else I told you. I can change. In the future, any help I give will be on your terms, not mine. And only if you ask for it.'

'Thank you.' A pause. 'I've always loved you, despite how badly I've behaved. Can I say something, though?'

'Anything.'

'You were awfully bossy at times. Sorry, but it's the truth.'

Ouch. She was right though. 'Shades of Mum, hey? Seems I've inherited her controlling streak.'

'I realise you meant well, but it often got a bit much.'

'I get that.'

Another pause. 'Can I admit something else? I've always been jealous of you.'

'Why? Because you thought Dad preferred me?'

'Partly. But also because of Caroline, the closeness you share. I don't have any friends, so I enjoyed causing trouble between you two. How warped is that?'

'It doesn't matter. Not now.' I'd already realised Scott had manipulated Ellie into telling Caroline - and Mum - about losing money to Steven Simmons. All part of his plan to sow discord.

'There's more. I hated the fact you're so switched on about money. That day we ate lunch at your new place? I was almost sick with envy. My little flat seemed so poky in comparison. When I told Steven, he said we'd soon be living in luxury in America.' She shook her head. 'How could I have been so gullible?'

'He was very persuasive, Els.'

She burst into tears again. 'I can't cope with any of this. Falling so hard for Steven, his betrayal, then him dying the way he did.'

I hesitated, unsure whether my words would be well received. 'You want my opinion?'

'What is it?'

'You've never come to terms with Alyson's death. Until you do, you'll always struggle mentally.'

Fear crossed her face. *Tread carefully*, I warned myself. 'Have you told your counsellor the full story?'

She shook her head, her eyes stricken. 'I lied to her about what happened, like I did with everyone else. I can't think about that night. If I do, I end up wanting to kill myself.'

'If you don't, the guilt will continue to fester. Haven't you punished yourself enough?'

'No. My best friend died because of me.'

I took her hands. 'Can I make a suggestion?' She nodded.

'How about seeing a psychiatrist instead?' Panic flitted into her eyes, but I carried on regardless. 'One experienced in dealing with guilt issues.'

'I'm not sure.' She pulled away.

'Steven convinced you to feel better about Alyson, even if only temporarily. If that bastard could manage it, so can a trained professional. But only if you tell the truth. No more bottling stuff up. Mum and I will support you all the way.'

'You will?'

'We're both here for you. You spend too much time on your own, and that's not healthy.'

She nodded. 'You're right. I get so lonely sometimes.'

Time to play my trump card. 'Mum asked me last night whether she should sell the cottage. What do you think?'

My words had taken her by surprise, I could tell. 'You want my opinion?'

'Of course. You've loved it there every bit as much as we have. Now, though ...' I shook my head. 'All my happy memories are tainted.'

'And Mum feels the same?'

'Yes.'

'I do too. But how does this relate to me needing help?'

'She's rattling around in that house all by herself. It's way too big for her now Dad's dead and we've both left home. Mum suggested selling both it and the cottage and buying somewhere smaller.'

'I still don't understand how that benefits me.'

'In two ways. She's proposing to split the leftover funds three ways, so you'd get a third. More than enough to replace what Steven Simmons stole. And she wants you to live with her. She told me she gets lonely too. You'd be company for each other.'

Ellie didn't reply and worry nibbled at me. Did she think I was interfering again? But it was Mum's idea, not mine; I was only the messenger.

'You've always got on better with her than I have,' I said. 'And I'd be a frequent visitor. You'll get sick of the sight of me.'

'You live in Spain now. We'd only see you every couple of months, if that.'

'Wrong. I'm coming back to Bristol. For good.'

'You are?' Such hope in her voice.

'Yes.'

Tears filled her eyes. 'I've missed you so much. That was partly why I got so angry with you. I needed my big sister more than I wanted to admit.'

Relief swamped me. We'd come a long way since Ellie's fake suicide bid. We still had a difficult road to travel, sure. Psychiatric support for her, finding out whether one or both of us might face prosecution. We'd get there, though. Together.

'I could sell my flat,' Ellie said. 'Help contribute towards the new place.'

'Or maybe rent it out. Think of the extra income.' Too late, I heard myself. 'There I go again, trying to run your life. Seems it's a hard habit to break.'

To my relief, she laughed. 'You'll do your best. You always do.'

I stroked my fingers over the gold bracelet around her wrist. 'To new beginnings,' I said.

'To new beginnings,' Ellie echoed. Our father would have been proud. Of that I was sure.

EPILOGUE

ONE WEEK LATER

A glass of whisky in hand, I leaned back against my pillows, the day almost over. Only one thing remained for me to do. I took a sip of Lagavulin, then opened my laptop and logged on to Love Rats Exposed. After all that had happened, Broken and Betrayed and Anna deserved some closure.

By then, the police had contacted both women, of course. They would know Scott, a.k.a. Rick Montgomery and Michael Hammond to them, was dead. Not the finer details, though, in light of the ongoing investigation.

The radio button by Broken and Betrayed's profile indicated she was online. Not Anna, not yet.

No rush. I could afford to wait, or log on again tomorrow if necessary. The alcohol warmed my belly as I eyed the screen on my laptop. Twenty minutes later the radio button next to Anna's profile turned green.

I opened up the private message box, added their names, and began to type. No need to reveal everything, just the gist of what happened on the cliff edge that night.

'It's over,' I finished. 'He'll never fool any woman ever again.'

Within a few minutes Broken and Betrayed replied. 'I'm glad he's dead. Is that awful of me?'

'No,' I typed. 'Just human. I feel the same way, believe me. So does my sister.'

'How's she doing?'

'Pretty good, all things considered. I reckon she'll be fine, given time.'

A post from Anna. 'I feel as though Sophie got justice at last. Thanks to you.'

'That was all I ever wanted,' I posted. 'For that bastard to get what he deserved. Once the police enquiry has been wrapped up, I intend to delete my profile on this site.'

'I'll be doing the same,' Anna responded.

'Me too,' typed Broken and Betrayed. 'Like Sophie, I also got justice. It's time to move on.'

'I've not seen Heartbroken Helen on here for a while,' Anna posted. 'Maybe she's also moved on.'

'I hope so,' Broken and Betrayed replied. 'She was always so supportive, wasn't she?'

I had no idea whether to laugh or cry. I'd not told them everything, after all.

With a wry shake of my head, I drained my whisky. 'Goodnight, both of you,' I typed. 'And good luck.'

Lightning Source UK Ltd.
Milton Keynes UK
UKHW04f1957241018
331145UK00001B/165/P